---- ★ ----

Under the thin moustache his bloodless lips were moving. Brodie couldn't hear a word. She leant closer. "What happened? Who did this to you?"

She thought he was trying to say something. His eyes closed with the effort to concentrate. "D...D..."

He'd said all he could. The life was pouring out of him: five minutes was just too long to wait. He reached for her wrist with long thin fingers, and she hadn't the heart to deny him whatever comfort that gave him. He was a bad man; but perhaps even bad men shouldn't die alone. "D..." he whispered just once more, and then he was still.

So was Brodie. Not because a dead man gripped her wrist but because fear gripped her heart. She'd asked him who'd killed him, and he'd told her. Someone beginning with D.

---- ★ ----

JO BANNISTER

CLOSER STILL

WORLDWIDE®

TORONTO • NEW YORK • LONDON
AMSTERDAM • PARIS • SYDNEY • HAMBURG
STOCKHOLM • ATHENS • TOKYO • MILAN
MADRID • WARSAW • BUDAPEST • AUCKLAND

Recycling programs for this product may not exist in your area.

CLOSER STILL

A Worldwide Mystery/August 2009

First published by St. Martin's Press, LLC.

ISBN-13: 978-0-373-26681-4

Printed in U.S.A.

Keep your friends close, and your enemies closer still.
—Sun Tzu

ONE

IT WAS LATER THAN HE THOUGHT. He'd been in the back room of The Rose for hours, conducting business. Then he got talking, and more than talking, and now it was two o'clock on a wet autumn morning and people with homes to go to had long since gone. The rain-slick pavement shone under the street lamps but all the houses were dark. He grinned to himself as he hunched his collar about his ears. Most south coast towns took on a different kind of life after midnight. Dimmock just pulled the duvet over its head and went to sleep.

But that was to ignore the special qualities of the night. Some activities are best conducted after sundown. The kind, forgiving night had given him his best times. Everyone in a seaside town enjoys the summer season, but he liked the winter best. The long nights. It was September now, and already the evenings were getting darker. It was coming his time of year.

But there are things that are better done on a sunny day than a wet night, and changing a flat tyre is one of them. He stared at it in disbelief. The gutter was running and the cracked pavement was grimy; and the wheel nuts had undoubtedly been tightened by a gorilla with a metre-long spanner, and even if he could find a wheel brace in the deep recesses of his boot, all his instincts told him it would be the wrong size. He looked up and down the street. No one.

He could return to The Rose and sort it out in the morning. He could phone Colin to come and sort it out now—and see him hiding a grin every time they met for the next fortnight because he knew what it meant that he was leaving the pub at two in the morning. He might have been doing the accounts. But he wasn't, and Colin would know he wasn't.

He really wished he hadn't sworn at the last person who tried to sell him an AA membership.

A footstep on the pavement behind him made him look round hopefully. A lot of people in the same position would have felt a certain unease, but the night was his friend. And right now, someone willing to change a wheel for him would be too.

There were two of them. The older one was big, the younger one was tall. The older one had his hands fisted deep in the pockets of a dark raincoat. The younger one was wearing jeans and a leather jacket. Neither of them was smiling.

'Having a problem, Joe?' The older man's voice was as expressionless as the craggy face it issued from.

Joe Loomis expelled the startled breath he'd caught, but only halfway. Lots of people would be nervous to be approached on a deserted road in the middle of the night, but round here what they were most anxious about was being approached by Joe. Loomis himself generally felt pretty safe. There was only one shadow which, falling across his path, was enough to make him pause—but it was a big one. Just exactly this big.

'Mr Deacon?' he said, waiting for his heart to steady enough to do nonchalance. 'And you were doing so well for yourself. How long have you been back on the beat?'

The big man chuckled bleakly. 'You *are* my beat, Joe. I've a good team down at Battle Alley, they can deal with pretty well anything that comes up. Which leaves me free to deal with you.'

'Mr Deacon,' said Loomis again, reproachfully. 'I don't need dealing with. I'm not a problem.'

'You *feel* like a problem,' said the younger man softly.

Loomis peered into the darkness. 'Detective Sergeant Voss, is it? How are you? I haven't seen you since…'

It was a sentence he'd have been better not starting. Not when he was outnumbered two to one numerically and about four to one by weight. He let it peter out and hoped nobody'd noticed.

They noticed. Detective Superintendent Jack Deacon fin- ished the sentence for him. 'Not since you had your mates beat the living daylights out of him because you couldn't reach me.' You could have bent horseshoes round the iron in his voice.

'A misunderstanding,' demurred Loomis. 'Anyway, we cleared that up. I seem to remember that we cleared that up.' Possibly without knowing it, he rubbed his jaw with the side of his thumb.

Enjoying the recollection, Deacon took out his knuckles and blew on them. It isn't often that a senior police officer gets the chance to deck someone with impunity. Only the memory of Charlie Voss's broken face, and the fact that if Division ever learnt how he'd reacted he could wave goodbye to his pension, kept Deacon from bursting into song every time he thought of it.

'We did,' he agreed finally. 'This isn't about that.'

'What is it about?'

'The reason you're still on the streets, and I'm still a police- man, is that *that* was personal,' Deacon explained carefully. 'This isn't. This is about the fact that I'm *still* a policeman, and you're *still* a pimp, a drug dealer and a racketeer. A trader in human weakness and human misery. You're a ponce, a parasite and a thug—and you're doing it in my town. And you're not doing it for much longer.'

It was true, all of it. But it isn't often a man like Joe Loomis hears the unvarnished truth about himself. He felt himself flushing, even though there was nothing there he'd take issue with. 'Mr Deacon—are you threatening me?'

'Yes,' said Deacon immediately. 'Oh yes, Joe, that was def- initely a threat. I'm threatening to use every power at my disposal to put you where you should have been for the last ten years, and keep you there until old age and infirmity stop you posing a danger to my town and pissing me off. It's a threat, a warning, a promise and my birthday present to myself all wrapped up in one. Now.' He turned to his companion. 'Is that everything I wanted to say to Mr Loomis?'

DS Voss ticked off a mental checklist. 'Threat, warning, promise, gratuitous insults—yes, I think that's everything, sir. Unless you want to tell him to be on the next stage?'

Deacon shook his heavy head. 'I thought about that, Charlie Voss, but I decided against.' He spoke as if Loomis had not been standing right in front of them. 'I decided I'd sooner have him in Parkhurst than sunning himself on the Costa del Crime.'

'Then that's it.'

'Fine.' Deacon went to walk away, then something occurred to him. 'Oh, Joe—you're going to need some help changing that wheel. Some sod's broken a match in your valve. Lucky we came along, really. Lord only knows who you'd meet on these mean streets if it wasn't for the local police keeping an eye on things. But since we are here, I was going to suggest...'

He waited until he thought he detected a glimmer of hope in Loomis's eye. '...that you call a friend, if you've got any. Just don't dial 999. That's not what we're here for.' And with that he strolled fifty metres up Rye Lane, got into his own car and drove away, with a smile on his face that Joe Loomis would remember for the rest of his life.

DS VOSS HAD A FLAT in one of the red-brick Victorian villas in Pound Street. Deacon drove by on his way home. But when he stopped the car Voss didn't get out.

After a moment Deacon looked at him quizzically. 'You're thinking, Charlie Voss. I keep telling you, it's not a good habit to get into.'

Voss smiled dutifully. 'I'm just wondering if we did the right thing.'

'Marking Joe's card?' Voss nodded his ginger head. 'Didn't you enjoy it?'

'Of course I enjoyed it. That's the problem. Usually, if you're enjoying something that much you shouldn't be doing it.'

Deacon gave a crocodile grin. 'Everyone needs a little plea-sure in life.' But the last four years had taught him that Voss only looked like an overgrown barrow-boy; he was in fact an experienced police officer with good instincts. 'You think I shouldn't have told him I'm coming?'

'Maybe not. It's going to make him careful.'

'He's *been* careful,' said Deacon. 'That's why he's been a major player in Dimmock for five years; why I've *known* he was a major player for four years, three hundred and sixty-four days, and even knowing I haven't been able to nail him. He *is* careful. Let's see if he can go on being careful when he's rattled.'

Voss nodded slowly. 'It's worth a try. And on the bright side, even if it doesn't work...' He hesitated.

'What?'

His smile was sunny. 'It *was* fun, wasn't it?'

TWO

JONATHAN FARRELL HAD KEPT a lot of hospital appointments in the first six months of his life. He'd seen a lot of doctors. Or perhaps he hadn't. It still wasn't entirely clear how much of anything he could see.

Which, in a way, made the decisions that were coming easier. Easier to take, and easier to bear. If he'd had enough sight to be worth saving, even the toughest mother in the world—which Brodie Farrell was not, though she sometimes tried to give that impression—might have found it impossible to balance the loss of his eyes against the chance of protecting him from a life-threatening illness.

Because there were no certainties. The tumours in his eyes might never affect the central nervous system. It might be safe enough to let him enjoy what vision he had for as long as it would last. But even the oncologist couldn't tell her for sure. They could wait, but there was danger in the waiting. They could remove one eye, or both, but they would do it without being sure it was necessary. It was a matter of percentages, or considering what had been done, and how successfully, with similar cases around the world.

Retinoblastoma is a rare condition and it's hard to get a statistically significant sample. Dr Millership saw a handful of new cases a year, few of them directly comparable to Jonathan Farrell's. Jonathan was born with white eyes, the tumours in both already apparent. She could remember two similar patients. One had had no possibility of sight and they'd gone for early enucleation: he was growing up blind but healthy. In the other, the prospect of preserving some vision had led her to start chemotherapy and laser treatment. The initial response had been good, but in the end surgery became necessary when one of the tumours began moving outside the eye. These cases, and others she'd read about, were at the forefront of her mind as she tried to advise Brodie Farrell.

The two women had formed a good working relationship over the last five months. They used one another's first names. Anne Millership didn't assume that having a sick child automatically made Brodie an idiot, and Brodie tried not to blame the doctor for knowing so much and still, in the end, not enough.

With Jonathan on her knee sucking determinedly on his teddy's head, she said quietly, 'Not good news, then?'

The doctor shook her head. 'The tumours are definitely advancing—the left more than the right, but actually both of them. I'm sorry.'

Brodie didn't need sympathy so much as sound guidance. 'What do you want to do?'

'I think we should remove the left eye as soon as possible. He has no useful vision in it and he'll be much safer with it gone.'

'And the right one?'

'This isn't what I want to be telling you,' said Dr Millership quietly. 'But we should seriously consider removing it too. He has a little vision, but I don't think it'll last as the tumour advances. We can slow its progress with a number of different treatments. I don't think any of them will enable him to grow up both safe and sighted.'

She paused to let that sink in. 'One thing in favour of early enucleation is that if he doesn't remember seeing he won't miss it as much. He'll grow up using his other senses.'

'I thought that was a myth,' said Brodie bleakly. 'That blind people hear better to compensate.'

'Yes and no,' said the doctor. 'We don't think they hear any better. We think they use their hearing, and their other senses, more effectively.'

Like a defective vacuum cleaner, Jonathan switched abruptly from suck to blow. The soggy teddy landed on the floor. With a smile Anne Millership retrieved it for him, and having returned it let her hand linger on his plump thigh. She looked up at his mother. 'We don't have to make any decisions today. But we should make them soon.'

In fact Brodie didn't need more time. She'd understood the situation pretty thoroughly by the time Jonathan was a month old. She'd discussed the options with Anne Millership, with Jonathan's father and with close friends; and then discussed them again as the less radical solutions were tried and failed. She'd known this moment would come, and she knew what she had to do about it.

'I don't want him to lose his eyes,' she said, her voice under rigorous control. 'But most of all I don't want to lose him. If surgery is his best chance, do it. If losing both eyes is safer than losing one eye, do that.'

The doctor slipped back into her chair. She nodded. 'Yes. It's the right decision, at the right time. I'll set the wheels in motion.'

Brodie was determined not to cry. She held her amiable baby tight and mourned the life she'd imagined for him that now he could never have. She forced a brittle smile. 'So he's not going to play rugby for England after all. How *do* I tell his father?'

'You start by saying he probably wouldn't have done anyway,' said Dr Millership practically. 'How is Jack about this? Does he feel the same way you do?'

Brodie struggled to know how Deacon felt. About anything, but most of all about this. He'd never expected to have this child. Neither of them had. By the time she realised he was on the way, Brodie's relationship with Jack Deacon was on the rocks. Deacon's initial reaction to the news was more shock than delight.

After that, though, there was no doubting his pleasure. Dear God, he even proposed to her—in a Deaconish sort of way, not so much an outpouring of emotion as a practical solution. When the baby came, and his problems were immediately obvious, his distress was at least as great as Brodie's. But they never really talked about their feelings. About the future, the prognosis, the various treatments available and the decisions they might have to take, but not about how they felt. She assumed that Deacon too considered any sacrifice worth making to keep his son safe—but she didn't know. He hadn't said and she hadn't asked.

She answered obliquely. 'He'll back whatever decision I take.'

Millership bit her lip. 'I'd be happier if I thought you were taking decisions together.'

'In a perfect world, so would I,' said Brodie tartly. 'But Jonathan is my responsibility. Jack and I aren't married, and we aren't planning to get married.'

'Does that make you solely responsible?'

Brodie managed a wry grin at the memory. 'Actually, the precise manner of his conception probably does. Anyway, I've done the single parent thing before. Jack's new at this. Anything he has to say I'll listen to, but the bottom line is that I'm paying the piper so I'll call the tune. Some decisions are easier to take on your own.'

Anne Millership nodded her acceptance. Whatever problems Jonathan's parents had were for them to sort out. 'One thing you must tell him. That if your baby had to have this condition, this is the place to get it. In the UK, nine out of ten affected children survive. Over much of the world's surface, nine out of ten die.'

There was reassurance in that. There was also a warning. Brodie's eyes acknowledged it. 'This will keep him safe, won't it? If we do the ops?'

Anne Millership could promise nothing. 'There's a tiny risk that the tumours may already have moved into the central nervous system. I don't think they have. I think operating now will ensure they can't.'

Brodie heard what she wasn't saying out loud. 'But one

time in ten, good doctors in good hospitals do all the right things and still—?'

The doctor nodded sombrely. 'Yes. We can't get it down to zero risk.' She brightened. 'But you'd put your shirt on a horse that was running at ten to one on.'

But all Brodie knew about horses was that they were unreliable.

So HER MIND WAS FULL as she left the hospital, Jonathan leading the way in the souped-up buggy his father had insisted on buying for him. Full of thoughts and fears and images. She was resigned now to losing the funny white eyes that startled strangers who leant over the pram to coo at him, but which Brodie had grown rather fond of. She knew that after the op he could have blue eyes or brown eyes or grey eyes, and nobody would know he was blind until she told them. She knew—she'd told people repeatedly so it must be true—that even blindness isn't the end of the world. That her son would cope with his disability with strength, imagination and good humour, and if he couldn't be a world-class rugby player he'd learn to be a world-class cellist. He'd have a good and full life.

Unless he was that tenth child.

She was almost back at the car before she realised someone had fallen into step beside her. She was in a public place in the middle of the day: it didn't occur to her to be anxious. She assumed he was parked beside her. Even when he stood by as she fumbled for her keys she just thought he wanted to help her load the buggy, and mumbled, 'Thank you,' without even glancing at him.

But he went on standing there, saying nothing, between her and her car, until she realised something was amiss and looked up. Her heart turned over. Then she said with conviction, 'You have no business with me, Mr Loomis.'

He wasn't a big man. Much smaller than Deacon; not much bigger than Daniel. Unless you already knew who he was, there was nothing distinctive about him. He had dark hair cut a shade

longer than was fashionable, and ungenerous eyes and a thin
moustache; and a certain sallow cast to his skin suggested he
didn't get out enough, at least in daylight. But there was nothing
to make alarm bells ring. He wasn't wearing a fedora with the
brim pulled down or carrying a violin case. Brodie was perhaps
the only person within a quarter of a mile who'd have looked
at him twice.

But then, she knew who he was, and what he'd done. She
knew that, if he wasn't the biggest crook in Dimmock, he was
certainly the nastiest. (Dimmock wasn't like London or New
York. In a faded Victorian resort, a determined man can conduct
a reign of terror with a whoopee-whistle. It was a matter of
some surprise to Division how much serious crime occurred in
the town. His superiors were never entirely sure whether more
crime came to light because Jack Deacon was Senior Investigating Officer, or if his very presence was a provocation.)

'No business,' agreed Joe Loomis smoothly. He gave a thin-
lipped smile like a snake's. 'I just thought I'd say hello. I'm an
old…acquaintance of your partner's.'

'I know who you are,' she said, clipping the words off short.
'Acquaintance isn't the word he uses. But if you want to discuss
it with him, I have his number on speed-dial.'

She met his gaze full on, and had the satisfaction of seeing
him blink. People tended not to realise how tall she was. Her
manner could be unsettling too. Her forthright gaze and the con-
fidence that came of dealing with the world on her own terms
troubled men who thought that strong women had to be plain.
Brodie Farrell was born striking but she learnt to be strong.
Now she was head of her household and proprietor of a successful business, and not much scared her anymore.

And if Joe Loomis was the exception, she wasn't about to
let him know. She stared him down, expecting him to move.

He didn't. He said, 'What a nice baby.'

It was the sort of thing Deacon said before he was a father,
polite and totally uninterested. If she'd been holding a melon

he'd have said, 'What a nice melon.' Only Loomis went on looking at the sleepy child long enough to suggest that he did in fact have an interest, even if he wasn't prepared to declare it.

Brodie honed the edge on her voice. 'You're in my way, Mr Loomis.'

Joe Loomis smiled again, and nodded, and didn't move. Brodie suddenly realised he wasn't alone. A young man in jeans and an older one in a suit were waiting by a big silver car, looking at nothing with the studied blankness of professional minders.

'It's time Jack Deacon had a family,' said Loomis judiciously. 'A man gets to a certain age, he shouldn't be putting all his efforts into his work any more.'

And that was what this was about. Brodie knew as surely as if he'd slapped his agenda on the bonnet in front of her. He knew about her and Deacon, he knew that Deacon was the father of her child, and he wanted her to know. And he wanted her to tell Deacon that he knew.

You couldn't object to anything he'd said. Nothing he'd said or done could be described as a threat. But Brodie knew she was meant to feel threatened. No one in her right mind wanted Joe Loomis taking an interest in her family.

She breathed heavily. 'If there's something you want me to tell Jack, spit it out.'

But he raised his hands in denial. 'Nothing. Just that I said hello. You can tell him I like his baby, if you like…'

With Jack Deacon for a father and Brodie Farrell for a mother, this particular baby was always going to have a sense of dramatic timing. As Loomis leant over the buggy to smile at him, Jonathan opened his mouth and yawned. And then he opened his eyes.

THREE

'ARE YOU ALL RIGHT?' asked Daniel, his short-sighted eyes concerned.

'I'm fine,' said Brodie shortly.

'Really?'

She thought a moment longer. 'I *am* fine, but I can't say it didn't give me a shock.' Then she laughed, an altogether earthier laugh than people ever expected. 'But possibly less of a shock than Joe Loomis got when the Antichrist fixed him with the evil eye.'

It was her idea of a joke, calling him that. It began as a defence mechanism, but now she could invest it with genuine affection. Disasters affect different people in different ways: humour, even black humour, is a good way of coping. Jonathan didn't think his mother was insulting him. He beamed complacently at her tone of voice.

Nor did Daniel object, though he'd become quite proprietorial about Brodie's baby. He sat on the little sofa with Jonathan in his lap, both of them quite at ease, while Brodie roamed restlessly about her office, putting things back the way she liked them.

This wasn't how it had been meant to work. She'd put her business into Daniel's hands because she couldn't continue to run it and look after a new baby. They had both known they'd have to make compromises. Brodie was used to working alone, and the fairest thing that could be said of Daniel's interest in Looking for Something? was that he didn't have one until it was required of him. He was a maths teacher. Looking for Something? was a finding agency: clients hired Brodie to locate things they couldn't locate themselves. A kind of detective agency without the divorce work. Except that he had a problem-solving brain, Daniel Hood was cut out to be a detective the way King Herod was cut out to be a nanny.

But needs must when the devil drives. Although Brodie didn't know this—Brodie must never know this—Daniel had been offered a job at Dimmock High just an hour before she broke the news of her pregnancy, at which point all bets were off. She hadn't asked for help, but she needed it; and schools would always need maths teachers but if Brodie shut her doors for six months she mightn't have a business to come back to. He offered to keep it ticking over for her; and she, knowing the likely alternative was to lose something in which she'd invested a lot of time, energy and money, accepted.

Since then, though, she'd made every excuse she could think of to come to the little office in Shack Lane and sniff disapprovingly at everything Daniel had done that wasn't exactly how she'd have done it. She didn't mean to be ungrateful. She rationalised it as teaching him the business. But had circumstances—and the laws of nature—been otherwise, it would have made much more sense for her to go on running Looking for Something? and for Daniel to have the baby. For a single man, he looked oddly at ease with Jonathan on his knee. Much more so than the child's father did. Deacon held him like a rugby ball.

'What did Jack say?' asked Daniel. Unconsciously he flinched.

'Jack?' repeated Brodie, wide-eyed. 'I haven't told Jack. He'd go apeshit.'

The expression had frozen on Daniel's round, rather plain face. 'Brodie, he needs to know.'

Except when she was furious with one of them—which was, admittedly, a good part of the time—it amused Brodie how different the two men in her life were: her partner a refugee from Mount Rushmore, her best friend…well. Daniel was harder to categorise. Everything about him was small and delicate and self-effacing, with two exceptions: his hair, which was the yellow of bright sunshine and meant you could pick him out in any crowd that wasn't too tall to find him in, and his spirit, which was adamantine. He never went looking for trouble. But when trouble found him he seemed constitutionally unable to step aside. He had this thing about honesty. He thought it mattered more than the odd broken nose.

'That a man spoke to me in a public car park?' she said, feigning negligence. 'It's hardly a matter for CID.'

'*Anything* Joe Loomis does is a matter for CID,' said Daniel firmly. 'And anything he does that affects you and Jonathan is a matter for Jack. You said it yourself—it was meant as a threat. He *wanted* you to tell Jack. He was warning him off.'

She turned to face him, perching on the edge of the desk. 'That's why I don't want to pass it on. Right now, Loomis thinks he's marked Jack's card so he's happy; and Jack doesn't know about it so *he's* happy. If I tell Jack, he'll hit the wall— and he might not stop at the wall. If Joe's worried, that means Jack's after him—and *that* means he'll be behind bars soon enough, and then it won't matter what he wants. But if this gets personal, you and I both know Jack can't be trusted to keep his cool. Look what he did when Charlie Voss got beaten up. Now ask yourself what he'd do if he thought Jonathan was in danger.'

'He's a professional police officer,' demurred Daniel. 'He'd…'

'Yeah,' said Brodie ironically. 'Right.'

But Daniel was insistent. 'He needs to know. And he needs to hear it from you, when he has a chance to calm down before doing something he'll regret, rather than from Loomis somewhere public.'

Reluctantly, Brodie conceded that. If Deacon was going to lose his temper—and Deacon was going to lose his temper— it had to be far enough away from Loomis that he didn't flatten the man, bin his career and squander his best chance of putting the little thug away all in ten hot-headed seconds. 'All right,' she agreed, 'I'll tell him. I'll phone him now.'

But Daniel shook his yellow head. 'Not in his office. In yours. I'll take Jonathan back to my place. Pick him up on your way home.'

BRODIE WAS NEVER SURE if she was good at relationships or very bad at them. She'd had what she'd thought was the perfect marriage—but it ended when John Farrell was swept off his feet by a plump librarian. After that she'd tried friendship—and what she had with Daniel was as close as a friendship could be without turning into something else. Though it began with her doing him a great wrong, it developed into something of sweeping importance to both of them and restored her faith in humanity in general and men in particular.

But she was aware, even as she drew strength from it, that it was more what she wanted and needed than what Daniel did. Unable to persuade her that the next step was right for both of them, he'd quietly taken it alone. Brodie knew that if the need arose he would die for her. And if what she felt for him wasn't love too she didn't know what it was, but it wasn't the same love he felt for her. She felt sad about that, and guilty, and wished it were otherwise, but she wouldn't lie to him and he wouldn't want her to. He thought that truth was the silver bullet.

And then there was Deacon. What she got from Deacon was pretty much what she wanted as well. By some miracle, she thought their on/off, do-it-when-we've-time partnership met most of his needs too—certainly better than the full-on commitment of a marriage, family of four, mortgage, dog and timeshare in Ibiza would have done. She didn't feel guilty about Deacon, at least not often. But she wasn't sure if the relationship was a success or not.

It was getting to be a long time since she was a full-time wife and mother racing to have the house nice for when her husband came home. She would never be that girl again, and had no wish to be; but a tiny private voice at the back of her brain wondered if she was missing out. If it would be nice to do the suburban hostess-trolley thing again. And if it would, whether it would be even possible to do it with Deacon.

When Daniel left with the baby, pushing the fancy buggy the short distance along the Promenade to the netting shed he'd made his home, Brodie called Deacon's mobile. 'Can you talk? Or are you in hot pursuit?'

'Hot pursuit of last month's crime figures,' grunted Deacon, his phone sandwiched between shoulder and ear. 'And a decent cup of coffee.' From the way he raised his voice Brodie realised this wasn't addressed to her.

All the same… 'Can't help with the crime statistics. But I've got the kettle on. And I've something to tell you.'

Not until she saw his face at her door a scant six minutes later did it occur to her that what he thought she had to tell him was news from the hospital. He'd known about Jonathan's appointment, had cemented two and two together with a good dollop of fear and got twenty-two. 'What did Millership say? Are his eyes getting worse?'

Brodie had to do a quick switching of points to get back on the same track. 'Actually, yes. She doesn't think that anything we do will give him any useful sight. And that he'd be a lot safer without his eyes.'

Deacon flinched. It wasn't that he hadn't been expecting this moment. They'd talked about it regularly over the past months. At the beginning it had seemed only a horrid possibility; more recently it had started to look inevitable. Still when it came it landed like a fist in the belly. 'What did you tell her?'

'I told her I wanted him to be safe.'

Deacon nodded slowly. It was the only possible answer: in all their talks, neither of them had come up with an alternative. Still he felt that, as Jonathan's father, she might have included him in the final decision. Partly for his benefit, but partly for hers. 'When?'

'As soon as it can be arranged.' She poured hot water into the coffee mugs, handed him one.

'Will he…?' He wasn't sure how to put this. 'Will he miss them?'

Brodie shook her head, the black corkscrew curls brushing her shoulders. 'Anne doesn't think so. She thinks he can tell the difference between light and darkness. She doesn't think he can see objects.'

He breathed the steam coming off the coffee. 'There really isn't any choice, is there?'

'No,' Brodie said. 'Not unless we're prepared to risk losing him.'

Deacon looked around the little office, suddenly puzzled. 'So where is he? And why are you here?'

'Daniel took him for a walk on the front. There's something else I need to tell you about.' She related her encounter in the hospital car park with the man who was careful not to threaten her.

Deacon didn't leap to his feet and start throwing crockery. He went massively still. His lips tightened, pale with fury. His voice was a vicious whisper. 'Did he lay a finger on you? Or on Jonathan?'

'No,' Brodie said quickly. 'And he never looked like he might. He wasn't there to hurt us, or even to frighten us—he was there to send a message. To you. I wasn't inclined to oblige him, but Daniel felt you needed to know and I could see he was right.'

'Daniel did.' Twelve months ago that would have come out a lot angrier. Now he was almost reconciled to the fact that she talked things through with Daniel the way she might with a sister before telling her partner what she'd decided. He still didn't like it, but he knew it wasn't going to change, and at last he seemed to realise it posed no threat to their relationship. But that didn't stop it being very peculiar, and at heart Jack Deacon was a deeply conventional man.

'He didn't want Loomis ambushing you with it. He was afraid'—she kept her face straight—'you might overreact.'

'Whatever would make him think that?' said Deacon through clenched teeth.

'Beats me,' said Brodie ingenuously. 'You wouldn't be so stupid as to compromise an important investigation by decking the suspect in a public place, would you? Not when that was so obviously what he wanted you to do.'

'No-o-o,' agreed Deacon slowly. 'What would I do instead?'

Brodie grinned. The danger point was past. If Loomis stopped him in the street as he left here and asked him the time, Deacon would—well no, not tell him, he was never that kind of policeman, but at least not shove his watch somewhere the beeps would be seriously muffled. 'Oh, something much cleverer than that. You'd get him into court. Because you'd know that after that he wouldn't be in a position to hurt anyone.'

'Yes.' Deacon mulled it over. 'I expect that's what I'd do. I might have to keep Charlie Voss on a tight leash, though.'

'Charlie?' Brodie's eyebrows betrayed her surprise. DS Voss was in many ways an old-fashioned policeman. Polite. Considerate. If Joe Loomis asked him the time he might very well tell him.

'Oh yes,' said Deacon with conviction. 'Still waters run deep. That nice, quiet, thoughtful, intelligent exterior—that's just a guise. Underneath he's a mad dog.'

'OK,' said Brodie carefully. 'Well, you hang on tight to that leash. It'll stop Charlie Voss rushing off and doing something stupid.' She half-turned and planted a casual kiss on his cheek. 'It'll also stop you.'

FOUR

FROM THE DAY OF HIS BIRTH, when he was the wrong sex for a mother desperate for a daughter, to the present day when he wasn't the lover sought by the woman he loved, Daniel Hood's life had always strayed down unexplored paths. Though some of them should have been gated, wired up and marked with a sign saying Beware of the Alligator, overall he hadn't many complaints. If the great passion of his life was destined to be unrequited, at least he knew what it was like to care that much. If getting drawn into Brodie Farrell's orbit meant that sometimes he got hurt, it also meant he never got bored. For a secondary school maths teacher, that's an achievement in itself.

And if he had no children of his own, he took a lot of pleasure in Brodie's. He counted her seven-year-old daughter Paddy among his best friends. And he pushed her peaceable, strange-eyed baby in his Grand Prix buggy along the Promenade with a sense of contentment surprising in a single man of twenty-nine.

Then fate stepped in again.

As they ambled along the front he was pointing out the sights to Jonathan, blithely ignoring the facts that (a) Jonathan couldn't see any sights, and (b) at six months old he probably didn't care that Scandinavian pine is the correct wood to weatherboard a netting shed. But he liked listening to Daniel's voice—pleasant and light grey like his eyes—and Daniel was a born teacher, he liked talking, so the short walk from Shack Lane to the odd little house beside the ruined pier passed happily enough.

Right up to the point that their way was blocked by a man and a woman engaged in heated argument. At least, the woman was heated—red in the face and shouting. The man seemed mostly to be laughing at her. Once, when she leant angrily into his face, he pushed her away—not violently, but also without much regard.

It was none of Daniel's business. He didn't know either party. No one was getting hurt, and the road was quiet enough now the summer season had ended that it was no hazard to drop the buggy down the kerb for a few paces to pass them. He kept his eyes carefully averted and kept telling Jonathan about the problems of finding a builder who was interested in using traditional materials.

He almost made it. He was back on the pavement, with the argument behind him and his odd little home ahead, and all he had to do was keep walking. Then the woman yelled, 'I don't care *who* knows I slept with a Pakistani! It's *you* I feel the need to keep quiet about!' And the man hit her.

It wasn't exactly a haymaker. The woman staggered back but didn't fall. If it had been two young men—or even two young women—arguing on the footpath and one of them had slapped the other across the face like that, probably even Daniel would have managed to stay out of it. Probably. After all, he was pushing a buggy with a baby in it; and the woman was free to walk away and go to the police; and if she needed help there were other people around better equipped to offer it.

But Daniel Hood was raised by his grandfather and had old-fashioned views on a number of things. One was that men don't hit women. Not in public, not in private; not at all. And none of the other people on the Promenade was acknowledging what they'd seen. Daniel gave a resigned little sigh. He knew what was going to happen. It had happened before. But knowing altered nothing. A man on the tenth floor of a burning building knows what's going to happen when he hits the ground. But the point comes when he still has to jump.

He picked out a young couple with a child of their own and blocked their way with an apologetic smile. 'I'm sorry, but would you look after Jonathan for me? I shan't be a minute.' He turned away before they had the chance to object.

Which put him behind the man's right shoulder. He was taller than Daniel but not much: over his shoulder Daniel could see the woman, her face startled, one hand to her flaming cheek. Daniel cleared his throat. 'Excuse me.'

The man turned slowly, with the air of someone who wasn't accustomed to interruptions. His tone managed to inject offensiveness into a one-word query. 'What?'

'I'm sure that was a mistake,' said Daniel politely. 'You saw a fly on the lady's cheek and, aware of concerns that global warming might bring tropical diseases such as sleeping sickness and beri-beri to the south coast of England, thought it best to swat it before it could bite her. I'm sure if you apologised now no one would think any more about it.'

The man's brow gathered as he tried to process this new information. Not just what Daniel had said, but that Daniel had said it. In his eyes a war was going on between irritation, amusement and downright disbelief. '*What?*' he said again.

Daniel's pale eyes behind their thick glasses didn't blink. 'Apologise,' he said quietly. 'And then leave.'

The man glanced up and down the Promenade. The little confrontation was attracting interest in a way that the woman's plight had not. The couple with the child, and now Jonathan, had edged within earshot; two middle-aged women walking their dogs had stopped, sturdy bodies rigid with curiosity; a group of boys on bikes had gathered round to jeer whoever seemed to be losing. In all probability the man could have flattened Daniel with a single blow; but with so many witnesses that was unlikely to be the end of the matter. In his eyes irritation was giving way to anger and a very personal dislike, and his voice to a low growl. 'I don't think you have any idea who I am.'

'You're right,' Daniel agreed readily. 'I have no idea who you are. But I know *what* you are. Whatever you call it, if it looks like a rat and it smells like a rat and it behaves like a rat, it's a rat.'

The impulse to smash his fists into the solemn bespectacled face and damn the consequences was almost overwhelming. The muscles of the man's back, shoulders and arms twitched as the old primitive in his brain told them to act and the smarter new bit urged caution. The colour rose in his sallow cheeks as his heart thumped and the oxygen packing his blood remained unneeded.

Another minute and the primitive would have won, and Daniel would have been sitting on a pavement with a bloody nose. Again. But the woman had had the moment she needed to gather her shock-scattered wits, and she came back fierce and defensive. Admittedly, she didn't know what the young man with the yellow hair and the expression of a slightly simple choirboy was capable of. But she did know what the man who'd struck her was capable of.

'Lay a finger on him, Joe,' she said sharply, 'and we'll finish this in the police station. I don't have a problem with that. I don't expect he'—she indicated Daniel with a jerk of her head—'has a problem with that. You have a problem with that?'

The man sneered at her. But the muscles of his arms stopped twitching. The old primitive had lost the argument, for now. He turned back to his car, something long and silver parked along the Promenade, kicking one of the bikes out of his way to get at it. The couple with the buggy were in the way too. He wasn't quite angry enough to kick a baby into touch, but he did snarl at it.

And got the shock of his life when it looked back at him.

He stood there frozen with surprise until the woman pushed herself between him and the buggy and broke the spell. As if she didn't even trust him with someone else's baby.

The man shook his head as if to dislodge an unwelcome thought, and got into the back of his car. But the woman wasn't quite done with him. As the driver went to move off she leant into the rear window. 'Do as I ask. Or I swear to God you'll be sorry.'

The car drove off while she was still leaning on the door.

By now Daniel had retrieved Jonathan. He waited patiently while the woman composed herself and turned back to him. 'Are you all right?' he asked.

She flashed him a brave if somewhat shaky smile. She was older than he'd first thought—fifteen years older than him. The ebullient red-brown hair tamed by a gypsy scarf and the calf-length dress under her hip-length jacket had misled him. *But then,* he thought, *that's not how young women dress now. It's how they dressed when she was twenty.*

'I'm fine,' she said. Her voice held a husky note that made Daniel blink. 'You?'

He smiled. 'Me too. And Jonathan positively enjoyed it.' He introduced himself and the baby.

'Faith Stretton,' responded the woman. 'Listen, thanks for your help. I think it would have got nasty if you hadn't intervened.'

'It *did* get nasty,' said Daniel. 'Who is he?'

Faith Stretton looked surprised. 'You mean, you really don't know?' Daniel shook his head. 'Keep it that way,' she advised him. 'His name's Joe Loomis, and he's bad news. And I wish someone had told me that twenty years ago.'

Daniel stared. 'That's Joe Loomis?'

Faith's head tipped, bird-like, to one side. 'You've heard of him, then.'

'Yes. He… Yes. In a way.'

There was another car parked on the front: not long and silver but an elderly capacious estate with a liberal dusting of road dirt. She went to get in. But her hand was shaking too much to make the key fit. Gently Daniel took it from her. 'You shouldn't be driving. My house is just here—come in for a coffee and wash your face, then I'll call you a taxi.'

'That's very kind of you, Mr Hood,' she said gratefully. 'If it wouldn't be too much trouble.' But when she looked around her eyebrows gathered in a frown. 'What house?' He pointed. 'Oh. I always thought that was derelict.' When she heard herself she flushed again with embarrassment.

Daniel chuckled, quite untroubled. 'It cost me a small fortune to get that look. The builder kept wanting to cheer it up for me. He wanted to paint it in blue and white stripes, like a beach hut.' Pushing the buggy ahead of him he steered Faith Stretton down the shingle shore to the iron steps which led up to his front door.

FIVE

AFTER DEACON LEFT IT WAS PAST noon. Brodie weighed up the chances of someone coming by in the next hour to offer her a valuable commission, and deciding they were slim she shut up shop. She thought she'd take Daniel out to lunch and quiz him discreetly about all the mistakes he was making with her business. She didn't know she was as discreet as a drill sergeant faced with a platoon of raw recruits.

Daniel had company. Brodie heard a woman's voice as she climbed the steps to his front door. (Extending the little house had done nothing to regularise its odd layout. Though there was now a second bedroom on the ground floor, the living room was still on the first floor so you had to climb in order to knock at the door.)

In ruthlessly honest moments, Brodie acknowledged that she had ambivalent feelings about Daniel. He was her best friend, her twin soul; he was not and could never be her lover, she simply couldn't see him in that light; at the same time, her heart refused to set him free to find someone who might feel about him the way he felt about Brodie. So when she found him alone—in this context a baby doesn't count—with an unexpected woman, she felt a surge of something bilious which she declined to identify but which anyone else would have recognised as jealousy. She gave a perfunctory knock and didn't wait for an invitation before walking in.

It didn't appear to be a secret tryst she was interrupting. Daniel was cradling the baby on his knee. The woman was holding a pack of frozen peas to her cheek.

'Brodie.' He didn't even sound surprised. Experience had

taught him that, if something was afoot, it wasn't going to be afoot for long before Brodie became involved.

'Daniel.' He heard the brittle note that implies the words, *You want to tell me what's going on here?*

He edged up on the sofa to make room for her. 'Ms Stretton had a bit of a shock. I brought her in for a coffee. Faith, this is my friend and Jonathan's mum, Mrs Brodie Farrell.'

Faith lowered the peas long enough to nod a greeting; and Brodie, returning it, couldn't see anything to justify a cold compress. 'Anything I can do?' she asked coolly.

'Thanks, but no,' said Faith. 'My son's picking me up in a few minutes. Daniel thought I shouldn't drive. I'll come back for the car later.'

'Yes? Fine,' said Brodie dismissively. Faith Stretton looked at her in surprise, but didn't care enough to pursue it.

Before any of them had to break the awkward silence there was the sound from outside of the shingle shifting under approaching feet. A man's feet: Daniel had lived here long enough to know from the chiming of the tiny stones displaced. The iron steps rang too, then a large fist was rapping on the door.

Daniel gave Jonathan to his mother and went to open it. 'Mr Stretton? Come in, your mother's in here.'

Before she rose to meet him, Brodie noticed that Faith Stretton not only stopped nursing the pack of peas but dropped it to the back of the sofa and pulled a cushion over it. 'It's all right, love, I'm fine. I just had…a bit of an accident. I'll tell you on the way home.'

When he saw Stretton, Daniel understood what he'd heard on the Promenade. Faith's son was Eurasian, a strong broad-shouldered man in his mid-twenties, as tall as Brodie with fine dark hair and chocolate-coloured eyes. A good-looking man, though right now he looked anxious as well. 'An accident? In the car?'

'Not exactly.' Faith linked her arm through her son's and steered him back towards the steps. 'Please, take me home. I've imposed on my Good Samaritan long enough.' She cast Daniel a grateful smile. 'Thanks again. It would have been even more unpleasant but for you. I'll see you again, I hope?'

Daniel gave an amiable shrug. 'I'm always around.'

He and Brodie went out onto the iron gallery from which he did his star-gazing to see the Strettons off. Probably before they were out of earshot Brodie demanded, 'Well, what have I missed? Who gave her the shiner?'

But Daniel made her wait until they were back inside with the door closed before he told her.

Her first instinct was to try to connect this event to what had gone before. But the closer she peered, the more it looked like coincidence. An odd coincidence, to be sure, but it's the nature of coincidence to look like a mind at work. The likeliest explanation was simply that Joe Loomis was a bad man with more than one enemy. That was probably the only connection between Deacon's inquiry and Faith Stretton's bruised face.

In particular, Brodie saw no reason to read into this new episode any danger to herself and her baby. 'He might go and throw stones at Faith Stretton's window. He might even come and throw them at yours. I can't see why he'd throw them at mine.'

'No,' said Daniel slowly. He was playing the action again at the back of his eyes. 'But he recognised Jonathan.'

At that Brodie felt a little stab of anxiety. But it was maternal instinct in overdrive. So what if Joe Loomis saw Deacon's baby on the Promenade? He could hardly hold the infant to blame for Faith's outburst. If Jonathan was in any danger from Loomis—and Brodie didn't think he was, but if he was—it was because Jack Deacon was after him, not because the child was passing when an old flame made a scene.

She forced a gruff little laugh. 'He must think he's being haunted by white-eyed babies. Well—not for much longer.'

Daniel looked at her with compassion. She had the child tucked up in his buggy again, ready to leave. As she bent over him, Daniel could almost see the dome of protectiveness she spread over him like a magnetosphere. He said softly, 'It's all right to grieve, you know.'

Brodie didn't glance at him. But for a second she froze, and the room froze around her. Her lips quivered, then firmed. 'I know. But not yet. If I deal with this as a practical problem, I can get through it. I'll grieve later. When he's safe.' Then she straightened up with a bright, brittle smile. 'Lunch? My treat.'

OCCASIONALLY PEOPLE wandered into The Rose in Rye Lane looking for a white wine spritzer and a pork pie. Mostly they left quite quickly. From the outside it looked a good copy of an ancient seafarers' inn, all black oak and tarry barrels and enough dust for Blind Pew to have lost his Black Spot in. But actually, it was all real. The oak was real, the age was real, the dust was real, even the disreputable customers leaning on the bar and the ferrety Wally Briggs serving them were all the genuine article. The Rose wasn't expensively modelled on a set from *Treasure Island*. Downstairs it was exactly what it appeared, a dark and dirty old pub with a clientele to match. Upstairs it was a brothel. The point about the painted sign above the door was not that it depicted a clipper's figurehead but that it showed a buxom young woman parting company with her chemise.

The sign was probably the best thing about The Rose. It wasn't even the best cathouse in Dimmock. The décor was grimy, the drinks were sour and the girls were tired. The place really only had two things to recommend it. One was a sea view from the front rooms upstairs. The other was a decent snooker table.

Joe Loomis was a good snooker player. If he'd wanted—if he hadn't opted for work that paid better and didn't require hours of practice—he could have turned professional. His first job had been as a bouncer in a pool hall, and he'd promised himself a decent table when he had somewhere to put it. He preferred snooker to pool because he thought it was classier.

He was playing tonight. He'd been sitting alone in his office at the back, bringing his books up to date—he kept two sets of accounts: one for the tax man, one for himself—and brooding darkly on Dimmock CID's most unreasonable determination to restrain his trade. But Wally had put his head round the door to say a couple of punters were playing for money, and Joe never had so much that he didn't want more. Within ten minutes the first fifty-pound note had changed hands.

The third fifty-pound note was just about to change hands when the door of The Rose opened and shut, the bar fell suddenly quiet, and someone said, 'It's closing time.'

Wally checked the clock above the optics. 'No, there's another ten…'

'It's closing time,' Jack Deacon said again, a weight in his voice like wet sand in a sock; and as a man the customers rose and headed obediently for the door. Every one of them knew him. Most of them had had their collars felt at some point in the last ten years. In normal circumstances this did not incline them to do as he asked; but there was a timbre in his voice and a steely look in his eye that warned them these were not normal circumstances. They drank up and left, and only one muttered, 'Catch you later, Joe,' over his shoulder as he went.

Where five minutes before a dozen men had been drinking, now there were Joe Loomis and Jack Deacon and Wally Briggs. And this didn't concern Wally Briggs.

Deacon came straight to the point. 'You've been bothering my family, Joe.'

Loomis wasn't surprised to see him. He'd meant for what he said to Brodie to get back to Deacon, and he'd known Deacon wouldn't take it well. But he was gambling that, after Deacon had done the shouting and stamping around required of a man in his position, he'd remember that his partner and child were still out there and so was Joe, and he'd back off. An armed truce: no harm, no foul. Joe Loomis knew a lot about men like himself. He didn't know much about men like Deacon.

Loomis thought he might be in for a bloody nose. He thought

it was worth it if afterwards Deacon decided to harass someone else. He thought that Deacon coming here showed his plan was working, and all he had to worry about now was getting through the next five minutes with his front teeth intact.

He tried for injured innocence. 'I haven't been bothering anybody, Mr Deacon. I bumped into Mrs Farrell at the hospital. I admired her baby. Where's the harm in that?'

Here's a tip: don't feign innocence in front of an irritable senior detective. They have enough trouble believing in genuine innocence. Deacon's brow lowered like a portcullis. Loomis had to remind himself that they were in his pub, and if he shouted two or three men would storm in here. Knowing that should have made him feel safer than it did.

Deacon's voice was so low that it rumbled—like an elephant's, or the voice of a storm. 'You know, I know and Mrs Farrell knows exactly what you had in mind. Don't insult my intelligence by pretending it was anything other than a threat.'

Loomis had the sense to keep quiet. He didn't need to speak. His point had been made.

After a moment the detective nodded. It seemed his business was all but done. He let his attention stray to the snooker table. 'You any good at this?'

'Not bad, Mr Deacon,' said Loomis modestly. 'Fancy a game?'

Deacon shook his heavy head. 'No patience with little balls. I used to play rugby, but I had to stop.'

Loomis pretended sympathy. 'The knees?'

Deacon nodded. 'In a way. I kept breaking other people's.'

Loomis, too, knew when he was being threatened. 'I thought there were rules against that…'

'Oh, there are,' agreed Deacon. 'I'm a big believer in rules. No low punches, no high tackles—and no bringing people's families into professional disputes.' He looked Loomis full in the eye. 'Don't do it again, Joe. If you did, I'd have to do something about it.'

Loomis wriggled a little shrug that was meant, *I don't know what you're talking about, really I don't, but if I did I expect I'd agree with every word of it.* 'I'm sorry if there's been some misunderstanding…'

Deacon smiled. He didn't do it very often, and this is why— it frightened children, it frightened villains and it set dogs barking half a street away. It wasn't a nice smile. 'No misunderstanding, Joe. We understand one another perfectly. Oh.' He reached for the cue Loomis had left lying on the table. 'I know one thing about snooker.'

'Yes? What?'

It wasn't that long since Deacon gave up playing rugby. He could still move astonishingly fast if the incentive was there. He had his arm around Loomis's throat, pinning the smaller man to his bulky body, and the tip of the cue up his right nostril before Loomis realised what he intended. He tried to yell but couldn't manage more than a strangled squawk. Even someone listening at the keyhole wouldn't have heard it.

'I know,' said Deacon deliberately, 'that the tip of a snooker cue, if propelled with enough force, will go straight up someone's nose into their brain. At which point they stop worrying about minor details like whether they'll be celebrating Christmas in Parkhurst.'

Joe Loomis was too scared even to struggle. Logically he knew that Dimmock's senior detective was not going to commit cold-blooded murder in the public bar of the victim's own hostelry. But his instincts told him that if something happened to startle Deacon, or if someone jogged his elbow, Loomis was just centimetres from being spoon-fed for the rest of his life. He froze rigid in Deacon's embrace. He could feel the big man's heart thumping.

As quickly as Deacon had grabbed him he let Loomis go, spilling him carelessly onto the table. He put the cue back in the rack. 'So, like I say,' he said conversationally, 'no misunderstanding. You didn't threaten Brodie, and I haven't been here. It must have been three other people.' And with that he walked out of The Rose and into the dark.

SIX

EVENTS MOVED QUICKLY, which suited Brodie fine. The less time she had to think about this the better. She trusted the advice she was getting, it accorded with her own best instincts, and if Deacon felt otherwise he hadn't said so. Now all she wanted was to have the operation over and Jonathan safely home again, and to start enjoying him free of the worries that had beset her since the day of his birth.

Even so, the summons came quicker than she was expecting. She'd had a bag packed for days. A favourite toy, a favourite blanket—things that would feel and smell the same when the baby woke up unable to see them. She'd also prepared a few necessities for herself, though she was determined not to do the whole anxious-mother-hovering-over-cot thing. Right now Jonathan needed Anne Millership more than he needed his parents.

'I might go into the office for a couple of hours,' she said to Deacon in the car.

He started so violently he almost ran into the back of a bus. *'Now?'*

'Not now,' said Brodie, in what she thought was a reasonable manner. 'After he goes down to theatre. It's going to take a while, and if we sit staring at one another it'll feel even longer. Let's do shifts. I'll stick around while you go to work for a couple of hours, and you can stay while I do.'

It was getting dangerous, driving in one direction while staring in the other. Deacon stopped the car on a double yellow line. 'I'm not going to work,' he said with a kind of forcible restraint. 'I'm waiting until my son's operation is over and he's recovering. However long that takes.'

'OK,' said Brodie negligently. 'Then you take the first shift. You've got my number, I'm five minutes away if anything happens. I'll be back before he's out of theatre.'

Deacon couldn't believe what he was hearing. 'Brodie— your baby is having an operation to remove his eyes. And you want to work on your VAT returns?'

She shrugged irritably. 'There's nothing I can do at the hospital except worry. In the office I can take my mind off it, at least for a while. Don't look at me like that, Jack. You deal with this your way, let me deal with it mine.'

He shook his head and steered back into the traffic. His voice was thick. 'I will never understand you as long as I live.'

'I know,' she said tartly. 'Isn't it a good job we aren't married?'

That shut him up. It always did.

In fact it was harder to leave than she'd expected. She carried Jonathan down to the theatre and held him in her arms while the anaesthetic took effect, only parting with him after he was asleep. She'd been afraid, thinking about it before, that she'd break down at that point. It was half the reason she'd wanted to be on her own, striding swiftly towards the busy anonymity of the car park where no one would see her cry. For some reason this mattered to her.

But when the moment came, the ties that bound them—not much longer than the umbilicus that had bound them for nine months—kept her close to the door that had shut between them. She wasn't crying. But all her muscles were clenched tight, because all her instincts were to do the one thing she mustn't do: barge through that door, grab her child and run.

In the end it was Deacon who steered her gently and firmly away. He sat her down in the waiting area, and sat beside her saying nothing until he saw the defensive rigidity of her long body begin to soften. Then he stood up. 'I'll bring some coffee. Stay here.' He caught her eye and said it again. '*Stay* here.'

He knew where every coffee machine in Dimmock General was located. He headed for the one under the stairs that was known only to staff and the occasional Munchausen's patient, and was back inside two minutes. Still he was mildly surprised to find she'd waited.

They drank the coffee in silence. When it was done Deacon looked at his watch, and was astonished to find a scant fifteen minutes had passed since he'd given up his son to the surgeon.

Brodie said quietly, 'He'll be all right, you know.'

'Yes. Of course he will.' Deacon looked at his watch again. Sixteen minutes.

For two hours this was what they did: look at their watches, get coffee, watch it go cold, look at their watches again. Brodie never found herself in tears. But nor, in the event, did she feel the urge to leave. There was nothing she could do here, but she could be here. She did that.

After two hours they stopped checking their watches—and, in Deacon's case, tapping it impatiently—and started watching the corridor that led to the theatres. That was the way news would come. Every time someone in theatre scrubs appeared, both of them tensed. But a lot of people wear scrubs in a big general hospital, and none of them had news of Jonathan.

Until finally one had. It was Anne Millership: Brodie recognised her immediately despite the anonymous outfit. She was on her feet, Deacon right behind her.

Millership's smile was reassuring. 'He's in recovery. It went fine—copybook, no complications. He's a sturdy little lad. He'll sleep the rest of today, and tomorrow he'll wake up.'

'Can we see him?' asked Deacon—in the tone of voice he used when he was investigating a spate of muggings and the suspect's mother was standing between him and a bedroom door. Brodie made a note to be amused later.

Dr Millership shook her head. 'There's not a lot of point. Between dressings and monitors, there's not much baby showing. You'll only upset yourselves, and there's no need.

He's doing well. Tomorrow morning you'll be able to see how well he's doing.'

'How did the operation go? Did you get all of the…?' Brodie looked at him in surprise as Deacon struggled with the word *cancer.*

'The operation went well,' said Millership confidently. 'Both tumours came away cleanly. We'll keep monitoring, of course, but I'm well pleased. One thing you should know. It was absolutely the right decision. If we'd left them, six months from now he'd have been in trouble.'

Brodie felt chill fingers stroke her spine. But that, she reminded herself, was good news. The doctor's advice, and her own instincts, had been right. In all probability today's work had saved a little life.

They walked out to Deacon's car. 'The office?' he asked. His voice was low.

She shook her head wearily. 'Home.'

She asked him in but was glad he declined. They were both too shattered by the day's events to want to chat.

The lights in her flat were on. Brodie had arranged with her upstairs neighbour to collect Paddy from school, but when she got inside it wasn't Marta babysitting, it was Daniel.

'I hope you don't mind,' he said, shamefaced. 'I couldn't settle to anything. I shut the office and came over here to wait. How is he?'

Brodie dropped into a chair. 'OK. Everything went well. He's sleeping if off, so I thought I'd come home.' She stretched out her arms and Paddy, quiet for once, slipped into them, creeping onto her knee. 'Be with my big kid.'

Daniel stood up. 'OK. Well, I'll leave you to it…'

She didn't let him finish. 'Oh, sit down again, you're not going anywhere. If we're all going to sit around moping all evening we might as well do it together. Let me get my breath back and I'll make some supper.' But she didn't. She fell asleep in the chair, her daughter cradled in her lap.

It was after nine when she woke. Paddy was gone, and some-one had spread a duvet over her. 'Daniel?'

He was in the kitchen. He'd fed Paddy and got her off to bed while her mother slept; now he was doing the washing-up. 'I'm here. Everything's fine.'

She thought for a moment. 'I'm going to call the hospital.'

There was nothing new. Jonathan was sleeping soundly, all his readings optimal. When she relayed the information to Daniel he looked as relieved as she felt.

Which reminded her that Jonathan had another parent, and it wasn't Daniel, and Deacon was undoubtedly as anxious as she was. Brodie picked up the phone again. 'I'm going to call Jack.'

Before she'd even dialled she thought better of it. 'No, I'm not. I've spent all day indoors: I need some fresh air. I think I'll drive over there. I'll be back in an hour. Will you stay with Paddy?'

'Of course,' said Daniel.

Though the evening was cold she drove with the window down, the chill breeze reviving her. She found herself feeling more positive about the day's events, even buoyant. Her son had his operation behind him: from now on he'd be a little better every day instead of a little worse.

The first reaction of people who didn't know him well was surprise at where Deacon lived. He didn't seem to have the imagination, or the time, to have converted a utilitarian building into a home. But as they thought about it, these people, they realised it was a match made in estate-agency heaven. Where else *would* Jack Deacon live except Dimmock's old jail? A low Georgian building, it squatted under the looming mass of the Firestone Cliffs, and still had bars at the windows.

In fact, not much conversion had been attempted. An earlier owner had installed plumbing and electricity, and at intervals Deacon slapped on another coat of limewash. Otherwise he lived in it much as its original inhabitants had, except that nobody locked him in at night.

There was a yard and outbuildings round the back—the jail

was also the town's pound—but Deacon invariably parked his
car at the front door, ready for a quick departure if news came
of a juicy crime. It wasn't there now. Sometimes he called in
at The Belted Galloway on his way home, leaving the car there
and walking the last quarter of a mile. So Brodie went to the
door and knocked.

She had a key, and Deacon would have expected her to use
it. She tended not to because that wasn't the kind of relationship they had. If she'd asked he'd have moved in with her
tomorrow, or sold this grim little house that could have been
made for him and bought something bland and child-friendly
and suitable for a family of four. But until she was ready to make
that kind of commitment she felt she had no right to let herself
into his home. The time might come, but it hadn't come yet.

He didn't answer her knock. Perhaps he was still at work,
making up the hours lost at the hospital. Brodie breathed
heavily, her breath momentarily visible as a white cloud on the
night air. But in fact it pleased her to know that kind of thing
mattered to him. He was a good man. He wasn't always a nice
man, but she could forgive a lot of his mistakes because she
knew that he was fundamentally a good, brave, honest, decent
man. A man who did the job he was paid for even when no one
expected him to.

She thought about phoning him—but then he'd feel obliged
to leave what he was doing to come and cheer her up. And there
was no need. She glanced at her watch. Nine-thirty-five. Shack
Lane was two minutes away. An unworthy thought occurred to
her. She could go into the office for half an hour in the absolute
confidence that Daniel wouldn't catch her checking up on him.

She knew it was childish. She knew that if she asked to go
over the last month's business with him—the approaches he'd
received, how many had turned into commissions, how he'd
carried them out and with what degree of success—he'd do it,
and if he felt hurt that she didn't trust him he'd keep it to himself.

But she was conscious that Daniel was doing her much more

of a favour by working for her than she was by employing him.
And she didn't want to seem ungrateful. Her business would
have folded if he hadn't stepped into the breach when she found
she was pregnant; and stayed here, holding the fort, when it
became evident that Jonathan's problems would make it hard
to find him a childminder. She'd expected to be back to work
before now. Instead of which that day seemed remoter now than
it had a year ago. So she couldn't afford to offend Daniel. But
also, she didn't want to offend him. She owed him.

But if he didn't *know* she was rooting around in his in tray…

She put the kettle on. But it boiled unnoticed as she studied
the evidence for the prosecution.

He was a tidy worker. That didn't surprise her, and it did
make it easier for her to follow the paper trail. Some of his commissions were well advanced, others in the early stages. More
cranberry glass for Mrs. Campbell-Wheeler; a Reliant Robin
for a television company; photographs from the early years of
a local boatyard to illustrate a commemorative volume for its
forthcoming centenary. Brodie noted with approval the small
stack of invoices ready to post. She'd have to find a way of
praising his diligence that didn't make it patently obvious she'd
been spying on him.

Shack Lane wasn't a major thoroughfare even in Dimmock.
And in Dimmock, even major thoroughfares were growing
quiet by ten in the evening. So when she heard a footstep on
the pavement outside she knew it was someone looking for her.
Guilt sent her first thought shooting to Daniel. But she'd left
him looking after Paddy: wild horses wouldn't have brought
him out. More likely it was Deacon, on his way home now,
who'd spotted the light in her window and guessed what it
meant. She went to the door to meet him.

You can get spyholes for a front door, so you need never
open it without knowing what's on the other side. Brodie had
considered installing one, and dismissed the idea. She was in
business here, she was constantly admitting people she didn't

recognise—a covert glance at them first would tell her nothing. And instinct warned her that the best defence against most dangers is the kind of tangible self-confidence that's undermined by nervous measures like spyholes.

So she got no warning, when she opened the door, that it wasn't Deacon on her front step with his knuckles raised to knock. It wasn't a potential customer either, or a passing friend looking for her or for Daniel. It was Joe Loomis, and he was drunk.

He staggered in as she opened the door, and Brodie gave a little breathy yelp of alarm. But immediately she knew she was in no danger from him. He could hardly stay on his feet. Unless he had a gun, and some superglue to keep the business end stuck to her anatomy, there was nothing he could do that she couldn't deal with. As the shock subsided she felt the surge of adrenalin diverting to its default function, which was anger.

'What the hell to you think you're doing here?' she demanded, her voice shaking with fury.

Loomis either couldn't remember or couldn't string enough words together to reply. He leant on one arm on the wall and shook his head slowly, as if trying to dislodge the fog without rattling his brain.

There wasn't much room in the entrance hall—there wasn't much room in the entire office—so Brodie squeezed past him to check outside. But he was alone. He must have given the minders the night off, assuming he could cope alone with a mother of two. *But in that case,* she wondered, *why the Dutch courage?*

She had to duck her head to snarl into his face. 'You've got ten seconds to leave under your own steam. After ten seconds I throw you out. Is that clear?' All the response she got was a mumble she couldn't interpret. She amended her ultimatum. 'Unless you fall over before your ten seconds is up, in which case I'll get Jack Deacon to help me throw you out.'

As if it wasn't bad enough that he'd given her a turn and was now cluttering up her doorway, he was also leaving dirty fingerprints on the wallpaper. It was a dark red flock, to go with the burgundy front door and the velvet curtain, so she hadn't noticed immediately; but he'd obviously been in the gutter on his way here and brought some of it with him. With a cluck of disgust she pulled out a tissue to try to mitigate the damage.

She stared in frozen disbelief as the tissue turned crimson.

She looked at him again. And smelt him. He didn't smell of drink; at least, not enough to explain his condition. His face was white and beaded with sweat, his eyes half-hooded, and his breath came fast and faint between his teeth. If it hadn't been Joe Loomis leaning on her wall, if she hadn't known who he was and what he was capable of and in consequence been just a little afraid of him, she'd have recognised shock the moment she saw him.

'Joe?' It didn't come naturally, calling a gangster by his first name, but anything else seemed odder. 'Are you hurt? Come and sit down. I'll get some help.'

But he didn't want to move. And when she put her arm round him to steer him inside he let out a thin wail that shivered along her nerve endings.

'What is it?' she gasped. 'Where are you hurt?'

He couldn't tell her. But when she looked closer she saw it emerging from his left armpit like a monstrous growth: the hilt of a knife, gleaming softly with mother-of-pearl. However long the blade was, the whole thing was buried inside him. The blood was a thick flood down his left side, soaking the cloth of his jacket and his trouser-leg and even his shoe, pooling on the navy carpet where he stood.

'Oh, dear God!' She hesitated no longer but flew inside and snatched the phone off her desk. She didn't even phone Deacon: she called 999 and asked for an ambulance and the police. Then she hurried back to Loomis.

'They're on their way,' she said, speaking clearly into his face. 'Five minutes, that's all. You just have to hang on for five minutes. You need to lie down, Joe—right here, just slide down the wall and…'

It may have been her help and guidance; it might simply have been that he'd lost the strength to stay upright. He did as she said, slumping slowly to the floor. Brodie suspected he'd have been better lying flat, but he stayed hunched up against the wall and she was afraid of doing him more damage by moving him. She fetched cushions from the office sofa and tried to make him comfortable. When her fingers brushed accidentally against the knife, Loomis keened again.

'I'm sorry! I'm sorry,' she stammered, recoiling.

Under the thin moustache his bloodless lips were moving. Brodie couldn't hear a word. She leant closer. 'What happened? Who did this to you?'

She thought he was trying to say something. His eyes closed with the effort to concentrate. 'D...D...'

'A doctor?' she hazarded. 'The ambulance is on its way. Just a few minutes more, Joe. They'll sort you out—you'll be all right. Just hang on in there.'

Joe Loomis shook his head. There were things he knew that she didn't, and one of them may well have been how long it takes to bleed to death. He tried again, as hard as he could, but still couldn't get past that stuttered initial.

Brodie nodded encouragingly. 'Detectives? Yes, I called them too, they're on their way. Tell me who stabbed you, Joe. They're going to want to know who did this.'

But he'd said all he could. The life was pouring out of him: five minutes was just too long to wait. He reached for her wrist with long thin fingers, and she hadn't the heart to deny him whatever comfort that gave him. He was a bad man; but perhaps even bad men shouldn't die alone. 'D...' he whispered just once more, and then he was still.

So was Brodie. Not because a dead man gripped her wrist but because fear gripped her heart. She'd asked him who killed him, and he'd told her. Someone beginning with D.

SEVEN

BRODIE'S OFFICE WAS BARELY BIG enough for the job it had to do normally. If clients arrived two at a time they had to share the sofa, and it wasn't a big sofa.

When Charlie Voss arrived, with Detective Constable Jill Meadows in tow, one of them had to step over Joe Loomis and view the scene from the other side. When the ambulance arrived a minute later, paramedics and their kit pouring into the narrow hall, the detectives were displaced into the inner office and Brodie was shunted into the kitchen.

They had to try—even for Joe Loomis they had to try—but Brodie was as sure as she could be that the man had gone where no warrant could follow. Within a couple of minutes the paramedics had reached the same conclusion. But anyone can be wrong, and Loomis was alive too recently to be sure he was irretrievable. They threw him onto a stretcher and into the back of the ambulance, and screeched off with the siren wailing.

Which made a bit more space in Brodie's office. Conveniently, because when Jack Deacon arrived as the ambulance wailed off he expanded with sheer fury. Because Voss was handy, Voss took the brunt of it.

'You let them take my body? You let them *take* my body?'

Voss, who'd been shouted at before, remained stoic. 'No one was prepared to say it *was* a body. They thought there was just a chance it was still a patient.'

'It was Joe Loomis,' yelled Deacon. 'Even if he *was* alive, who's going to want their blood donations wasted on *him*?'

Charlie Voss filled the same role for Deacon that Jiminy

Cricket filled for Pinocchio. If he'd thought it mattered he'd have put the moral argument and risked his superior's wrath. But nothing hung on it. Voss had seen a number of dead bodies by now—not as many as Deacon, but more than most people—and Loomis had looked as dead as any of them. He wasn't coming back. The paramedics could in good conscience have left him on Brodie's hall carpet to have a chalk-line drawn round him.

But in fact Deacon was yelling from habit. No vital evidence had been compromised by the decision to give Joe Loomis one last chance. Brodie's office may have been where he died but it wasn't where he met his death. When Deacon looked he found Loomis had left a route-map marked with his own blood. It ended on the bit of waste ground behind Shack Lane which Brodie used as a car park. Loomis's car was there, painted like a Comanche steed with bloody palm prints.

By now Billy Mills, the Scene of Crime Officer, had arrived, resplendent in his white suit, and he set about preserving it. He was the only man in Dimmock—possibly the only man in Christendom—brave enough to shoo Jack Deacon away from a bloodstain.

Finally Deacon remembered Brodie. She'd been barricaded in the kitchen when he arrived. When he returned to the office he found her sitting at her desk.

She saw him ponder how to approach this. Where to start. The angel that looks after fools and children steered him in the right direction so that at least his first question was the correct one. 'Are you all right?'

She nodded weakly. 'Fine.'

'He didn't hurt you. That's not…?' He was indicating her hand.

She looked, without surprise or any other emotion. 'It's not my blood. He didn't touch me. I touched him.'

'We found where it happened. In the car park. Was his car there when you arrived?' Brodie shook her head. 'What time was that?'

'About twenty to ten.'

'Were you expecting him?'

Her brow lowered at that. 'You mean, did I come here to meet him? No, Jack, I didn't. Actually I came to see you, but you weren't at home. I came in here to'—she did a bit of editing—'pass a few minutes, then I heard him outside. I thought that was you too, so I opened the door and he fell inside. I thought he was drunk. Until I saw the knife.'

'Would he have known you were here?'

Brodie shrugged. 'He could have seen the light on. I suppose he just might have been following me, but it's a hell of a coincidence— he was following me and someone was following him. Maybe he used the car park to meet someone because it's dark and it's private and nine times out of ten there's no one there after the shops shut.'

Deacon nodded slowly. It seemed probable. And when Loomis found himself in need of help, he staggered into Shack Lane and made for the first light he saw. 'You didn't see anyone else? Someone running off? Or a car?'

'Nothing.' She gave an apologetic little smile. 'But then, I was kind of occupied.'

'Did he say anything?'

Brodie hesitated. 'He…was trying to.'

'What did he say? A name? Think, Brodie. Maybe he was trying to name his killer.'

'Maybe he was,' she agreed softly. 'He was certainly trying to say something. He tried several times before he died.'

'A word? A syllable? A letter? Give me something, for God's sake.'

She thought before she replied, but she didn't think long. They weren't alone. Voss was there, so was Jill Meadows. Both of them would have heard what she said.

'I'm sorry, Jack. I couldn't make any sense of it.'

BY THE TIME SHE GOT HOME Daniel was asleep on her sofa. Brodie didn't want to disturb him, quietly turned the lights off. But then, instead of going to bed, after she'd checked that

Paddy, too, was sleeping she went back to the living room and curled up in one of the armchairs. Even unconscious, Daniel was balm for her soul.

And this was how they'd met—almost four years ago—him lying unconscious and her watching over him, worried sick and feeling guilty. And if the reason for it was different, the feeling of guilt was the same.

Perhaps because he always—so far as Brodie knew—slept alone, awareness of her proximity percolated down to him and Daniel stirred. Her dark-adjusted eyes saw him groping blindly for the lamp switch and his glasses.

'It's all right,' she said quietly, 'it's only me.' Because there had been an occasion when he'd woken like this, not alone, and it had been people who hurt him.

By the time he had his glasses on he was fully functional and his concern was only for her. 'Are you all right?'

She smiled tiredly. 'I'm fine.'

Which was what she'd told Deacon. Unlike Deacon, though, Daniel didn't move on to his next question but waited for her to answer this one honestly.

'No,' she admitted then, 'not fine. But not hurt. By the time he got to me he wasn't capable of hurting anyone. At least, not…'

She hadn't decided to tell him. In fact, she'd decided not to—Daniel's devotion to the truth made him a difficult confidant on occasions when Brodie considered dishonesty the best policy. But a part of her needed to share her fears. And Daniel never needed an open door, just a crack to push against.

He leant forward earnestly, mild grey eyes searching her face. 'Not what? Not physically?'

Brodie shrugged uncomfortably. 'He wasn't a nice man, Daniel. Dimmock's a better place without him.'

'Except that now there's a killer running round. I'm not sure that's much better.'

'Oh, it is,' she said, too quickly. 'Believe me.'

Daniel went on watching her, not crowding her into confiding in him, just somehow expecting it. These last three years, of course. If they'd taught him anything, it was that he and Brodie couldn't keep secrets from one another and shouldn't try. 'Of course I believe you. What's bothering me is how you know.'

If she really hadn't wanted to talk about this she'd have been more careful. She let out a long, broken sigh. 'I spy, with my little eye, someone beginning with D…'

Whatever she was doing, Daniel knew it wasn't a game. 'Me,' he said immediately.

Brodie shook her head. 'You've got an alibi. You were with Paddy. Someone else.'

She saw the answer lodge in his head, widening his eyes. '*Jack?*'

So she told him everything. Everything she hadn't told Deacon. Which was also a recurring theme these last three years.

Daniel heard her out, then shook his yellow head firmly. 'No. Jack wouldn't do that.'

'Sometimes,' she whispered, 'Jack's not a nice man either.'

She didn't need to remind Daniel. At the same time, he wasn't emotionally involved; or not with Deacon. 'Jack has a temper,' he acknowledged. 'One day he could kill someone. But it would be with his fists, not a knife.'

'He was angry. Loomis threatened us—me and Jonathan. I think, if he thought we were in danger…'

'That he'd ambush him in a dark alley and stick a knife in him?' But he did her the courtesy of thinking about it. Perhaps it wasn't absurd. Deacon had had as difficult a day as Brodie had. She'd gone home to friends and family: he'd gone home alone. Was it beyond the bounds of possibility that the fury at Loomis's threats had built up in him until he could sit still no longer, had to do something about it?

With a knife?

'You need to talk to Jack.'

Brodie's eyes flared in alarm. 'No!'

'You have to. He needs to know what Loomis said.'

'He didn't say anything! He couldn't. He couldn't get past the first letter…'

'Which was a D. Jack may have had a motive of sorts, but if he was at Battle Alley between nine-thirty and ten, someone else killed Joe Loomis. And Jack needs to know that Loomis recognised his killer, and tried to say his name.'

Brodie mumbled something that he didn't hear. 'Hm?'

'I said, Jack wasn't at Battle Alley. Charlie Voss arrived five minutes before Jack did.'

'OK, so he was at home. Someone may have seen him leaving.'

'He wasn't at home earlier. Not when I knocked on his door twenty minutes earlier.'

'Then…' Daniel couldn't come up with another alternative. 'He could have been anywhere. He could have been in The Belted Galloway. He could have been walking on the Promenade. Wherever he was, he can probably prove it if he knows he has to.'

She made one last attempt at avoidance. 'No one else was there. No one else heard it. If we're sure Jack's not responsible for this, why bring it up at all?'

It really didn't need saying but he said it anyway. 'Because it's evidence. Because at some point that one letter Loomis was able to say will mean something to someone. Because Jack needs to play this with a full deck. And because he doesn't need you to compromise yourself to protect him.'

Brodie was nodding slowly. She managed a wry smile. 'You're right. I'll call him in the morning.'

'Call him now.'

WHEN HE ASKED WHAT she wanted, she refused to say over the phone. He asked if it was important enough to drag him away from a murder inquiry and she said it was. Naturally, his first thought flew to his son.

When Brodie met him on the front steps of the big Victorian house in Chiffney Road, his big craggy face was fish-belly white. 'There's some news? What? Is he all right? Brodie, tell me!'

It was reassuring that his first thought, his immediate fear, was not for himself. 'Jonathan's fine, Jack. This is about Loomis. Come inside, we need to talk.'

Daniel offered to leave them to it. But both for their different reasons wanted him to stay: Brodie because his quiet presence helped her stay focused, restrained her from saying things she didn't mean and would later regret; and Deacon because this was business and he'd listen to anything anyone had to contribute. And he knew from bitter experience that Brodie would have discussed this with her friend before coming to him. Daniel might remember details she'd forgotten.

But since he was there, Daniel made a point of watching Deacon's face as Brodie spoke. So far as he could tell the big man never saw the punch-line coming. Even after she'd repeated Loomis's abbreviated last words, it took a moment for their import to sink in.

Then his jaw dropped slowly. His heavy, intelligent eyes saucered. There was a long silence, perhaps half a minute, while he considered the implications of what she'd said. Then:

'You thought I stabbed him.'

'No!' And then, 'Really, I didn't. But in all the circumstances I didn't feel I could keep it to myself. Only I didn't want to say anything in front of anyone else, just in case...'

'In case I'd lured Joe Loomis to a dark car park and buried a knife in his armpit?' finished Deacon tartly. 'Thanks, Brodie. I appreciate your consideration.'

'Don't be like that.' Increasingly she was convinced it was a coincidence, that Deacon had nothing to hide. For the moment it made her tone conciliatory. Before long, though, that would give way to the annoyance that was her default position. 'I was shocked and scared. I wasn't thinking clearly. I needed to talk to you alone first. Just in case. I'm sorry if that feels like an insult. It wasn't meant as one. I just... Dead or alive, Joe Loomis means nothing to me. You do. I wanted to be sure.'

But Deacon was shaking his head in disbelief. 'You really

thought I could have settled an argument like that. With a knife, in the dark. We've known each other for three and a half years, Brodie. We've had a child together. And you haven't the foggiest notion who I am.'

Daniel winced at the spark in Brodie's eye that said she'd done apologetic quite long enough. 'Or maybe,' she retorted, 'I have a better idea who you are than you do. Don't tell me you've never got physical with a thug before. Don't tell me you've never got physical with *this* thug before! I didn't think it was likely—I thought it was possible. I didn't want to put something on record if there was even an outside chance it would come back to haunt you. Hate me for that if you must. All I knew was what Loomis had said, and that you weren't at home when I knocked at your door and you weren't with Charlie Voss when *he* arrived. Motive and opportunity. *You'd* have suspected you in the same circumstances!'

Her angry eyes held his. Deacon broke the contact first. He looked away and, shoving his hands deep in his trouser pockets, muttered something to the wall.

'What?' demanded Brodie.

'I said, I was at the hospital. In the car park, underneath his window. I didn't go in because I knew there was nothing I could do. But I wanted to be near him for a bit. That's where I was when Charlie called.'

He'd managed to startle her to silence. He was not a sentimental man. He was in many ways the antithesis of a family man. That act of quiet devotion told Brodie something about Jack Deacon that she hadn't discovered even in three and a half years; and reminded her what it was about him that she liked enough to put up with all the things that she didn't. She bowed her head. 'What do you want me to do?'

He didn't hesitate. 'I want you to call Charlie Voss right now. He's still at the office. Tell him everything.'

EIGHT

AT FIRST THE INVESTIGATION proceeded along well-worn lines. Forensics. Interviews with people who might, but probably hadn't, seen anything significant. The establishment of a timeline.

The autopsy revealed, unsurprisingly, that Joe Loomis died of a knife driven deep enough into his armpit to sever two major arteries. The assailant was a right-handed man who'd attacked him from the front—or, just possibly, a left-handed man who'd attacked him from the rear.

The knife itself had a ten-centimetre blade and a fancy mother-of-pearl handle that was covered with fingerprints. Unfortunately, half of them were Joe's and the others were Brodie's. No record survived of the killer's hand.

Diligent police work—in this case, looming threateningly over Wally Briggs—established that the knife belonged to Loomis. That he always carried it, and often pulled it out to emphasise a point or simply to toy with. Raising the distinct, and unsurprising, possibility that Joe himself started the altercation that led to his death.

So far, so predictable. The murder of a decent law-abiding citizen is extremely unusual; of someone like Joe Loomis, less so. People who knew him only casually spent the next few days nodding sagely at one another and agreeing it had only been a matter of time. There was no real public interest in who'd done it. The general feeling on the darker streets of Dimmock was that someone had been bound to do it sooner or later.

Events then took an unexpected turn, signalled by the visit to Battle Alley Police Station of Assistant Chief Constable

(Crime) Emily Blake. She arrived without warning and asked to see Detective Superintendent Deacon, and the radio room became a flurry of activity as people who generally had no idea where he was until a complaint came in tried to track him down.

In fact he wasn't far away—up on the Firestone Cliffs, interviewing the town's other significant unconvicted criminal, Terry Walsh, about the death of his rival. Deacon and Walsh were old sparring partners: Walsh didn't mind when Deacon said he'd have to take a rain check and hurried away.

Driving back to town, he tried to work out which infringement of police procedure he was being accused of now. Not because he hadn't infringed any, but because he infringed lots of them all the time. It made it hard to prepare a defence. He didn't want to find himself explaining to the ACC some incident she didn't actually know about.

Probably, he thought, *it was the snooker cue.* Joe may not have reported it widely—it had done little for his reputation—but there was a witness, and the bartender had little reason to be discreet after his employer was dead. All it needed was for the story to have reached someone with an interest in embarrassing Deacon— professionally: personally he remembered the moment with enormous satisfaction—and there was a wide choice. One of them could easily have made an anonymous phone call to Division.

He toyed briefly, hurrying up the back steps from the car park, with the idea of claiming it was an accident. That he and Loomis were enjoying a friendly game of snooker when he got a thick contact and the tip shot off the ball and up Joe's nose… But Emily Blake hadn't reached the pinnacle of her profession by believing lies, even lies that were better constructed than that one. Deacon thought she'd staple his ear to his own blotter for trying it. He settled for the defence that had served him best down the years: silence and a dumb expression until he knew who had what on him.

And in a way it served him this time too. She didn't know about the snooker cue. She did know about Joe Loomis's last words.

And the way she knew was that he'd reported them. He'd made a full report of everything he knew or could surmise, then he'd got on with his job which was trying to find the killer. Not for a moment did he expect what was now on its way.

'Jack'—if she'd been about to tear strips off him she'd have given him his full title—'when you were making this report, didn't it occur to you how it was going to look?'

Deacon genuinely didn't understand. He frowned. 'You mean, my typing…?'

Blake breathed heavily at him. She was a couple of years younger than him, and better groomed, but otherwise they had a lot in common. She'd come up through the ranks by sheer hard work and a leavening of inspiration, and was one of the few people that Deacon acknowledged as being capable of doing his job as well as he did. It might have been tacit, but they'd always had a lot of respect for one another.

'No,' she said with heavy patience, 'not the typing. The fact that, to someone who doesn't know you—or rather, who knows you but not as well as I do—it might look as if Joe Loomis with his dying breath was trying to accuse you.'

Deacon dismissed that with an impatient hand. 'Of course he wasn't accusing me. He may or may not have been trying to accuse someone, but since he never got further than the first letter and we don't have holding cells for one twenty-sixth of the population, I didn't think it would be much help until we had a suspect.'

'The problem is,' explained Blake carefully, 'to certain sections of the community it might look as if you *are* the suspect.'

It was only then that he realised she was treating this seriously. His frown turned to a deep lowering scowl. 'Me? You think I stabbed Joe Loomis?'

Now the ACC was dismissive. 'Of course I don't think that. Even those at Division who are not fully paid up members of your fan club don't think it. What we do think is that it looks bad, having you as Senior Investigating Officer when Joe Public might reasonably wonder if you *should* be a suspect. That this particular investigation should be led by someone else.'

Deacon stared at her in frank astonishment. 'Who? Charlie Voss is a *sergeant*. But if I go on gardening leave, he's still the best detective in Dimmock.'

Blake shook her head. Her hair was as long as Brodie's, but tamed in a businesslike pleat at the back of her head. 'It's not just a question of rank. As you well know, we have reservations about DS Voss's judgement. Well, he's a young man, he may prove us wrong—but he's not getting the chance to do it on a murder investigation where his own superintendent could be in the frame. We'll bus someone in.'

'Who?' Already outraged, Deacon was ready to be offended as well.

'No one you know,' said Blake briskly. 'Someone with no connections to Dimmock. Someone you've never worked with and who doesn't owe you any favours. I want this clearly above board.'

Deacon didn't know what to say. If Blake had been a man he'd have got inventively unpleasant; but after that he'd have come to where he was now, seeing that she was probably right and it was stupid of him not to have expected this. 'Do you want me off the premises?'

Her point won, Blake could afford a little kindness. 'That's really up to you, Jack. If you think you can spend a couple of weeks looking for pirate videos and stolen bicycles, and stay out of the Loomis investigation, do it. But my guess is you'd be happier off-stage. Do a bit of decorating. Take Mrs Farrell on holiday.'

Deacon regarded her coldly. 'Our son is in hospital. Neither of us is in the mood for seeing the Costa del Something-or-other from an inflatable banana.'

Blake winced. That was something she hadn't known. 'Jack, I'm sorry. I hadn't heard. Is he all right—is he going to be all right?'

'Hopefully,' conceded Deacon. He brought her up to date,

briefly. 'He's getting over the op pretty well. We're hoping to get him home tomorrow.'

'Good. I hope he keeps doing well.' Blake nodded decisively. 'So you'll need some time off anyway. Give Mrs Farrell my best wishes. Tell her I'll get you back to work as soon as I can.' And when Deacon gave a puzzled frown the ACC responded with a little feminist chuckle.

DETECTIVE INSPECTOR Dave Salmon arrived on Friday morning. Voss helped him to move in, then brought him up to speed on the investigation. But it was a cool welcome. Salmon thought he understood. He was here because Division had decided to act on a wildly improbable suspicion: naturally Deacon's sergeant was resentful. But that was, in fact, only half the story. Last time Voss was loaned to a visiting fireman he got his fingers burnt. He was a professional, he'd work on what he was told to with who he was told to—but this time he'd be watching his back.

Salmon was younger than Deacon, a man in his late thirties with dark hair and a tan he appeared to put slightly too much effort into. He had a pleasant voice and an easy manner, but Voss detected a certain intensity in his dark brown eyes. Bush telegraph said he'd been working in London, in which case he probably thought Dimmock would be a sinecure. Voss hid a little smirk. He'd learn.

As soon as he was settled in, Salmon wanted to interview Brodie. He asked her to meet him at Shack Lane and talk him through what happened.

The waspishness she felt on meeting him surprised Brodie. She'd known someone else was taking over the inquiry; and she could see why; and she'd told Deacon it was a good idea, that any suspicions about his role would be dissipated quicker by someone else's investigation than his own. So she wasn't sure why her hackles rose when DI Salmon walked into her office. A kind of misplaced loyalty to Deacon, she supposed. She tried not to let it affect her dealings with him.

She'd already made a full statement, and Salmon had read it. All Brodie had to do was recount what had happened— and not enough time had passed for her to have trouble re- membering. She wasn't sure there was that much time left to the world.

Daniel offered to leave them alone. But Salmon had read his statement too, about the altercation at the seafront, and asked him to stay. He heard them out in attentive silence, only moving into the hall when Brodie described going to the door.

He wanted to establish exactly what Loomis had been trying to say as he bled to death on her carpet. Brodie couldn't tell him, only what she thought he'd been trying to say.

'Something beginning with D,' echoed Salmon.

'I think so,' nodded Brodie.

'Only think?'

She bristled and shrugged. 'He was dying. He wasn't ex- pressing himself very clearly. I think it was a D. But I'm not a qualified lip-reader.'

'But you thought it was a D.' Salmon's gaze on her was steady. 'And you said so.'

That pricked her conscience. 'Yes.' Her jaw came up, defi- antly. 'But I wouldn't have done if I'd thought he was accusing Jack Deacon.'

With the ghost of a smile Salmon turned to Daniel. 'I don't suppose you had any reason to murder Mr Loomis?'

Daniel flicked him a little smile in return. 'I have an alibi. I was baby-sitting.'

The detective nodded. One letter wasn't much of a case against anyone: not Daniel and not Deacon. 'Going back to the squabble you witnessed at the Promenade. You say it was Ms Stretton who was angry with Loomis, not the other way round?'

'That's how it looked. I think she wanted him to do some- thing for her. Or maybe to *not* do something for her. She needed a favour, and he thought it was funny.'

'And then he hit her.'

Daniel was at pains to be fair even to Joe Loomis. 'He slapped her. It wasn't a right hook.'

'*Why* did he slap her? If he was amused.'

'I think she insulted him.'

'What did she say?'

Daniel remembered word for word. 'That she didn't care who knew she'd slept with a Pakistani. That it was Loomis she felt the need to keep quiet about.'

Salmon blinked. 'Do you know what she meant by that?'

Daniel had thought it was pretty obvious. 'Her son is of mixed race. I think she was saying she didn't mind who knew that she'd had a relationship with his father, she just hoped no one knew she'd also had one with Loomis. Twenty years ago.'

The Inspector raised an eyebrow. 'You know the family?'

'No. But she told me. That she wished she'd known twenty years ago what she knew now. And I met her son when he picked her up at my house.'

'And he's a Pakistani?'

'No, Inspector,' said Daniel, with that quiet precision that Brodie recognised as marking one of his lines in the sand, 'he's English. He's also Eurasian.'

Salmon nodded. 'I'll need to talk to Faith Stretton. Do you know where I'd find her?'

'I'm sorry, I don't.'

Charlie Voss, who had contributed nothing since performing the introductions, cleared his throat. 'They have a cottage up on the Downs. On the far side of Cheyne Warren.'

'They?'

'The Strettons. Faith, and her son and daughter. No husband or partner in evidence.'

'OK, Sergeant,' said Salmon, 'we'll pay them a visit next. Thanks for your time, Mrs Farrell—Mr Hood. I'll try not to bother you again, but if I have to…'

'We're always around,' said Daniel.

The detectives returned to their car, parked exactly where Joe Loomis had parked his. Voss drove.

'This cottage,' said Salmon. 'Is it far?'

'Twenty minutes,' said Voss. 'Do you want to phone ahead and check she's in?'

It's not good policy to warn suspects that you're on your way, but not many career criminals are murdered by middle-aged women and Salmon thought he'd take the risk.

A man answered. 'I'm afraid my mother's out at the moment. This is Dev Stretton—can I help?'

MOST OF THE COTTAGES scattered across the Three Downs had been built for agricultural workers, at a time when agricultural work meant walking eleven miles behind a plough to break one acre of ground. Now it meant sitting in forty thousand pounds' worth of machinery that did the job inside the hour and there were more cottages than labourers. Faith Stretton bought this one when she had two young children to raise and only her skill as a potter to raise them on. She'd converted a stable into a workshop, installed a kiln and set about supplying the souvenir and curio shops of the south coast with mugs and salad bowls.

Today, though, she'd strayed from her wheel. She still wasn't home when the policemen arrived. Her son met them at the door. So presumably the Land Rover outside, with Crichton Construction stencilled on the doors, was his.

He seemed unsure what they wanted. Detective Inspector Salmon was deliberately vague, in case the way his mind turned might tell them something. Mostly a man is anxious about what he feels guilty about.

But Stretton only shrugged. 'You're wasting your time on me. I didn't see the incident—my mother only called me after it was over.'

Dave Salmon nodded equably. 'So I understand. Well, we're still trying to get a picture of where Joe Loomis was and what he was doing in the days before his death. We're not sure what's relevant at this point so we're talking to everyone.' He jerked his head towards the drive. 'You're in the construction industry?'

'I'm a civil engineer.'

'Bridges, dams—that kind of thing?'

'Sometimes. Right now we're laying a main sewer out to Menner Down.'

'Ah. The glamorous end of the business.'

Stretton didn't return his smile. That didn't mean he was guilty of something: on the whole, innocent people are more nervous around the police than those who see them regularly. The inspector cleared his throat. 'Your mother knew Joe Loomis years ago, didn't she?'

Her son bristled just perceptibly. 'She made a statement about this.'

'Yes, she did. But finding a murderer involves getting a lot of people to repeat themselves.'

'I'm sure she'll repeat it as often as you need,' said Stretton calmly. 'Shall I phone her and tell her to hurry home?'

'In a minute,' said Salmon. 'Mr Stretton, you're not telling me you don't know about her relationship with Loomis?'

'I know about it. I don't remember it. I was a small child. My mother didn't share the secrets of her love life with me then, and she doesn't now.'

'She didn't tell you about the incident on the seafront?'

Stretton shrugged. 'Yes, of course—but… Look, it was unpleasant, but neither of us thought we'd end up answering police questions about it. She bumped into an old flame, they argued, she snapped at him and he slapped her. Not very edifying, but not that big a deal.'

'He assaulted her.' It was Charlie Voss's first contribution. 'She could have told us. We'd have thought it was a big deal.'

'Well, maybe.' Stretton's tone was sceptical. 'Or maybe someone would have made a note on a blotter and she'd never have heard any more about it. Anyway, she didn't want to see Loomis in court. She wanted never to see him again. It was personal, and it was over. It never occurred to us that a week later he'd be dead. I don't think he died because he slapped my mother's face, Inspector. Nothing I've read in anybody's bible suggests God's a feminist.'

'What was the argument about?' asked Salmon.

But Stretton shook his head. His expression was turning slowly—not stubborn, exactly, more immovable. Without saying or doing anything objectionable he was able to convey the message that they could lean on him as much as they liked, it wasn't going to get them anywhere. 'I told you, I wasn't there.'

'Didn't she tell you?'

'No.'

'And you didn't ask?'

'No. It was personal. And these are questions you should be asking her. My mother's an honest woman, she'll tell you anything you want to know, so don't ask me to talk behind her back.'

Salmon shrugged, unabashed. 'My whole job's about asking people to talk behind one another's backs. So your mother knew Loomis twenty years ago but they didn't stay friends. Did she see him much in that time?'

'Dimmock's a small town,' Stretton said loftily, 'it would be odd if they didn't clap eyes on one another in twenty years. He never came here. If she met him, she never said anything to me.'

'Did she talk about him?'

Shutters closed behind Stretton's eyes. 'Hardly at all, and never with any fondness. It was a mistake. She was glad to put it behind her.'

They were interrupted by the sound of a car pulling up outside, then by voices. The front door of the cottage opened and Faith Stretton came in, accompanied by her daughter. There wasn't much of a family resemblance between any of the three of them. Dev was dark and six-foot tall, Faith was tawny and sturdy, the girl was a slender brunette.

Faith's lips framed a question mark. 'Dev?'

'They're policemen, Ma. They want to ask you about Joe Loomis.'

'Ah.' She thought for a moment, then turned to her daughter. 'Evie, take the shopping upstairs.' Then, laughing at the girl's expression: 'Don't look so worried! They're not here to arrest me. I haven't done anything you can get arrested for. Dev, give her a hand. I swear to God, we've emptied the shops the length and breadth of Dimmock.'

When they were alone she addressed the detectives. 'Now, what can I tell you about the late and unlamented slimeball that you don't already know?'

Voss blinked. Nicely spoken middle-aged women don't usually call people slimeballs even when it's accurate.

Detective Inspector Salmon met her honesty with some of his own. 'I don't know what you were arguing about that resulted in him striking you in a public street.'

'Ghosts,' said Faith Stretton succinctly. 'The shade of a foolish girl not much older than my own daughter, who thought she could polish up a rough diamond and broke both her nails and her heart.'

'Then why did you want to see him again?' asked Salmon.

'I didn't. I bumped into him on the Promenade. If there'd been time to cross the road I would have done. But he'd seen me and I wouldn't give him the satisfaction of running away.'

'What did he say?'

'He asked after Dev. I told him he was fine—qualified and working for a big company. I enjoyed telling him that,' she added with a secret smile.

'Why?'

She shrugged. 'I'm a proud mother.'

'Yes. And?'

She tipped her head to one side like a bird, assessing him. 'Inspector, you've met my son. I presume you noticed he's what polite people call mixed-race and the less couth call a half-breed? Well, Joe Loomis was always less couth than anyone else. When I first knew him he resented the fact that I had a half-Asian child, and the intervening years did nothing to mellow him. Within about three sentences he was getting nasty. I should have walked away. Instead I told him I didn't care who knew I'd once had an Asian lover as long as no one knew I'd slept with Joe! That's when he hit me.'

Which was pretty much the story told by the witness statements. 'Did you see him after that?'

Faith Stretton shook her head. 'A week later he was dead. And all I could think was, *Good riddance.*'

DS Voss said, 'Mr Loomis was stabbed around ten o'clock on Tuesday evening. Do you remember what you were doing about then?'

'Tuesday night? I was here, filling the kiln. But I don't think I can prove it.' She caught him with a faintly provocative eye. 'Do I need to?'

'Not at the moment,' said Salmon cheerfully. 'What about Dev? Was he here too?'

'You mean, can we alibi one another? As a matter of fact he was. Working in the upstairs office. The same as he does every weekday evening. My son works hard, Inspector. He works long hours, and when he gets home he's tired and he's dirty. He goes out socialising on a Saturday night, maybe sees friends on a Sunday. But weekday evenings he's at home, either on the computer or with his feet up in front of the television.'

'What about you?' asked Voss. 'Do you do much socialising?'

'Even less than Dev,' she said cheerfully. 'I've got a good excuse for not bothering any more. I'm forty-six.'

Voss said, 'If Dev was on the computer we can probably substantiate that.'

'If you feel the need to,' said Faith tartly.

He met her gaze unblinking and gave her the stock answer. 'Routine procedure, Ms Stretton. It always helps to eliminate people from an inquiry.'

Back in the car he said to Salmon, 'Do you want to get his hard drive checked?'

Salmon was thinking. 'He doesn't seem the type. Except…'

Voss nodded. 'D-d-d-Dev,' he said.

NINE

'D-D-D-DEV,' STAMMERED Inspector Salmon pensively. 'D-d-d-Deacon.'

'D-d-d-Dave,' murmured Charlie Voss. They'd stopped off for a ploughman's lunch in The Belted Galloway.

Dave Salmon chuckled. 'It's not much to base a case on, is it?'

'Unless the D in question happens to be a policeman,' said Voss sourly.

'Well—the senior investigating officer,' amended Salmon reasonably. 'Look, Charlie—you know Deacon's a good cop, I know Deacon's a good cop, Division knows Deacon's a good cop. Nobody thinks he killed Joe Loomis. But it would look like a conflict of interests if he handled this one. Deacon was after Loomis and Loomis was fighting back. It had already got personal, it was about to get nasty. And Deacon can't prove where he was when Loomis walked sideways into a sharp instrument. Of course it means nothing—except that he should leave this one to someone else.'

'You.'

'Us,' Salmon corrected him. 'You know the people involved, I know something about murder. We'll find out who did it, then I can go home and Jack Deacon can come back to work. Thus pleasing both my wife and Mr Deacon's partner.'

That made Voss grin. Salmon may not have been in Dimmock long but he'd quickly tuned in to how things worked here. Of course, he'd spoken to Deacon and interviewed Brodie. Perhaps it didn't take a world-class detective to see the potential for friction.

Last time Voss was liaison between Dimmock CID and a blow-in he was made the scapegoat when things went pear-shaped. He didn't want to be put in that position again. It wasn't just that Deacon was the devil he knew: he trusted the man. Voss wasn't blind to his faults, but his virtues were important ones. Honesty. Integrity. Strength of mind, character and purpose. It would be a while before Voss let himself be swayed by charm again. He said, 'What do you do in London?'

'Recently, this,' said Salmon, attacking his Stilton baguette. (The landlord at The Belted Galloway had a rather up-market view of what ploughmen ate.) 'Filling in where a gap has opened up. Illness, injury, guys taking gardening leave—basically, any job that no one else wants, send Salmon. Murder today, drugs tomorrow, counter-terrorism next week. You know the biggest problem? You're never anywhere long enough to work out which coffee machine makes the best brew.'

'Shouldn't be a problem here,' sniffed Voss. 'We've only got one, and it doesn't know the difference between coffee and oxtail soup.' He backed up a step. 'Counter-terrorism?'

Salmon nodded calmly. 'That's really my field. I was at it for four years. And then my face got known and it was safer to move on. Now I'm the Scotland Yard equivalent of a supply teacher.'

You can't have a casual conversation with a detective. They always read between the lines. Voss's eyes widened. 'You were undercover?'

'Yes.'

'Wasn't that…pretty scary?'

'Yes,' said Salmon again, briefly. He changed the subject. 'How's the CCTV scan coming?'

Voss rolled his eyes. 'The way they always do—slowly. I got Jill Meadows to take over this morning, but I'll have to relieve her when we go back. It's like air traffic control: no one should be expected to do it for too long.'

'Anything helpful?'

'Not yet. I've got Loomis leaving The Rose and getting into

his car at quarter to ten. He heads up Rye Lane, we see him driving down Fisher Hill, then he disappears off the monitors. There are no cameras covering Shack Lane. But the timings suggest he went straight to the car park and met whoever killed him.'

'So who do we see driving *up* Fisher Hill at quarter to ten?'

Voss shrugged. 'A lot of people. It's the main thoroughfare at that end of town. If you're on the Promenade and heading for a pub, chances are you'll go up Fisher Hill. There's also a gym, and you can go that way to the cash machine outside the bank. We're not going to ID every car on the tapes. The best we can do is look for one behaving suspiciously.'

Salmon nodded. That was realistic. CCTV has proved an excellent weapon in combating town-centre crime but—like every weapon—it has limitations. You can see where someone goes, as long as they stay in sight of the cameras. You can see who they speak to; you can't know what they say. And a man who obeyed speed limits and traffic lights after burying a knife in someone's lung might never be spotted.

'Go back a bit,' suggested the DI, 'see who Loomis met earlier that evening. Maybe he went to Shack Lane as a consequence of some earlier event.'

In fact Voss had already thought of that. It was what he was planning to do this afternoon.

WHEN DIVISION SENT Deacon on gardening leave they overlooked the fact that he didn't have a garden. So while it was possible to replace him as senior investigating officer on the Loomis case, they couldn't stop him thinking about it.

Brodie didn't mind him thinking about it. She minded him thinking about it in her house, getting under her feet. He'd come with her this morning to bring Jonathan home, and she understood that he wanted to spend time with his son. He was holding him now. But he held the baby as he might have stacked a bunch of box-files on his knee, and instead of talking to him, or even about him, rumbled on endlessly about what was now somebody else's murder case. Jonathan didn't seem to mind. He smiled complacently, his bandaged eyes shaded by the peak of a jaunty cap, but Brodie minded for him. Her fund of patience, never bottomless, was lower by the day.

Oblivious of her train of thought, Deacon tried stammering his way through all the options. He'd bought a pocket dictionary to help. 'D-d-d-drugs?'

'That's a dying man's last utterance?' said Brodie sceptically. 'That cost him blood and just about the last breath he ever drew? He might try that hard to give us a name but not the motive. Especially when it tells us nothing new. *Everyone* knows Joe Loomis was dealing drugs. The dogs in the street knew it. How would it help to tell us that?'

Deacon nodded. It was something no one would ever say. The dying man would have tried to name his killer if he could; or if he didn't know his name, to describe him or something distinctive about him. 'The make of his car? Daihatsu, Daewoo—Daimler?'

Brodie shook her head. 'That's pretty sophisticated thinking for a man running on empty. It would be nice if he'd got the number plate, but I don't think it was that either. I think he knew his killer. I think we were right all along—we're looking for someone beginning with D.'

Deacon had got used to the fact that Brodie treated his work as if it were a little sideline of hers, to be toyed with when she had time. He no longer bothered to challenge that *we*. 'D-d-d…Dev?'

'Dev Stretton is a man in his mid-twenties,' said Brodie dismissively, 'Loomis would call him by his surname. If he'd stabbed Loomis, Joe would have been stammering *S-s-s…*'

It wasn't enough for Deacon to eliminate Stretton from his inquiries. But he knew Brodie was better at people than he was, and she had a good instinct for probabilities. 'There just aren't that many names beginning with D,' he complained. 'There's me. There's Daniel. There's Dev Stretton. I can't think of anyone else.'

Brodie turned just long enough to fix him with a cool eye. 'If that's your choice, your next move is clear. Arrest yourself on suspicion. Lock yourself up where you'll no longer be a danger to the public. And in the meantime, will you for pity's sake straighten that child's hat? He can't see a thing…'

The echo of the words rocked her heart, filling the room like the dust and silence after an explosion. Her cheeks drew thin and her eyes filled with grief and tears.

Clumsy as always in the realm of the emotions, Deacon tried to comfort her. 'Don't punish yourself. It isn't—it doesn't… It doesn't matter. We're going to say stupid things. This is new to us. We haven't had a blind child before. Hell, I haven't had a *child* before—I don't know what you say when they're normal!'

The problem with Jack Deacon and Brodie Farrell as a couple—their tragedy, if you like—was that they only worked as lovers, not as friends. If they'd been two men, or two women, they'd never have sought out one another's company. They didn't understand one another well enough, had no tolerance for each other's mistakes. The same words from Daniel would have drawn a watery smile and Brodie would have taken reassurance from them. But on Deacon's lips they grated, and she slapped at the irritation like swatting a wasp.

'Don't tell me how to feel! You want to know what's normal? *This* is normal—hurting when they hurt, wanting to protect them from harm, feeling a failure when you can't. He's just a little boy, Jack! He's six months old. He was born with problems, and things have gone downhill since. And it *feels* like it's my fault. For eight months everything he is, everything he's ever going to be, was in my hands. And I couldn't keep him safe. Just eight months. He didn't even demand the full penalty that the law allows—he gave me time off for bad behaviour! But in those eight months I conceived him when I didn't mean to, I exposed him to the dangers of my business and I damn near delivered him in someone's front garden! Don't tell me none of that matters. My son is suffering, and is going to go on suffering, because of it.'

'Even if all that was true,' said Deacon quietly, 'it still wouldn't make it your fault. He played contraception roulette and won—which made him one in a thousand before he was even born. It also makes him a determined little sod: remember that. And we don't know if the attack on you was responsible for his eyes or not. Even if it was, so what? The drugs weren't something jolly for the weekend, they were an attempt on your life. You did nothing wrong. You didn't even do anything stupid. You were unlucky. Jonathan was unlucky. Now we deal with it. But we don't deal with it by blaming ourselves.'

But Brodie wouldn't be mollified. 'That's easy for you to say. You can walk away tomorrow. Any time this gets too difficult you can find yourself a nice serial killer somewhere and switch off. I can't. Jonathan can't. We're in it for the long haul. And yes, maybe that means I find it hard to be objective. I'm sorry to be such a bore.'

Deacon couldn't believe she'd used that against him. He'd have married her two years ago if she'd been willing. He tried very hard to marry her before Jonathan was born. The continued regularity of their situation was entirely her choice. It was impertinence on a jaw-dropping scale to accuse him of lack of commitment now.

'Brodie—I'm going nowhere,' he managed. 'I'm here for you, as long as you want me; and I'm here for Jonathan whether you want me or not. What do you want me to do—weep into my hanky every time I look at him? Of course I'm sorry he's got problems. But with or without them, he's my son and I love him. I love just sitting here with him on my knee, and if his stupid little hat falls in his face of course I'll straighten it. But I don't want to load everything that happens to us from now on with tragic significance because he's blind. He's not a burden, and he's not a freak. He's just a baby who can't see.'

By now Brodie was feeling ashamed of herself. Which

didn't help: she didn't handle self-criticism well, perhaps because she didn't practise enough. She should have been touched, not only by how he felt but that he would try to explain it to her. Deacon was a notoriously private man: saying what he just had must have been terribly difficult. But instead of applauding his effort Brodie felt diminished by it. As if parenthood was a competitive sport and there could only be one winner.

'I don't even know what you're doing here,' she snarled. 'A man died in my office—why aren't you out looking for the killer?'

She did know: he'd told her. Clinging on to his patience, he told her again. 'They wanted me off the case. *Because* he died in your office; and because he'd threatened you, and because of what you heard him say. D-d-d…'

Brodie had to grit her teeth quite hard to keep from screaming.

And then she had a stroke of absolute genius. Her whole face changed. She went from wanting to deck him with the iron and bury him under the patio to seeing hope for the future in the blink of an eye. 'Jack,' she said, and even her voice was different, 'you're not going anywhere for ten minutes, are you?'

Two sentences ago she'd been ready to throw him out. Deacon had every reason to be confused. 'No-o-o…'

'Good,' she beamed. 'Then will you look after Jonathan? I need to see Daniel.'

He might not have been in. The job took him out and about a lot. She didn't phone first because she couldn't face the disappointment if she'd got the answering machine. If he was out she could find something to do in the office while she waited for him to get back. It was better than listening to Deacon stammering.

Luck was with her. Daniel was on the phone. He raised an eyebrow in a slightly puzzled greeting but finished the call. He was on the scent of some cranberry glass for Mrs Campbell-Wheeler.

'Where's Jonathan?' he asked when he put the phone down.

'He's fine,' said Brodie airily. 'He's with his father. Daniel, I have a question for you. I want you to answer it honestly, not tell me what you think I want to hear. The question is, do you like doing this job?'

She'd succeeded in surprising him. Again. He had to think quite quickly to remember what he'd said when he asked her to trust him with her business. Because he almost never lied, it didn't come naturally. He'd said he needed a job, and she needed someone to cover her maternity leave, and could they kill two birds with one stone? He *hadn't* said that he'd already been offered the job he really wanted at Dimmock High School. That was the bit he had to avoid letting slip.

'Er…sure. I mean, it's not what I trained for, it maybe wouldn't have been my first choice, but it's interesting and I like working with you. Why?' he asked then, his face clouding. 'Am I making a mess of it?'

Brodie smiled. 'Of course you aren't. You've done what no one else could have done for me—kept it safe and ticking over while I couldn't be in two places at once. I'd have lost it without you, Daniel. I'd have had to shut the door and see everything I'd built fall down. I know it isn't what you want to do with your life. I'll always be grateful that you were willing to put your own hopes on hold till I was able to come back to work.'

He wasn't sure what she was telling him. 'You mean, now?'

She nodded. 'If we can sort out the details. I've imposed on you once: I'm not going to steamroller you now. If you're thoroughly enjoying the work I'll think again. But if you're not— if you're really only doing it because I needed you to…'

Like a mirage before a man dying in the desert, Daniel saw the image of a classroom, the scrawl of maths symbols on a board, floating in front of him, almost within reach. But if he snatched, would it disappear? And anyway, was it practical?

'Brodie—nothing's changed. You've still got a baby who needs looking after. What are you proposing to do—bring him to work with you? Cart him round the salerooms? Park him in a corner of the Public Records Office?'

Brodie beamed. 'Of course not. Jonathan will still need

looking after. But maybe he doesn't need me looking after him all the time now. Now he's had his op and hopefully he's on the mend, maybe he'd be just as happy with someone else.'

'Like who? Jack's not going to be on leave forever. They'll find out who killed Loomis, or at least eliminate Jack from the inquiry, and then he'll be back. And Jonathan's not just any baby. He needs special consideration. People whose voices he knows. Would he get that at a nursery, or with a childminder? Would you be happy with that?'

'No,' she admitted.

'Then who's going to look after him if you come back to work?'

You could have started forest fires with the sparkle in her eyes. 'I hope you are.'

TEN

'DON'T BE ABSURD!' exclaimed Daniel.

'What's absurd about it?' demanded Brodie. 'You like him, he likes you. You *don't* particularly like this job. I, on the other hand, love this job and—without wishing to sound ungrateful— I'm better at it than you. It makes sense for us to swap.'

'I'm not a childminder!'

'Neither's Marta, but she's had Paddy often enough. Come to that, so have you. You don't need qualifications to look after a child in its own home.'

'But...I don't *know* anything about babies. I teach secondary level maths. What am I supposed to do with a six-month-old baby?'

'Very basic maths?' hazarded Brodie. 'One rusk plus one rusk equals two rusks? Daniel, you don't have to do anything with him. Feed him. Change him. Talk to him. Stick him in his buggy and take him for walks. You've been doing all those things since he was born. All I'm suggesting now is that we make it official.'

'And what's Jack going to say?'

'Well—Jack's going to be a bit surprised,' conceded Brodie. 'Look, Jack's the problem. He's driving me insane. He's got nothing to do all day so he thinks he'll spend time with me. But all he talks about is work. I know every D in the *Oxford English Dictionary* by heart! Daniel, if you don't help me *I'm* going to end up committing murder!'

Daniel shook his yellow head in bemusement. 'I don't know what to say. Of course I don't mind looking after Jonathan. And yes, I know you run Looking for Something? better than I do. I was only ever filling in until you were able to come back. Only…will it work?'

'It'll work if we make it work,' insisted Brodie. 'You will do it, won't you? You'll enjoy it. You can take him to the Science Museum. You can set up your telescope and describe sunspots to him. He'll be much more interested than anyone else. Also, a pram is a real babe magnet.'

Daniel looked at her. She looked at Daniel. Finally he said, deadpan, 'And that's what you reckon I need, is it? A babe?'

Brodie shrugged. 'Couldn't hurt. Come on—what do you say?'

'You want me to be your nanny.'

She gave up the unequal struggle with a smile. 'I suppose that's exactly what I want. We could come up with another job description if that's what's bothering you. Home Management Executive. Infant Care Operative. Please, Daniel? Can we at least try it? For a week, say? Or until Jack goes back to work, whichever comes soonest.'

When it came right down to it, he could never refuse her anything, and both of them knew it. Brodie was aware that she exploited his love shamelessly, and always had it in mind to stop. But there was always one thing more he could do for her first.

Nor was Daniel blind to the way she used him. It wasn't cynical, it was just how she was—if there was something she needed she asked for it. He could always say no. But his relationship with Brodie had become the most important thing in his life. It was even when they both still thought of it as a friendship, and it still was now that—at least on his side—it had grown into something more. He didn't want to say no to her.

'I am *not,*' he said firmly, 'positively not, wearing a starched pinny.'

DETECTIVE SERGEANT Voss was slumped in front of the screen when DI Salmon checked in on him. Before his eyes flickered a succession of staccato images of such unsurpassed ordinariness they could have been used to cure insomnia.

Salmon came bearing coffee. 'Thought you might need a break.'

Voss accepted the polystyrene cup gratefully. Though it was impossible to make a positive ID, the liquid inside was brown and hot and if he told himself it was coffee it would taste something like coffee. Anyway, he appreciated the gesture. He leant back in his chair and stretched like an old stiff horse.

'Any luck?' asked Salmon.

'Yes,' said Voss, sipping cautiously, 'and no. I've got Loomis going into The Rose, I've got him coming out of The Rose. Four separate times on the day he died. Well, that's no surprise, it's where he worked. Except in the eyes of the licensing authority, which thinks it's owned by a respectable elderly aunt of his, The Rose was Joe Loomis's pub. As well as Joe, and what you might laughingly call his normal clientele, I've got other people coming and going. Some I recognise, some I don't. One of them may know what happened to him, but none of them's going to knock on our door and tell us about it.'

'Anyone beginning with D?'

Voss shook his ginger head. 'Not among those I recognise. We could send the others to the PNC, see if anybody knows them. Though the images aren't great. The camera's at the bottom end of Rye Lane.'

'Why? When one of the local godfathers is doing business out of the pub in the middle?'

'Because when it was positioned closer to The Rose it kept getting broken,' said Voss, deadpan. 'Local kids found out that a well-aimed bottle was worth twenty quid a time.'

'And now Loomis is dead and we may have a picture of his killer but the camera wasn't close enough to ID him,' said Dave Salmon with some satisfaction. 'Who says there is no God?' He pulled over a spare chair. 'Want to run some of the mystery men for me?'

Voss's fingers skipped over the keyboard. 'These are just that day. If you want to go back further, you'll need a more comfortable chair.'

In a perfect world, he thought, watching the little figures hurry Chaplinesque across his screen, DI Salmon would immediately stiffen, point and say, 'But that's Mac *The Knife* McManus, I arrested him last year for stabbing a rival East End gangster, he only got off on a technicality!' Unfortunately, real life is seldom that elegant. Most unidentified bystanders who might know something about a crime remain unidentified and you just have to hope they didn't know much.

Only a few minutes into their joint vigil, though, Salmon did indeed stiffen and lean closer to the screen. 'Can you run that again?' Voss obliged; and again when Salmon had watched the five-second clip intently and wanted to see it again. Then he had it frozen.

'Well now,' he said softly, 'what are you doing here?'

Voss looked at him in astonishment. 'You know him?'

'Yes,' said Salmon. If he remained in any doubt it didn't show. 'He's an Arab called Daoud. I first came across him when I was working with Drugs Squad.'

'Daoud with a D?' Voss gave a whistle. 'So it was about the drugs after all. Except…' He scrolled back and forward a few times. 'That isn't a drugs delivery. He doesn't take anything in and he doesn't bring anything out. Joe Loomis wouldn't be interested in the sort of quantities you can carry in your pockets.' He checked the time. 'That's a couple of hours before Joe got stabbed. If there was a problem with the deal, maybe they arranged to meet later on neutral ground. But then Joe would have taken backup…'

'I don't think it's anything to do with drugs,' said Dave Salmon.

Voss was surprised. 'What else? We know Loomis was distributing the stuff, and we know he was doing it from The Rose. And you know the mule. But he hadn't got the goods with him. He'd stashed them somewhere while he tried to renegotiate the price. Joe wouldn't play ball, and they ended up in a knife fight in which Joe came second.'

'Well—maybe,' said Salmon. 'If we're very, very lucky, maybe that's all it is.'

Voss felt his skin prickle and his blood slowly freeze. Dimmock was no metropolis: it wasn't often the war on drugs produced a salient here. If Battle Alley made a breakthrough and apprehended a murderous drug-runner, that was going to be a big news day. He was afraid to ask what Salmon suspected that was even bigger.

But he had to. 'And if we aren't that lucky?'

Salmon looked at him like a doctor breaking bad news. 'It's five or six years since I was with Drugs Squad. I moved on, so did Daoud. Last time I saw him he was up north, recruiting suicide bombers for al-Qaeda.'

ELEVEN

JACK DEACON HAD BEEN ACCUSED of many things in his time, but terrorism wasn't one of them. The new information cast the Loomis case in an entirely new light. He hadn't died because he'd made threatening noises about anyone's family. He'd died because somehow he'd got involved in the war on terror.

A couple of Saturday morning phone calls was all it took to bring Deacon's gardening leave to an abrupt end. Division recognised, however grudgingly, that if Dimmock was facing real danger there was no one better equipped or more ready to defend the dowdy old broad than Jack Deacon.

The first thing he did was pull Dave Salmon and Charlie Voss into his office and shut the door. 'Who knows what?'

'In this nick? You're looking at them,' said Salmon. 'As soon as I realised what we'd got I went straight up the line. You'll want to go public at some point, but when is your call.'

Deacon nodded his approval. 'Good. I don't want this descending into a general panic. I don't want Mrs Aziz's 8-Till-Late on the corner of Edgehill Road burnt to the ground because, although she speaks with a Birmingham accent, her father came from Pakistan. I don't want brown kids having to fight their way home from school and white kids scared to use the buses for fear of what's been left under a seat.'

'The problem is,' murmured Voss, 'if someone's intending to plant a bomb here, people need to know. General vigilance is our best chance of finding the terrorists before they're just an interesting pattern on the side of a broken building. Also, they have a right to know.'

Deacon scowled. Not because he disagreed with anything Voss had said, but because he didn't like hearing the words *people* and *rights* in the same sentence. To Deacon, the general public was an animal very much like a sheep. It needed looking after. It needed protecting. It needed saving from its own stupidity, and very often the task fell to him. But it only confused matters if you started thinking of it as an intelligent creature with rights and obligations. Deacon saw no reason to invest it with the former until it proved better at shouldering the latter.

'They'll panic. They'll all decide to visit their Auntie Vera in Wigan, and jam the road so none of them can go anywhere. And we won't be able to get about either.'

Salmon nodded. 'There's no such thing as an orderly evacuation. Once this is common knowledge, life won't go on as before except that people will be a bit more alert. There will be panic and there will be accidents. People will probably die. We want to be sure there's a credible threat before we go that route.'

'Is it our call?' asked Voss. 'Won't Division decide when to make the announcement?'

'Division are doing what we're doing right now,' rumbled Deacon: 'trying to work out if the threat justifies the cost of going public. Only, being Division, they'll talk a lot more, and break off for lunch, and they won't reach a consensus much before tonight. And hell, it's the weekend—they might not actually get round to doing anything before Monday morning. That's our time. Until they call the play, we can do our job without interference. Blowing yourself up in a built-up area is a crime, and we're detectives. Let's get out there and find ourselves a criminal.'

He raised a questioning eyebrow at DI Salmon. Though Deacon was the senior officer, Salmon was the expert in the field—if he'd argued for a different approach Deacon would listen. But Salmon only nodded.

Voss said, 'How many bodies do we need? Who are we going to tell?'

Deacon looked at him as if he was mad. 'Nobody. You know what it's like trying to keep a secret in a police station. We tell Uniform—hell, we tell the rest of CID—and yes, they'll be a big help getting out and door-stepping people. But most of them will tell their nearest and dearest first. They'll tell them not to pass it on, but they will. They'll tell their mothers and their sisters, and that nice old lady across the road who's going to need a taxi, and half an hour after I stand up in the canteen it's going to be public knowledge.

'We'll do that—we'll have to—if we think there's going to be a terror attack in the next forty-eight hours. But it's not a cost-free option. People will be terrified, and frightened people do stupid things. We'll have road accidents as they try to leave town, we'll have fights over tinned food in the supermarkets, we'll have normally responsible citizens attacking one another because of the colour of their skin. If we have to do it, I want us to be ready. We'll have to manage the announcement—tell people not just about the threat, but what we're doing to counter it. Until we have a plan in place, we keep this between ourselves. You, me, him.' He stabbed his thumb at each in turn. 'Yes?'

He didn't expect an argument and he didn't get one. But he'd been in this job a long time, he'd seen good people make bad mistakes. 'Charlie, what will you tell Helen?'

'Just…' He caught the treacherous sentence in a word, but even one word could have been too much if it had been his fiancée he'd been talking to. He coloured to the roots of his ginger hair. 'Nothing, boss.'

'Right. If this goes pear-shaped she'll be as safe in the hospital as anywhere else. And even if she wasn't, we both know she'd stay there. Helen hears when Uniform hears, and the rest of Dimmock hears soon afterwards.' He turned to Salmon. 'I don't know what your chief'll want you to do. But I'd like you to stay. This isn't something I've any experience of, thank God. Anything you can tell me, any advice you can give, I'll be glad of.'

Salmon nodded. 'You've got it. But there's something I should put on record first. The reason I recognised Daoud is that I was five months in deep cover with Counter Terrorism Command. He's the reason I had to come out—four years earlier I arrested him for drug-running. I don't think he remembered me, but I'd taken enough risks for one lifetime. It's always a bit hairy under cover—staying down when one of my marks could have a Damascus moment at any time would have been plain crazy.

'That's not what I was going to say,' he said with a hint of impatience. 'The reason I was in deep with these guys—the reason I got away with it for five months—is, it wasn't all an act. My family are Sunni Moslems from Iran. My father's name was Suleiman—he changed it when he came to this country, to make things easier for his children.' He looked at his forearm, between the white of his cuff and the strap of his watch, then up again. In his dark eyes was a kind of humorous challenge. 'That didn't come from a sunbed.'

There were people who had known Deacon longer than Charlie Voss but not many knew him better. But even Voss couldn't tell what he was thinking. His expression had shut down entirely. It was like looking at the Sphinx.

Finally he said, 'Is it going to be a problem for you?'

Salmon shook his head. 'No.'

'Are these people gunning for you?'

'No,' he said again. 'As far as I know they never made me. Even if they did, I'm no more at risk from them now than you are. If there's a terror cell in Dimmock, we're all in danger. It isn't personal, it's a numbers game—they just want to kill as many people as they can.'

Deacon nodded slowly. 'OK. Well, it sounds like I need you more than ever.' He sniffed. 'Forty-eight hours may be a generous assessment. What are our priorities?'

Salmon was in no doubt. 'Right now Loomis's death is of no consequence. The only thing that matters is finding out what

Daoud was doing here. Who he saw, where he stayed, and where he went after he left a knife in Loomis's lung.'

'Yes,' agreed Deacon. 'Charlie, you're going to have to stick with the CCTV. I want all the info you can get on Daoud. All of it—follow him round town from when he arrives until he leaves.' He turned to Salmon. 'Meanwhile, you and me go back to being woodentops for a day and knock on some doors. Let's see who'll open up to us and what they have to say.'

'If we're approaching the Asian community, let me do the talking,' suggested Salmon.

Deacon favoured him with a mirthless grin. 'Why do you think I kept you?'

'MR TARAR WILL SEE you now,' said the girl with the long blond hair; and while Deacon was thinking grumpily, *Damn right he will,* Salmon was already thinking Pervez Tarar was not just a successful businessman, he was a clever one. Most immigrants who get a foot on the ladder make a point of employing other immigrants—family if they have enough, countrymen if they haven't. Mr Tarar of the Green & Pleasant Leisure Company had been cunning enough to find a receptionist who, if you'd sawed her leg off, would have had *English Rose* written right through it.

Knowing he'd be at a certain disadvantage, the name he'd given his company and the face he'd given its front desk were deliberate ploys to raise no questions in customers' minds until they met the chief executive. Most people, even the surprised ones, were too polite immediately to make their excuses and leave; and those who stayed quickly realised they were dealing with a highly effective entrepreneur and the colour of his skin mattered less than the colour of his balance sheet.

And his balance sheet was very healthy, thank you. The office the policemen were shown to demonstrated the fact in the best possible way, i.e. subtly. Less subtle but equally good at conveying the message was the executive helicopter parked on the lawn outside.

Tarar saw them seated before pulling up his own chair. 'If you have time I'll order tea.'

'This is pretty urgent,' said Salmon. 'We need your help. This town needs your help.'

Tarar's eyebrows arched. He wasn't a big man, although success and time—he was in his mid-fifties—had added a comfort zone around his midriff. 'That sounds serious, Inspector.'

'Hard to overemphasise just how serious it could be,' said Salmon. 'Which is why we're going to tell you things we haven't told our own colleagues yet. We're relying on your discretion. We have no choice.'

'Tell me how I can help.'

As he'd promised, Deacon left the talking to Dave Salmon. They'd discussed on the way here—Green & Pleasant had as their base a small Georgian manor house on the edge of Peyton Parvo—how much they should tell Tarar, decided they'd have to tell him most of it to ensure he'd help if he was able to.

So Salmon told him that an Arab known to have associated with terror suspects in Britain had been spotted in Dimmock. 'It's vitally important that we trace his movements. Find out who he met in Dimmock and where he stayed. One man he went to see is already dead. We need to find Daoud before anyone else dies.'

Dark eyes are not always warm. Those of Pervez Tarar were as chill as the wind coming off the Hindu Kush. 'Gentlemen—you think I'm the kind of man who knows terrorists?'

Salmon shook his head. 'Nothing we've been told about you suggests any such thing. But you're in a unique situation in this area. You've created a successful business by beating the locals at their own game; at the same time you've remained in close touch with the Asian community around Dimmock. You don't so much straddle the fence as own it. You're respected by both your own countrymen and the English. You don't need me or anyone to tell you the right thing to do.

'Correct me if I'm wrong, but I think you know the face of every regular at the mosque in…'

He glanced to Deacon, and Deacon didn't let him down. 'Romney Road,' he said woodenly.

'The mosque in Romney Road,' nodded Salmon, 'and therefore every stranger who turns up there. If this man Daoud was at Friday prayers, you probably saw him. I expect others did too, but most people living in a country they don't entirely think of as their own try to avoid trouble. It's always easier to keep your head down and say you saw nothing, and who can prove otherwise?'

'You could do that too, sir,' said Detective Inspector Salmon. 'But I don't think you will. This isn't an *us* and *them* situation— or rather, the *us* is normal decent law-abiding people of whatever racial background, and the *them* is a bunch of moral bankrupts with no philosophy beyond an explosive belt. And I think you're *us*. Tell me I'm wrong.'

There was a long pause. Pervez Tarar scrutinised Dave Salmon closely enough to know where he bought his shirts and how much he paid for them. Then he said, 'You're not wrong, Inspector.'

TWELVE

THE BLISS OF SOLITUDE issued from Brodie like an aura, expanding until it filled the little office with happiness. She couldn't stop smiling. She felt like a scene from a Disney cartoon, full of twinkle-dust and blossom. She feared that if an orphan puppy were to wander past she'd adopt it on the spot.

She realised, of course, that it didn't say good things about her, that she'd rather be running her business than looking after her baby. It wasn't that she begrudged the time she spent with Jonathan. He was a lovely baby—she was lucky enough to have two lovely children—but still motherhood was something that she did rather than who she was. She'd enjoy her children all the more tonight for having done something else during the day. She'd enjoy Deacon's company the more when she'd sought it rather than because he had nothing better to do. And she'd missed the intellectual stimulation of work.

So she settled back into her poky little office like sinking back in a favourite armchair. In the old days she'd made a point of spending Saturday mornings combing the flea markets or looking at houses and taking Paddy along; and the little girl had clearly expected to drop back immediately into the old routine. She was disappointed when Brodie made an excuse.

'Next week, darling. I've no idea what needs doing. I really need to spend the morning at my desk. We'll do something nice this afternoon.' Huffily, the child agreed.

Alone in the office, hoping not even clients would come to disturb her just yet, Brodie did a bit of filing, made a few phone calls, made some notes; but mostly what she did was breathe deeply and treasure the peace that was hers until she chose to break it.

So it was a minor irritation to her that there were notes in the diary that she couldn't make sense of. Of course, Daniel hadn't had much notice of his forthcoming career shift: when he made those notes he'd expected to be dealing with them himself. But she wished she could have got through at least the first morning without needing to consult him.

She dialled his mobile. 'Where are you?'

He sounded as if he'd been expecting her to check. 'My place.'

That made her grin. So Deacon was driving Daniel mad too. Unlike her, though, he had somewhere else to go. 'Are the kids with you?'

'No, I left them at the dog pound,' he said indignantly. 'Of course they're with me.'

'No need to be ratty,' chided Brodie. 'All I was going to say was, let's meet for lunch.'

He sounded faintly surprised, as if he might have misjudged her. 'Sure. Where?'

'Well, if you're already there...'

The resignation was back in his voice. 'So what you mean is, will I make you some lunch?'

'That would be lovely,' said Brodie sweetly. 'If you insist.'

Daniel was oddly tidy. He didn't surround himself with many belongings, and those he had were always in their allotted places. So when she opened the front door of the netting shed— he only locked it at night, during the day visitors just knocked and entered—she thought he'd had burglars. There were jars and cans all over the floor. 'Good grief!'

Daniel's head shot round the kitchen door. 'What's the matter?' But he saw Jonathan still snoozing in his buggy and immediately relaxed. 'Oh—the orchestra.' He smiled.

'The *what?*'

He sent Paddy to demonstrate while he watched his cooking. Each of the jars held a quantity of shingle off the beach, and made a different sound when shaken depending on the quantity or size of the stones. 'Daniel made them,' said the little girl proudly. 'For Jonathan.'

Brodie knew exactly what he'd done: found a way to add texture and richness to the world for a child who could no longer see it. She picked a way through the chaos into the kitchen, slipped a long arm around her friend's waist and lightly kissed his cheek. 'That is some lucky baby.'

She and Paddy tidied up. Jonathan was still asleep. 'Have you fed him?'

'Before his snooze. Like it says on the list.' When she'd entrusted Daniel with her business she'd written out a schedule of what to do when. She'd done the same before handing over her baby.

While they ate she asked about the cryptic notes in the office diary. Then she glanced up at him slyly. 'It didn't take long for Jack to chase you away.'

'Jack wasn't there. I just thought it would be nice to bring the kids down to the beach.'

Brodie was frowning. 'Not there? Daniel—Jack's *always* there. Since they took him off the Loomis case, he's been like that albatross in the poem—*always* hanging around. Did you tell him I'd gone back to work?'

Daniel shook his head. 'Did you?'

'No. I thought it would be a'—again the slightly malicious glance—'nice surprise.'

'He must have had something else to do today.' Daniel wasn't above a slightly malicious smile of his own. 'Perhaps he'll pop round tonight.'

It wasn't even that thought that widened her eyes. 'He's gone back to work!'

For Daniel that was an inference too far. 'He's probably shopping. Or getting the car serviced. Or…'

Brodie shook her head with certainty. 'Daniel, if you'd seen him these last few days you'd know that the only thing that would have got him out of my hair was being called back to work. Which means developments in the Loomis case. They know who killed Joe.' She was already reaching for her phone.

The instant Deacon answered Brodie knew something was wrong. 'Is this really urgent?'

'No,' she said honestly. 'I just wondered…'

He wasn't interested. 'I'll get back to you when I can.' And then he was gone.

She sat staring at the phone in astonishment. Often enough in the past they'd argued, they'd shouted, they'd made up. She couldn't remember him refusing to speak to her. 'Well,' she said to Daniel. 'I think we can safely say he's busy.'

'At work?'

'He'd *better* be,' said Brodie firmly. 'It sounded like he'd not only got guy who killed Joe Loomis, he'd got him pinned against the wall and was answering the phone with his other hand.'

'Then, in due course, we'll hear all about it,' Daniel said pointedly.

Brodie had never thought that *in due course* applied to her. 'I wonder where they are…'

'Sit down,' insisted Daniel, 'and finish your dinner.'

His tone surprised her. 'This may have been a mistake,' she said waspishly. 'You're starting to sound like a nanny already.'

People who knew him came up the iron stairs to knock on the door. People who didn't mostly hovered on the lower steps clearing their throats. As Daniel cleared away the plates Brodie heard first the crunch of the shingle, then a foot on the steps, then a voice. A female voice.

'You've got a visitor,' she said. Then, with a grin: 'I *told* you kids are a babe magnet.'

It was Faith Stretton. When Daniel opened the door she started to come inside, then saw Brodie and blinked. 'I'm sorry. You have company. I'll come back later.'

Brodie waved a breezy invitation exactly as if it had been her house. 'Not on my account.'

'Come in,' said Daniel. 'I'm just making coffee.' He seemed unaware of the cagey way the two women were regarding one another.

If she'd got no further than the gallery Faith would indeed have gone away again. But turning round this far into the room would have meant a retreat, and Faith didn't seem like someone who retreated.

And what made it possible for Brodie to judge a woman she hardly knew was the instinctive recognition that the age gap was the only significant difference between them. Faith was a redhead while Brodie was dark; Faith favored the casual look while Brodie would look smart in a towel; Faith's children were grown up while Brodie's were still small. But these were things of no account. They were two strong, determined women who were beholden to no one for their lives or happiness, and like dogs on a beach they could spot one another a long way off. Sometimes it was with wagging tails, sometimes with teeth.

So Faith moved deliberately towards the armchair, took the cup Daniel offered her and sat down. And Brodie thought that was exactly what she'd have done too.

'I just wanted to drop by and thank you properly for your help,' she said. 'But for you it would have been a deeply unpleasant incident.'

'It wasn't exactly a bundle of laughs anyway,' said Brodie. 'As I heard it.'

Daniel forbore to comment. He knew what she was doing, possibly better than she did. Though she'd have denied it with her dying breath, the idea of him having female friends troubled her. She had no need to be jealous, for two reasons. She didn't want him the way he wanted her; and he didn't want any other woman that way either. But pointing out how illogical she was would have incurred her wrath without achieving anything, so he let it go.

'Are you all right?' he asked Faith, and she nodded.

'I'm fine. I was fine the next day. I'd have come round

sooner, but I was a bit—taken aback, I suppose—when I heard he was dead.' She pursed her lips. 'But I honestly can't say I was sorry.'

She was in the right company. Neither of them had felt moved to send a wreath.

Brodie said, 'Anyway, the bruise has gone.'

Faith gave a surprised little laugh. 'Yes. The last thing he'll ever give me. When I heard he was dead I wondered if I ought to try to keep it. Then I thought, why would you want to?' Her gaze travelled from Brodie to Daniel and back. 'Do the police know who killed him? Or why?'

Brodie shook her head. 'He had a finger is so many pies, all of them unsavoury, that any number of people might have wanted him dead. Well, that's not the trick—there are probably people who want me dead too. The trick is pissing off the sort of person who's liable to do something about it.'

'You think that's what it was? A gangland killing?'

'It wasn't a professional hit,' said Brodie dismissively. She never needed more than a bit of background information to set herself up as an expert on anything. 'A pro wouldn't have left him till he was dead. OK, he didn't manage much in the way of last words, but he was still alive when he reached me and he was trying to say something. The little I got might still prove helpful.'

Faith looked startled. 'I didn't realise. The police came to see me, but they didn't tell me any of this.'

'Probably because…' She shut up abruptly.

They were too alike. Faith did what Brodie would have done in her situation: put what she knew together with the sudden gap in the conversation and made an intelligent guess about what the words would have been. 'Because I'm a suspect?' Her eyebrows rocketed. 'No—because Dev is. The police suspect *Dev?*'

Brodie gave an apologetic shrug. 'They were looking for someone whose name begins with D. And there'd been this scene between Joe Loomis and you. They had to wonder if your son had gone round to mark his card and things got out of hand.'

'Dev wouldn't *kill* anybody! Not even Joe Loomis. If he'd been there when it happened he might have thumped him, but he'd never have used a knife. I don't think he owns a knife.'

'I don't suppose he does,' said Daniel soothingly. 'Faith, you don't need to convince us.'

But she seemed to think she did. 'He's a civil engineer. Do you know where he's spent the last two years? In Pakistan, working to repair the damage of the Kashmir earthquake. I don't mean he got a job out there—I mean, he packed a ruck-sack and lived in a corrugated iron shack for two years and helped rebuild the place. While the students he graduated with were getting their careers on track, Dev was digging out rubble, and bodies, and designing water systems, and pouring concrete. For nothing. For his own satisfaction. Because that's who he is. If he can help he wants to, and he doesn't much care how much it costs him.'

'And you're proud of him,' added Daniel with a smile.

'I'm proud of both my children,' said Faith firmly. 'I don't think this is an easy time to be young. When I was their age we still talked about free love. Kids now know that love doesn't come free, and neither does anything else.'

Brodie had been thinking. 'Here's something for free. Take out your phone right now and ask Dev where he is.'

'He's at home. I left him there half an hour ago.'

'Humour me.'

Even Daniel looked puzzled, and Faith looked at Brodie as if she was mad; but then she did it. 'He's still at home. He's working on the computer.' Her eyebrows sketched a question mark.

'Well, if the police still suspected him of anything, eBay would be the last thing on his mind. They're in hot pursuit of whoever killed Joe Loomis right now, and since being pursued by Jack Deacon is like being chased by a bull buffalo at the height of the rutting season, I'm pretty sure he knows it.'

It took Faith a moment to work out what she was being told. Then she gave a tremulous smile and stood up. 'Thank you.

Again. I've taken up enough of your time—I'll leave you to finish your coffee in peace.'

Brodie watched from the window as the woman hurried up the skittering shingle towards her car. 'Five gets you ten that she calls him back, just to be sure.'

She thought for a moment she was going to lose her bet. But as Faith reached the Promenade, out came the phone again. 'You lose,' said Brodie with satisfaction.

Daniel was clearing away the pots. 'Who'd have guessed?' he murmured.

THIRTEEN

ALL AT ONCE IN THE MIDDLE of the afternoon, things started happening.

By now DS Voss had a gallery of shots of the man Daoud, taken on various cameras located in different parts of Dimmock in the twenty-four hours before Joe Loomis met his un-maker. He made a timeline of them. He wasn't sure what it would tell him. But he needed something to tell him something soon.

And as he stared at the screen, it started to. He reached slowly for the phone and called Deacon. 'I've got nineteen shots here, of Daoud in and around town on the eleventh and twelfth. Nothing after that. But ten of them are in and around Romney Road, in spite of the fact that we've only got two cameras up there.'

'Times?' grunted Deacon.

Voss read them out. 'That's a lot of coming and going for a visitor. Either he had business in the area or he was staying nearby.'

'The business he had with Joe Loomis was in Rye Lane,' said Deacon.

'And we've got him going into The Rose and coming out. But if someone's planning to blow something up, it wasn't Joe,' said Voss. 'I'd believe you were a suicide bomber before I'd believe Loomis was.'

Deacon thought the same. 'And yet they had business together. Well, Loomis handled large quantities of drugs. Maybe Daoud used the same pipeline to get explosives in. It would make it a lot safer for him to travel around. Then, once he'd got his hands on them, he needed to shut up the guy who knew.'

It made sense. Except… 'So why would he visit him, leave him alive, then kill him later?' asked Voss 'And on the whole, suicide bombers don't use ready-made explosives. They cook up a brew out of locally available ingredients. Flour and bleach and stuff. They don't need to smuggle anything in.'

Deacon hated it when Voss knew something he didn't. He himself had learnt the job when a good general education was considered an obstacle to effective policing. Though he was neither stupid nor unlettered, his default position was that criminal detection was about people, not science. 'What's the last shot you have of him in the evening and the first shot the next morning?'

Voss checked the screen. 'Eleven-twenty-two p.m., and six-fifty-five on Tuesday the twelfth.'

'He was staying in the area,' said Deacon with conviction.

'I'll try the hotels and guest houses.'

'He wouldn't need a hotel room. There'd be people waiting for him who'd put him up. Safer for all concerned.'

'I still don't see how Loomis got involved,' said Voss, puzzled. 'This is not his scene.'

'Maybe he wasn't involved,' said Deacon. 'Salmon says the first time he came across Daoud he was muling drugs. Maybe that's how Loomis knew him. Daoud realised he'd been spotted and couldn't risk Loomis blowing his cover. Maybe that's what happened.'

It made more sense than Joe Loomis as a sudden convert to Islamic radicalism. He hadn't died because he was an up-and-coming crime lord. He died because he was inconvenient.

'So Salmon's right. We really have got a terror cell in this town. If we don't find them, lots of people are going to die.' Deacon rolled his eyes—a gesture lost on the man at the other end of the phone. 'Who are we looking for? Young Moslem men who take adventure holidays in Pakistan? And live within a couple of streets of Romney Road.'

Voss winced. Every fibre of his liberal soul rebelled at ca-tegorising people according to the shape of steeple they worshipped under. He believed that people were people, and bad things were done by bad people and good things were done by good people, and the colour of their skin and where or whether they prayed had very little to do with it. He was engaged to a Chinese girl, for heaven's sake! Racism was anathema to him.

'Yes…' he said slowly. 'But a lot of young Moslem men will live within walking distance of their mosque. On it's own that's not suspicious behaviour. We have to be careful…'

Deacon was getting angry. 'Right now, Charlie Voss, political correctness is a luxury we can't afford. We're looking for a bunch of fanatics who think it's not enough to live for their religion, they have to die for it as well. And take as many people with them as they can. They may have been born here, they may be immigrants, they may be visitors. They may be black, brown or white. But we can be pretty sure they're Moslems. Salmon knows that, and he's one of them. It's not tactful to avoid saying the words, it's just downright stupid.'

Voss knew he was right. But knowing didn't make him feel any better. 'I don't think I'm going to get any more out of these tapes. Shall I join you down there?'

Deacon was tempted. It would up the task force by fifty per cent. But the critical factor was not how many houses they could doorstep in an hour, it was how many hours they had before either the secret got out or Division took over, whichever came first. 'Better not. We need someone to field any calls that come in about this. If they go to the Squad Room we can forget about managed disclosure.'

Voss was accustomed to Deacon shouting, to Deacon being snide, even to Deacon being pleasant which made his toes curl. He couldn't remember hearing that particular tone in his superintendent's voice before. Deacon probably thought it was irony, but to Voss it sounded like despair.

THE SECOND THING that happened was that Pervez Tarar phoned Deacon. 'I have spoken to a number of people—discreetly,

Superintendent, do not be concerned. None of them mentioned a stranger at the mosque or anywhere else. Nevertheless, I have some information. I cannot judge how helpful it may be. Two cousins who live in Balfour Terrace, halfway up Romney Road, had recently altered their usual shopping patterns.'

Deacon's heart skipped a beat. 'Flour? Bleach?'

Mr Tarar sounded puzzled. 'No. Chillis, chick peas, garam masala and tamarind paste. Mrs Aziz says they were making *khatee channe*. Which is not in itself a criminal offence, unless you overdo the chillis, but the Dhazi cousins are not known for their culinary expertise. Usually they buy ready-meals. Mrs Aziz thinks they had visitors from home.'

'What kind of visitors?' Deacon didn't want to hit the house with three Armed Response teams only to surprise someone's auntie.

'No one saw them,' said Tarar. 'Which is strange in itself. If I have visitors from home, I show them around and introduce them to my friends here. I would be considered a very poor host to do anything less. So visitors whom no one has seen are not common.'

It could mean nothing at all, and Deacon knew it. It could have been the kind of duty visit that was an embarrassment to both parties— 'Your mother told my mother I had to look you up while I was here so hello, thanks for the *khatee channe* and goodbye.' But it was a disturbance in the normal pattern of someone's life that was sufficient for someone else to notice, so the detectives got back in Deacon's car and drove down Romney Road, away from the mosque and towards Balfour Terrace.

Dave Salmon knocked on the front door at 4.15 p.m. There was no response. But someone threw a shadow on an upstairs window, and someone's feet made the bare stairs creak, and a keen ear at the letterbox heard a key turn in the back door lock. 'Quick, round the back,' yelled Salmon.

Deacon could still do quick if he had to, but he couldn't keep it up as long as younger, leaner men. He let Salmon pass him then got back in his car and headed the other way, stopping round the corner where the back entry emerged. Rafiq Dhazi hit the car full tilt and sprawled across the bonnet.

Deacon had him handcuffed before Dave Salmon came panting down the entry. He pushed his big, craggy face into the young man's with such force that Dhazi flinched. 'Now then, Mr Dhazi,' he rumbled, 'explain to me why a law-abiding citizen would run like the clappers rather than answer a knock at his front door.'

'We will have the money next week,' wailed Rafiq Dhazi. 'I promise.'

'Will you indeed? And what money's this? And why do you think I care?'

A little of the terror in Dhazi's eyes moved over to make way for uncertainty. 'You are not from Mr Loomis?'

'I am not even slightly from Mr Loomis,' agreed Deacon. 'I am a police officer. And Mr Loomis is dead. Mr Loomis carelessly walked sideways into a sharp instrument.'

English was not Rafiq Dhazi's first language. Nonetheless, he was fluent enough for all normal purposes. A conversation with Jack Deacon didn't come into that category. 'I beg your pardon?'

There was this about dealing with foreign miscreants, thought Deacon: they were more polite than home-grown ones. 'Somebody stabbed him.'

'Oh yes, I know.' In the young man's eyes the fear flared again. 'It was not me!'

'No?' Deacon sounded distinctly skeptical. 'Tell you what. You come down to my nick and convince me. While you're at it, you can tell me about this money you owed Mr Loomis and would probably have had to pay him if he hadn't conveniently died.'

Dave Salmon had caught just enough breath to speak. 'Or,' he suggested, 'you could tell us about Daoud.'

Rafiq Dhazi was twenty-two, and slender enough to look younger. His eyes dipped. 'It was not good. We needed the money.'

'What wasn't good?' frowned Deacon.

'My cousin and I, we have a large family. At home. We

came here to make money for them. People here earn good money. But it also costs much money to live here. There was not enough. And someone suggested…' His voice petered out.

'What?' demanded Deacon. 'Blowing up the bank? What?'

'Oh no!' He seemed genuinely startled. 'It was never our intention to blow anything up. But there is a demand here for substances which may be acquired quite cheaply at home. We know it is not legal. But we have a large family.'

'Heroin,' said Salmon. His gaze on the other man's face was needle-sharp.

'Yes.' The boy looked puzzled. 'You are police officers—is this not what you wish to talk about?'

'We want to talk about Daoud,' repeated Salmon.

'Yes. He was travelling from Multan. Mr Loomis gave us money to pay him a deposit on the…supplies. But there was a problem. His luggage went astray. A foolishness on the part of the airline. So Mr Loomis wanted his money back. But Mr Daoud also wanted *his* money. He had paid for the supplies, and he said his suitcase would arrive at our house within a few days and we could pass it on to Mr Loomis then. Only…'

'Only?'

'The suitcase did not arrive. And Mr Loomis was stabbed. And people think it was because of us!'

'Funny,' said DI Salmon, 'that's what I think too. I don't think there are any…supplies. I think you took Loomis's money all right, but not to spend on drugs. I think when Loomis guessed what you were up to, Daoud went round to shut him up. Because it takes forty-eight hours to produce a useful quantity of HMTD, and you wouldn't afford to have anyone rocking the boat while you were making it.'

Rafiq Dhazi was doing puzzled again. 'Please—what is a chemtidee?'

Salmon slapped his face. 'Don't piss me around, sunshine.' He indicated Deacon with a jerk of the head. 'You're scared of him? He's big, he looks mean? You've no reason to be scared of him. He's a nice English policeman and he goes by the book. I'm not, and I don't. Don't you dare tell me a young Pakistani doesn't know what HMTD is.'

'I don't know how to make it!'

'I didn't ask if you knew how to make it. But while we're on the subject, let's see if you're lying about that too.'

Deacon felt like the man in the 3-D cinema who's dropped his special specs. There was a lot going on around him and he wasn't sure he was getting it all. 'You want me to call Forensics?'

But Salmon shook his head. 'I know what to look for.'

They returned to the house the back way, to avoid attracting attention. Salmon pushed Dhazi ahead of him into every room. Deacon saw him looking at the windows and wondered why. He opened every door, every cupboard, but then he shook his head. 'Nobody's been cooking up explosives here.'

Deacon's brow lowered. 'You're sure?'

'Positive. The fumes are so toxic they bleach your eyebrows—you have to work with all the windows open, and then they'll kill your garden plants. Can you smell anything like that? And half the windows don't even open—they're painted up. He'—he gave Dhazi a contemptuous shove—'may know about HMTD but he hasn't been making it. No one's been making it here.'

Deacon felt as if someone had burst his balloon. They'd seemed to be onto something. Now they were back to square one. 'So—what? They have a factory somewhere else? Or were we wrong about this?'

'I wasn't wrong about Daoud,' swore Salmon. 'And Mrs Farrell didn't imagine Joe Loomis bleeding to death on her carpet. Yes, I imagine there's a factory somewhere else. Maybe Mr Dhazi here knows. If he does, I bet I can get him to tell me.'

Deacon regarded him with misgivings. He was accustomed to being the Rottweiler in the petting zoo; when suspects were being threatened, mostly what they were being threatened with was him. Now he had that uneasy feeling that you get with the first shift of the ground at the start of an earthquake. It could just be an act, but he suspected Dave Salmon meant every word of it.

'No, sir,' said Rafiq Dhazi urgently. This conversation had produced a dew of sweat on his upper lip that even running for his life had not. 'I know nothing about explosives. My cousin knows nothing about explosives. Perhaps we are not good men, but we are not *that* bad!'

'Your friend Daoud is that bad,' said Salmon. 'I know he is.'

'Then you know him better than I do,' insisted Dhazi. 'I never met him before. He was to carry supplies from Pakistan and we were to hold them for Mr Loomis. Only it went wrong.'

'Damn right it went wrong,' snorted Salmon. 'You and your cousin are going to prison for conspiracy to commit terrorist offences. You'll be middle-aged men when you come out. *If* you come out. The men inside have families too. Families who use buses and trains and banks and offices, and are as likely as anyone else to be beside him when some nut yells a slogan and blows himself to buggery. You'll *get* fifteen years. You'll *serve* life.'

'But—truly—I don't understand…' The boy was close to tears.

Deacon said gruffly, 'Where's Daoud now?'

'W-what?'

'Daoud. Where is he now? If we can get hold of him, maybe he can clear you. Maybe all we're talking about is a drugs bust after all.'

'I— He— I…' Dhazi swallowed. 'I think he would kill me.'

'Yes,' agreed Salmon frankly, 'I think he probably would. If he got the chance. But he isn't here and we are. Not to put too fine a point on it, right now we're your problem. Give us Daoud, and either we'll put him away or he'll decorate a couple of shop fronts with his own intestines. Either way, you're in a better place than you are right now.'

'But I know *nothing!*' wailed Dhazi.

'You must know something. You put this guy up at your house for two days. You must have talked about something besides the *khatee channe*. Then he disappeared. Where did he go?'

'He asked about trains to Birmingham.'

'OK. What did you tell him?'

Rafiq Dhazi gave a tremulous shrug. 'I told him I ride a bicycle. How would I know?'

'SO HE WENT TO BIRMINGHAM. To blow up something there, or to fetch something he needed to cause an explosion here?'

Deacon was doing sums. They'd remained in the house on Romney Road when the Dhazi cousins were taken into custody. The Scene of Crime Officer was working methodically around them, otherwise it was quiet. A good place to think. 'Joe Loomis was stabbed four days ago. Daoud had been here for two days but he left the following morning, probably for Birmingham. Maybe he's just lying low till the heat dies down, and then he's going to come back and do what he originally came here for.'

'Not delivering drugs,' said Salmon.

'No, not delivering drugs,' agreed Deacon. 'He was using a way into the country that he was already familiar with, and the drugs were his cover story. But his bag was sent to Bangkok. That brought Joe Loomis down on the Dhazi boys, and the courier went round to explain. And when they met they both realised they knew one another. It didn't matter too much to Joe but it did to Daoud—because he knew your mates at Counter Terrorism were aware he'd graduated from Best Afghan White to things that go bang. So Daoud arranged to meet Joe somewhere quiet, on the pretext that he had the bag now and was cutting out the middlemen, and slid a knife between his ribs. As soon as the rush hour started the next morning he headed for Birmingham.'

'It fits,' nodded Salmon. 'Except that Loomis brought the knife.'

'I imagine they both brought knives,' said Deacon. 'Loomis pulled his when he realised he was in danger, and Daoud took it off him because it was quicker than pulling his own. You know the guy—would he be capable of that?'

'Oh yes,' said Salmon with conviction.

'If he'd been planning to blow up the Bull Ring we'd have heard the bang by now,' continued Deacon. 'So he's just staying out of the way until our investigation goes quiet. Hell, he knows as well as we do what kind of man Joe Loomis was—there'll be no shortage of suspects but the trail will go cold a lot quicker than if his only enemy was his mistress's husband. A couple of weeks, he thinks, and he can probably stroll back into Dimmock and no one'll give him a second glance.'

'And then he goes shopping,' murmured Dave Salmon.

FOURTEEN

'SO WE HAVE TIME,' SAID Dave Salmon. 'An attack may be planned but it isn't imminent. Putting the town on a full-scale alert right now would do more harm than good.'

'We have a little time,' amended Deacon, 'if we're reading this right.'

'Well, we're the guys on the ground. We're more likely to get it right than Division. Should we let them know what we've found, and what we think?'

Deacon made the call. He was asked a lot of questions he couldn't answer: questions beginning with *How certain are you?* and *What's your evidence?* He dismissed them as curtly as a man in a pensionable job should. 'I'm *not* certain. My only evidence is that there isn't any real evidence. This is what I think. If you think differently, if you think it makes more sense to risk a mass panic, go public with this. But I'm standing in the house where any explosives that were being cooked up would most probably be, and there's nothing here. Maybe I'm wrong. Maybe there's another house. Maybe there's a whole cell of other young men planning to blow up Dimmock. But this is where the trail led, and there's a scared kid here who's telling me what I think is the truth. I think we're safe until this man Daoud has been back in town for forty-eight hours.'

Division said they'd call him back. Half an hour later his phone went and it was ACC (Crime) Emily Blake. 'This is my call, Jack. If it's wrong it's my mistake. But we're going to hold off. Bring your team in on it now, but don't tell them the full story. Go with the drugs angle. Tell them Daoud's dangerous, they need to know that, but—correct me if I'm wrong—he's just another dangerous criminal until he's had forty-eight hours in a kitchen. The clock starts when he returns to Dimmock, so we need people watching for him. But if they miss him, the first thing we'll know is when he comes to the house. Is there anything to see from outside?'

Deacon was ahead of her. 'No. No tape, no cars, no uniforms. There's me and Salmon, and Billy Mills doing SOCO. And we took the Dhazi boys out the back way. With luck, nobody's even noticed.'

'Good. You'll need to keep a presence there, and you'll want armed response vehicles close but out of sight. Borrow a couple of garages—but be careful who you borrow them from, we don't want someone warning him off. And then watch, and wait.'

That made sense to Deacon. He told Salmon, 'I'm going to pull SOCO out. There's nothing for him to find here, and if there's going to be a fire-fight I don't want civilian staff in the middle. Will you stay? You'll spot Daoud before anyone else.'

Salmon nodded.

'I'll send Charlie Voss to keep you company. What about firearms? I'm guessing you're authorized?' Salmon nodded again, expressionless. 'Then that's probably all we can do right now.'

'Try to give me a bit of warning.'

'I'll have the train and bus stations watched,' said Deacon. 'And the Guildford Road, in case he's got himself a car by now. We'll invent some road works to slow the traffic and get a good look at everyone coming in.' He frowned. 'The railway station's going to be the weak spot. With a trainload of passengers all arriving at the same time we could miss him.'

'Put up a notice saying you're looking for a runaway child,' advised Salmon. 'Make people leave the platform in single file. That shouldn't warn him we're onto him.'

Deacon eyed the younger man with some admiration. 'You're good at this, aren't you?'

'I *was* good at this,' said Salmon. 'I had to be.'

DIVISION HELPED WITH EXTRA manpower. By Monday morning they were all in place, and all thinking they were watching for a dangerous drug trafficker. Deacon allowed himself space to breathe. When he dropped in to see Brodie he was surprised to find she, too, had gone back to work. He took his son on his knee, still handling him like a suspicious package, and regarded Daniel over the top of his head. 'So you're looking after Jonathan.'

Daniel nodded. 'Does that bother you?'

Deacon shook his head. 'No. I just wonder…' He let the sentence peter out.

'What?'

Deacon blew out his cheeks in exasperation. 'Why we let her do this to us. Both of us. Why we let her rearrange out lives at a moment's notice because it makes things more interesting for her. Why we don't, just occasionally, tell her to shove it.'

Daniel's smile was a gentle ghost. 'You know why.'

'Do I?' It was a policeman's trick, answering with a question, but it was also how Deacon dealt with the mystifying world of personal relationships. 'Remind me.'

'Because we love her.'

Quite severe torture wouldn't have dragged the words out of Deacon. He marvelled at how easily Daniel could say it. Of course, they'd known each other a while now, and for some of the time you'd have to say they'd been friends because there was no other word that got closer. But Deacon couldn't imagine exposing his feelings like that. Especially if he'd known, as Daniel did, that those feelings weren't reciprocated. He said, 'You're still…' And again, failed to finish the remark.

It was the honesty thing. Daniel didn't lie about anything. If he talked about his feelings at all, he told the truth. His smile broadened, became impish. 'What? Still holding a candle for her? Still waiting for my chance? Yes to the first, Jack, and no to the second. You know—you were the first to guess—how much I care for her. But you also know it's never going to happen. Brodie loves me too, as a friend, but she doesn't and she never will want me the way she wants you. And if you joined a circus tomorrow, she'd find someone else and it still wouldn't be me. I'm no threat to you. As far as Brodie's concerned, we occupy separate membranes of existence.'

If there was one thing worse than Voss being clever, it was Daniel using mathematical analogies. It made Deacon want to hit him with a brick. 'And you're…all right with that?'

'No,' confessed Daniel with a chuckle. 'But it's the best I'm going to do.'

'And she knows?'

'She knows. It doesn't suit her so she ignores it.'

'And you still…?'

'*Yes,* Jack,' said Daniel, amused. 'I still dot dot dot.'

Deacon shook his heavy head in disbelief. The better he knew Daniel Hood, he thought, the less he understood him. And that troubled him more than he could explain. A man much more in touch with his own emotions might have struggled with the relationships which had developed between these three: for Deacon it was *terra incognita.*

If someone had asked him about Daniel, his immediate response would have been: 'He's a geek, and a pain in the backside.' Except he wouldn't have said *backside.* If he'd felt the need to be more honest than that, he might have said: 'He's a geek and a pain in the backside, but…' But he would never have gone on to say, as a man of genuine insight might have done: 'There's something about him that touches people's lives. Even if I'm not sure what it is, I know it's touched mine too. You don't have to be a raving queer'—and he *would* have said *queer*—'to feel richer for knowing him. And because of that, to care about him.'

To Deacon, the C-word was almost as treacherous as the L-word. He avoided both like the plague. He cleared his throat. I'll—um…'

Daniel nodded amiably and took the baby. 'She should be in the office.'

Deacon headed out to his car, unloading discomfort with every step.

BRODIE HAD MADE the office her own again. It wasn't that Daniel had wrought any radical changes during his tenancy. But he kept the stapler in the wrong drawer. He'd hung the calendar on the back of the door instead of beneath the clock. And he always answered the phone with his right hand before switching it to his left in order to take notes, resulting in a tangled cord. Small things, all of them, but how they'd rankled! Putting them right had cheered her immediately.

'Back in the old routine, then?' Deacon said, and Brodie couldn't be sure if that note in his voice was censure or not. Which meant that it was, just not quite enough for her to object.

She grinned happily. 'This is more *me.*'

'Meaning, feeding and changing the baby is more Daniel?'

'Daniel doesn't mind. I think he was glad of a change too.'

'Daniel's doing what he always does: picking up the bits you can't be bothered with.'

That was definitely censure. Brodie frowned. 'Jonathan is *not* a bit I can't be bothered with.'

'Well, that's how it looks. Like anyone can look after a baby, but your business needs to be handled with care.'

Brodie breathed heavily at him. 'Jack, if you've come here to argue, make an appointment. Right now I've got better things to do. Actually,' she added, the hint of a challenge in her voice, 'I'd have thought you had too. Unless you've charged someone with the murder of Joe Loomis and just haven't thought to mention it.'

He dismissed that with a characteristic curl of the lip. 'As a matter of fact,' he growled, slashing a hand at eyebrow level, 'I'm up to here. And Joe Loomis is the least of my worries.'

In the days when they printed posters saying *Careless talk costs lives!* this is what they meant. If Brodie had been an enemy spy her bosses would have been fuelling the V2s by now. She could spot a deceit faster than anyone Deacon knew. What he'd said had hardly been a mistake. But her ears had pricked like those of a fox who's heard something tasty in the undergrowth, and his heart was leaden with the knowledge that she'd let it go only after she'd sucked the bones white.

'Really?' she said, watching him. 'We have so many murders in Dimmock these days that the victims have to take a number and wait? I know Joe Loomis was no loss, but that didn't make it all right for someone to stab him. You've got someone walking around this town thinking he got away with murder. And you don't know who, and you don't know why—and still it's the least of your worries? What's going on, Jack?'

He shook his head brusquely and avoided looking at her. 'Nothing. I'm busy, that's all. A drugs case.'

But Brodie wasn't wearing it. 'Drugs don't take precedence over murder, and you know that I know that. So why would you lie to me? Only one possible reason: there's something going on that's even more serious. And the only thing that's more serious than a murder that's happened is a murder that's about to happen—a murder that, if you throw everything at it, just could be averted.'

Her eyes were brilliant with curiosity. 'That's it, isn't it? They've brought you back to work because somebody's life depends on CID asking the right questions and getting the right answers, and doing it yesterday. You're somebody's last best chance.'

If she hadn't got the details exactly right, she had the essence of the thing and she knew it. Deacon realised with astonishment that she was proud of him. He didn't know what to say. 'Er...'

'It's all right,' she said lightly, 'I know you can't talk about it. Go on, get back to work, carry on saving the world. Tell me about it when you can.'

What she didn't say, and what Deacon never for a moment realised she was thinking, was that if Battle Alley was fully occupied with a crisis, and it was so sensitive even she had to be kept in the dark, perhaps there was another way she could help. Joe Loomis had come to her when he was dying on his feet. She hadn't been able to save him, but perhaps she could spare him the indignity of hanging around until his death was considered important enough to investigate.

'Go on,' she said again. 'There's stuff I need to do as well.'

FIFTEEN

BRODIE BEGAN WITH THE ONLY person she knew who'd known Joe Loomis personally. Faith Stretton had been his lover a couple of decades ago and was in contact with Loomis again shortly before his death. If the police were concentrating on the drugs angle, perhaps Faith could cast some light on the man's private life.

She didn't phone ahead to make an appointment. She found it paid not to. Sometimes it meant a wasted journey, but people found it harder to send you away from their door, there was a good chance of catching her in.

She was in, but she was busy. Through the open kitchen door Brodie could hear a washing machine at work. 'I won't keep you long,' she promised. 'I can see you're up to your eyes.'

'That's OK,' said Faith, running a distracted hand through her copper hair. 'My daughter's visiting friends for a couple of weeks—and *now* it turns out she's down to her last clean knickers! What is it with teenage girls, that they can't think one minute ahead of where they are right now?'

Brodie chuckled sympathetically. 'Be grateful. My daughter's seven. She doesn't care if her knickers are clean or not as long as her jodhpurs are.'

Faith passed on a universal truth. 'The longer they stay interested in ponies, the less time they have for boys.'

Brodie winced. 'They seem to grow up faster every year, don't they? It scares the life out of me—girls barely into their teens dolled up like scrubbers. We were still children at their age. Weren't we? Or am I forgetting?'

Faith shrugged. 'The world moves on. When I was Evie's age I was wearing bells and saving the planet.'

'Seems to have worked,' murmured Brodie, and Faith laughed. 'I'm afraid I never did good causes. In my teens I wanted to be a Success In Life. Good degree, good job, good marriage, pretty children.'

'I'm guessing that worked too,' said Faith.

'Well, yes,' said Brodie, 'and no. Fairly good degree, decent job, married the boss, lovely kid. Then I got dumped in favour of a fat librarian and had to start again. This time I chucked the book away and asked myself what I really wanted.'

'What was the answer?'

'To write my own rule book. I never wanted to be dependent on anyone again. And yes thanks, it's working fine.'

Faith nodded. They really did have a lot in common. 'So what can I do for you?'

'I'm almost embarrassed to admit it, because he was certainly trash and he didn't deserve much from society, but I'm worried Joe Loomis is getting a raw deal. No one cares that he's dead. Well, I don't care much either, or I won't once I've paid for the new carpet, but I kind of care that he was murdered. Even Joe didn't deserve that. And no one's trying to find out why. So far as I can make out, the police investigation consists of going into crowded places and asking people to put their hands up if they killed him.'

The older woman was watching her carefully. 'How do you think I can help?'

'You could put your hand up if you killed him,' said Brodie hopefully.

Faith gave a gusty little laugh. 'I didn't.'

'Oh well, back to the drawing board. I suppose I'm looking for some insight into who he was. I know *what* he was, I know what he did, and the likelihood is that's why he's dead. But he must have had a personal life like everyone else. Most murders are domestic affairs—the killer and the victim are family or close associates. I wondered if, since you'd known him on and off for twenty years, you knew anything about his private life.'

Faith Stretton was still looking wary. 'I'm sorry, have I missed something here? Why is this your concern?'

Brodie was untroubled. In her line of work it didn't pay to be sensitive. 'It isn't. Except that finding things is what I do, and it goes against the grain to give up when the search gets difficult. Look, I didn't like Joe Loomis any more than you did. He threatened me and my baby. Oh, he didn't produce a gun or anything, but I was meant to feel threatened and I did. So actually I'm not sorry the guy's dead.'

'But he came to me. About the last decision he made was to stagger to my door and ask for my help. And I feel under an obligation because of it. Because of who he was, the police aren't exerting themselves to find his killer. But everyone, even Joe, deserves for someone to know how and why they died. If I'm the best he could do it doesn't say much for his value as a human being—I disliked and despised him. Even so, maybe I should try to understand what happened.'

Faith shrugged. 'It's more than he'd do for you.'

Brodie smiled. 'Of course it is. But I like to think I'm a better person than Joe Loomis.'

Faith was unconvinced but she offered no more arguments. 'What do you want to know? Bearing in mind that I've hardly seen him since I was Dev's age.'

'Was he ever married?'

'Not that I know of. But I haven't been following his career through the social columns.'

'Any children?'

'No,' said Faith.

Brodie cocked an eyebrow. 'You seem pretty sure of that.'

'Did he strike *you* as fit to be swimming in the gene pool?'

'Put it like that,' chuckled Brodie, 'then no. Still, all sorts of unpromising men become fathers. But there were no children that you knew of. What about friends?'

Faith laughed out loud. 'Joe didn't have friends. I wasn't a friend: I was a stupid girl who, one mad summer, saw something glamorous in a dangerous man. Finally even I saw him for what he was and got out. *Joe* was the only friend Joe had.'

Brodie had brought out her notebook. She put it away unused. 'You're saying that Jack's probably right—it was a business deal that went wrong.'

'It had to be,' shrugged Faith. 'He didn't have personal relationships. Ask around, maybe you'll find someone who knew him better than me. But I think the only people Joe knew, the only people who'd have cared enough about him to want him dead, were those he did business with. Drug traffickers, and people wanting to score.'

'I believe he also ran a stable of prostitutes,' said Brodie.

Faith Stretton's expression shut up tight. 'Really.'

'You weren't aware of that?'

'He never told me. But I can't say I'm surprised.'

'Maybe that was the motive. A desperate girl, an angry father, a jealous boyfriend. A punter who went home with more than he paid for.'

'Who knows?' Faith was rigid with distaste. 'You know, nothing you're saying suggests he was worth the time you're giving to this. Not when there are lost dogs that need finding and broken tea sets that need matching.'

'I know. But still… Murder is a crime in any civilised society,' said Brodie. 'Not even because of the victim but because of the killer. There's someone wandering round out there who solves his problems with a knife. I don't want to be the next one who annoys him. I don't want anyone I care about bumping into him next time he's in a bad mood.'

'You're right, of course,' agreed Faith, chastened. 'What about the weapon? Was that any help? Were there any fingerprints?'

Brodie shook her head. 'They found Joe's prints on it—it was his knife—and they found mine. That was stupid, I shouldn't have touched it but I did, while I was trying to help him. And that meant any other fingerprints on it were spoilt.'

'Not the one with the pearl handle? He had that when I knew him,' remembered Faith. 'He was always playing with the damn thing. He seemed to think it was sexy.'

'Tell me again,' said Brodie, '*what* did you see in this man?'

Faith gave a grim little chuckle. 'Beats the hell out of me.'

THERE WAS NO WARNING. The man Daoud returned to Dimmock not by bus or train or even driving a car, but hitch-hiking with a long-distance lorry-driver. The first anyone knew was at two o'clock the next morning when DS Voss, watching from the front bedroom window, saw a figure walk down Romney Road and stop at Balfour Terrace, looking for the house he wanted.

Detective Inspector Salmon was sleeping in his clothes a metre away. Voss slapped his foot with one hand and pulled out his phone with the other. 'We're on.'

Daoud didn't knock: he must have had a key because they heard the front door opening. Salmon drew his weapon and crept, silent in his socks, to the bedroom door, listening for foot-steps on the stairs. But the new arrival had gone into the kitchen—they heard a tap running, then the click of the electric kettle. The man had been on the road for hours: he wanted a cup of tea.

This wasn't how they'd planned it. They'd expected to have a bit of warning and a lot of back-up, a net closing behind the suspect as he approached. But they outnumbered him two to one, Salmon was armed, and they had the advantage of surprise. Still they waited. If this was going to get messy, the closer Armed Response was when the action started the better. Or perhaps when Daoud had made his cup of tea and sat down in one of the threadbare armchairs, and kicked off his shoes and started to doze, they might take him without a fight.

The time of night was to their advantage. If he'd come by day he might have wondered at the silence of the house and gone from room to room checking out the situation. But at two in the morning he assumed the Dhazi cousins were asleep—even terrorists like to be considerate—tried not to disturb them.

But thirst is not the only physiological consequence of a long journey. Before the kettle had boiled Daoud was on his way upstairs, heading for the bathroom.

They might still have waited to see what happened. But there were more possibilities now. In a few seconds the suspect could be behind a locked door. Or he might stick his head into the bedrooms to check on the cousins. As the senior officer present Salmon had to call the play, but he hadn't much time to think about it. Right now he and Voss still held the initiative: ten seconds from now they might have lost it. 'We take him,' he breathed.

They positioned themselves so that Voss could yank open the bedroom door and leave Salmon just air between his weapon and Daoud's left ear. They waited for the sound of a hand on the bathroom door.

But a man who lives as Daoud lived has keen senses. If he doesn't have them at the start, he develops them or he dies. Natural Selection in action. They never knew what alerted him. He may have heard their breathing or smelt their aftershave. But something told him there was a problem, and even told him which door it was lurking behind. In the very act of reaching for the bathroom door he froze.

Then he pivoted on the ball of his left foot and exploded through the bedroom door while the men inside were still waiting their moment.

The leaping door hit Voss in the side of the head and knocked him halfway across the room, spilling him in a dizzy heap beside the bed. For a split second Dave Salmon's vision, ranged down the barrel of his gun, was entirely filled by the face—white in the moonlight and dark with fury—of the man bearing down on him. There was time to fire and he should have taken the shot. But one difference between police officers and terrorists is that the former consider killing someone the last resort, and he hesitated.

So the shot that boomed in the confines of the little room, that brought bedroom lights on in houses all along the street, wasn't his.

SIXTEEN

DEACON WORKED THROUGH to one in the morning before finally going home. He'd been asleep an hour when the phone startled him awake. This happened regularly enough that his fingers could take the call while his brain was still struggling with the whole concept of consciousness. 'What?'

It was Sergeant McKinney, calling from Battle Alley. 'Are you awake, Jack?'

'What?'

McKinney had known him for ten years. Long enough to call him by his given name; long enough to know he could do a good impression of a senior investigating officer while still technically sleepwalking. 'You need to be firing on all cylinders for this one. Tell me you're awake.'

'I'm awake, damn it,' growled Deacon. 'What's happened?'

'The shit's hit the fan at Romney Road. There was a firefight. The ambulance is there now, so's the Area Car and an Armed Response Unit. The story I'm getting is one dead, one critical, one hurt.'

Deacon's heart turned over and sank like a stone. It took an effort to get the word through his teeth. 'Who?'

But McKinney couldn't tell him. 'All I have is numbers. I'll get back to you when I have names to go with them. Or you could…' He stopped talking when he realised no one was listening. Deacon had thrown the phone down on his bed while he fought his way back into his clothes.

DETECTIVE INSPECTOR David Salmon had stared death in the face many times. And worse than death: his job had taken him into the company of men who used torture as a male bonding exercise and made videos of it as a kind of party bag to take home afterwards. His prime concern had never been whether he'd be killed if his cover was broken, because he knew he would. But some of these people were experts, and could make it last for hours.

In spite of which, he doubted he'd ever been closer to death than he was right now, staring down a gun barrel so still it might have been mounted on a tripod. Three, maybe four seconds ago the biggest problem on the man Daoud's immediate horizon was finding his way to the bathroom without waking his hosts. Now he was about to kill someone, and he'd made that massive mental leap without any sign of confusion. The face above the gun was as immobile as the gun itself: intelligent, focused. The eyes, one narrow, one wide, were asking *Now what?*—but Salmon had no sense that he was waiting for the answer. The only question that mattered right now was which of them was going down. Because one of them was. And Salmon's gun was halfway across the room, still spinning on the board floor, while Daoud's was in his hand.

Then Daoud blinked. 'I know you.'

For a second Salmon couldn't think if he was in more trouble or less. But actually that was a no-brainer: he couldn't *be* in any more trouble. So he nodded. Very slightly; very carefully. He spoke in Arabic. 'I know you too. Your name is Daoud. I'm Suleiman—we worked together in Leeds.' He rolled his eyes. 'And today we nearly killed one another. Stupid, stupid, stupid. Why do we need enemies when we're perfectly capable of destroying ourselves?'

The other man didn't lower his gun by a millimetre. But nor did he pull the trigger. He spared an instant's glance for Voss, sprawling dazed beside the bed. 'Who's he?'

'He's Irish,' said Salmon, inventing rapidly. 'The bomb-maker.'

Now Daoud's eyebrows rocketed. 'We need a foreign bomb-maker? We haven't bomb-makers of our own?'

'Theirs go off when they're supposed to,' said Salmon tartly.

'Look, will you get that gun off me? You know who I am. I'm sorry if I surprised you, but we weren't expecting you. I thought we were being raided.'

'I wasn't expecting you,' admitted Daoud. Finally he lowered the gun. Only a little, it stayed in his hand, but at least Salmon wasn't staring down the barrel any more. It made it easier to think. 'Or your Irish bomb-maker.' He stared at Voss as if his ginger hair was a personal affront.

'Let me tell him what's going on,' said Salmon. 'He doesn't speak Arabic. He probably still thinks we've got a problem here.'

After a moment Daoud nodded. 'We don't want anyone thinking we've got a problem.'

Voss mightn't speak Arabic but Daoud spoke good English. Salmon had to get this right. 'A misunderstanding,' he said, and hoped Voss was less groggy than he looked and capable of following not only what he was saying but also what he wasn't. 'This is my friend Daoud. We worked together in the past. I told him we thought he was the police.'

Voss laughed dutifully.

'He thought the same thing. I explained you're from Belfast, here to show us how to make a better bomb.'

'So tell me,' said Daoud quietly, in English, 'what is it you know about explosives that we don't?'

Voss sat up, leaning his back against the bed. 'I know Semtex is a damn sight more reliable than HMTD.' He wasn't sure about the accent. But Daoud was a Saudi—he might recognise an Irish accent when he heard one but probably wouldn't know the difference between a Belfast accent, a Dublin one and the kind of stage Irish brogue in which drunken Englishmen sing 'Danny Boy'.

'But also harder to get hold of. And reliability is less of an issue when your operatives are willing to martyr themselves,' said Daoud.

'You mean, the dumb shits don't mind fragging themselves and leaving the target standing?'

For a second Salmon thought he'd killed them both. But he'd

got the tone exactly right. The weary combativeness, the disrespect of the veteran terrorist for the upstart: exactly those things may be heard in the voices of IRA men who've outlived their war.

Daoud nodded slowly. 'What will you do about that?'

'The trigger mechanism,' said Voss immediately. 'I mean yeah, pulling a string is nice and simple, you wouldn't think much could go wrong. But you know, I think we can improve on it.'

Suddenly Daoud smiled. 'You know, I think you're right.' The gun in his hand seemed less like a weapon now and more like a piece of personal jewellery. Finally he took time to look around. 'Where are the Dhazi boys? Hiding under the bed?'

Salmon grinned. 'I didn't trust them to keep their nerve. I sent them away.'

'Permanently?'

Salmon's brows gathered in a frown of mild disapproval. 'To relatives in London.'

Daoud looked surprised. 'You trust them to keep quiet in London?'

'Will you guys talk English?' demanded Voss in his all-purpose Irish accent.

Salmon ignored him. 'I don't think they'll talk to anyone. I think they'll talk to one another by slipping notes under the door.'

Daoud laughed aloud. 'OK.' He cocked an eyebrow at Voss. 'That English enough for you—OK? Someone should bring me up to date. Things have moved on while I was in Birmingham.'

Salmon immediately looked wary. It required no acting at all. 'Then—forgive me—perhaps it's not me who should be bringing you up to date. Are you actually supposed to be here?'

'I don't know,' admitted Daoud. 'The Dhazis knew I was coming back. But the Dhazis aren't here now, and you are.' He considered. 'Are *you* supposed to be here?'

Even to himself, Salmon's chuckle sounded less than convincing. 'We're where we were sent. We were given a job to do and told to do it here. Maybe we were told wrong.'

'English,' insisted Voss. 'Talk frigging *English!'*

'We're upsetting your ethnic friend,' said Daoud in Arabic. Then to Voss: 'My apologies. Very well. How far have you got? You have the Semtex here?'

Voss hesitated. If he said *yes* the very next question would bring the whole subterfuge to a bloody end. But if he said *no* the Arab was entitled to wonder why not. He turned indignantly to his senior officer. 'I want to know exactly who this guy is before I tell him anything. You said we'd be alone here. Jesus, have you people *no* idea what's meant by the word *security?*'

Salmon gave an awkward little shrug. 'He has a point. Maybe we should call someone...?'

'That's probably best,' agreed Daoud. 'Call your contact. Listen.' He jerked his head towards the bathroom. 'I'm bursting. I'll be right back.' He closed the bedroom door behind him.

Salmon vented a long, silent breath to carry away some of the tension. But he held up a hand to warn Voss that they weren't safe yet. 'Call the boss,' he said aloud. 'Tell him what's happened.'

And because he was talking to Voss, who was still on the floor beside the bed, he had his back half-turned when the door opened again unexpectedly. The first thing that came in wasn't Daoud. It wasn't even Daoud's gun. It was a bullet. So was the second thing.

DEACON ARRIVED, wheels spitting grit, as the paramedic slammed the back door of the ambulance. Deacon's hand closed over his on the handle, inflicting instant paralysis. 'Who?'

But there hadn't been time to get names. 'Foreign-looking guy. Listen, we've got to go, right now. This is a straight-to-theatre job.'

Deacon stood back. 'Go.' The weight of shock kept him standing there a moment longer. He'd thought they'd done everything necessary to control the situation. But a fanatic with a gun had slipped through the cordon, and he'd lost one of them because of it. Dave Salmon, who'd survived deep cover with Anglophobe extremists only to go down protecting a dowdy little south coast town nobody'd ever heard of; or Charlie Voss, who'd had it all ahead of him, who'd have made an outstanding police officer and now wouldn't get the chance.

Deacon wasn't a man who prayed. What had happened had already happened and it was asking a lot even of omnipotence to turn the clock back. But he hoped briefly, guiltily, that it was Salmon who was dead and Voss who was alive. Then he went into the house.

Everyone was upstairs. They melted out of his way like magic. On the landing someone had, in defiance of best practice, perhaps as a mark of respect, spread a sheet over the body. Inside the bedroom another paramedic was bent over the third man, dispensing bandages and good advice. 'Sit there. Don't move. You're in shock—if you try to get up you'll fall over.'

Deacon tried to see past his shoulders and couldn't. So he fisted one hand on the man's collar and pulled him back like restraining an Airedale.

'Hi, boss,' said Charlie Voss weakly.

SEVENTEEN

ALL AT ONCE Deacon needed to sit down. Any evidence on the bed would need to be collected from the imprint of his backside. The springs creaked under him. 'What happened?'

Voss was cold. Someone had put a blanket round his shoulders. 'I'm not sure. He got the drop on us but Dave lied for England, told Daoud we were all on the same side. I thought he'd got away with it. But Daoud did the revolving door thing and nailed us while we were mopping the sweat from our brows.'

'He shot you?' Deacon's voice soared. 'Then what the hell are you sitting here for? Why aren't you in that ambulance?'

'I wanted to see you first. I'll catch the next one. They were in a hurry, I didn't want to hold them up. I'm OK.' He moved the corner of the blanket gingerly away from his leg and there was a blood-blackened tear in his jeans. 'He almost missed me. It's just, I'm a bit chilled.'

It was the middle of a mid-September night but that wasn't the reason. When Deacon put the back of his hand to Voss's forehead his skin was cold and waxy and dewed with an icy sweat. 'Tell me about it later. You need to be in hospital.' He turned on the paramedic, still rubbing his throat. 'What the hell were you thinking of? There's room in an ambulance for two. And if there wasn't, you could have left the other one on the pavement.'

It wasn't just professional ethics that made the paramedic's eyebrows climb. 'I thought…'

Voss realised there'd been a misunderstanding. 'Er—boss?' He actually flinched as Deacon's gaze seered round at him.

'You're not thinking that was Daoud in the ambulance, are you? It's Dave. He's got a bullet in his lung. Daoud's under the sheet.'

Deacon moved the impromptu shroud carefully and stood looking down at the man. He'd come within a gnat's whisker of killing two good officers but failure had cost him his own life. There were finger-sized craters in his left thigh and his left cheek, and Deacon knew that if he risked SOCO's wrath by rolling Daoud over he'd find fist-sized exit wounds on the other side. It was too late to hate him. But Deacon despised him. He despised all who talked loftily about causes but left the world poorer and in pain.

He had a number of regrets about tonight's work. A lot of man-hours and a big slice of budget had gone into spotting Daoud early enough to manage his arrest safely; but they'd missed him, and because of that Dave Salmon was being rushed to hospital with a chest wound, and Charlie Voss was shivering with shock, and a man who could have answered vital questions wasn't telling anybody anything ever again. All these things were regrettable. But at a personal level, all he felt about the violent death of a violent man was relief. Any way a wolf dies, the lambs breathe a little easier.

He turned and looked at Voss. 'If Daoud shot Salmon, who shot Daoud?'

'I did,' admitted Voss.

'You weren't armed.'

'Dave was armed. Daoud knocked the gun out of his hand.'

'And you picked it up.'

'Yes.'

'And shot him. Twice.'

Voss blinked. 'Did I? I fired a lot of rounds. I didn't know how many hit him. I just kept firing till he went down. I didn't think I had a choice. He'd have killed us both.'

'You don't have to explain it to me, lad,' said Deacon with a kind of gruff kindness. 'You did the right thing. Remember that. Anyone tells you otherwise, they're wrong. They weren't there, they don't know. You did what was necessary.' He sniffed. 'Now will you for God's sake get off to hospital and stop bleeding on my crime scene?'

IF JOE LOOMIS had had a wife, or a mistress, or even a casual companion, Brodie would have spoken to her. So far as she could discover he hadn't. She wondered about that. No one who knew him would have described Loomis as the answer to a maiden's prayer, but even the most unpromising men can usually find a partner if they play their cards right. And there are plenty of women for whom money, even dirty money, is the ace in the hole.

So his lack of attachment was a puzzle. Brodie wondered briefly if it wasn't women's names she should be looking for but men's. But nothing she knew about him suggested he was easily embarrassed, and when you rule a criminal empire—or perhaps more a criminal emporium—essentially by fear, you don't have to worry about people poking fun. If there'd been a man in Loomis's life Brodie was pretty sure she'd have got wind of it by now. There must be another explanation.

And there was; and it was so obvious she felt foolish for not spotting it sooner. The man didn't just deal in drugs, he dealt in prostitutes. And he was exactly the kind of man to think that you don't need to buy a box of chocolates when you've got the key to the pick-and-mix.

The Rose in Rye Lane was not the sort of pub where respectable unaccompanied women take lunch. It was the sort of pub where respectable women, and men, do an about-turn, mutter something about their parking meter and beat a hasty retreat if they wander in by accident. It was dark, it was dirty, and the best that could be said of the regular clientele was that when they were adding to the fug in The Rose they weren't making the rest of Dimmock nervous.

So when Brodie came inside, appropriated a high stool and slapped her handbag on the bar in front of Wally Briggs, the background mutter of nameless crimes being reminisced over stopped dead. Every eye in the place was on her.

She waited about ten seconds—which in such circumstances is longer than it sounds—before half-turning on her stool and saying calmly over her shoulder, 'Don't get your hopes up, guys. I'm here on business but not that kind of business.'

She turned back to the bartender and took from her bag a handkerchief that wasn't much more than a large, rusty stain with a lace edge. 'Do you want to guess what that is, Mr Briggs?'

For a lot of years Wally Briggs had stayed safe in dangerous company by never venturing an opinion on anything. He wasn't about to break the habit of a lifetime for a woman who looked like a princess, talked like a hooker and was clearly up to no good. He shook his head.

'It's Joe Loomis's blood. Your boss's blood, Wally. Someone stabbed him and he came to me for help. Do you know what his dying words were?'

Wally shook his head again, so quickly it looked like a tic.

'He said, "Find out who did this. Tell my old mate Wally to give you any help you need."'

Wally Briggs felt his jaw dropping. Being helpful was even worse than offering an opinion, even more likely to blow up in your face. But Joe Loomis was his boss. Well, strictly speaking *had been* his boss, but Wally wasn't a man who adjusted to change quickly. Other people had taken over the pub, and other aspects of the Loomis enterprise, but down at gut level where survival depended on jumping for the right voice, Wally still reckoned to work for Joe. In the man's unavoidable absence, he owed his allegiance to Joe's blood on a bit of cotton.

Brodie would have sworn the bartender was actually speaking to her handkerchief. 'What do you want to know?'

'Who's running his stable now?'

Wally avoided her eyes. 'I don't know what you mean.'

'Of course you know what I mean,' said Brodie impatiently. 'Joe kept a stable of prostitutes upstairs at The Rose. Every-

body knows that. Now, I don't believe they all went into con-
vents first thing last Wednesday morning, so someone's taken
up the reins. I want to speak to him.' She pushed the stained
handkerchief across the bar. Wally recoiled. 'It's what Joe
wants.'

'Her,' muttered Wally.

'Her?'

'The girls talked it over. They didn't want none of Mr
Loomis's minders telling them what to do. Donna Sugden's
keeping the book.'

'Then I'll talk to Donna.'

Nothing terrible had happened to him. Wally rallied a little.
'I'll see if she's free.'

'Good idea,' nodded Brodie. 'I'll come with you.'

Wally couldn't think how to stop her. The prostitutes worked
upstairs but the office was at the back of the rambling old inn.
As he led the way he said, with awe in his voice, 'Did Mr
Loomis really send you to me?'

'Of course he didn't, you stupid man,' said Brodie dismissively. 'That was soy sauce on the hanky.'

DONNA SUGDEN WAS OLDER than Brodie and no longer
boasted the kind of looks that make a certain kind of man
reach for his wallet. But her continued presence in a working
brothel didn't surprise Brodie. She could see immediately
what the woman had to offer. Her face was alive with expression, the eyes intelligent, a quirk of humour lifting one corner
of the mouth. Probably none of her clients came here looking
for a forty-year-old woman whose laughter lines were turning
inexorably into wrinkles. But men who would have trouble
distinguishing one pneumatic blonde from another after they
sobered up would remember Donna, and seek her out again.
And she had the girls' vote. Brodie had met several prostitutes
in the course of her career. They were canny about everything
except their own lives.

Donna nodded a cautious greeting. 'Wally said you wanted to see me.'

'Yes. Thanks.' Brodie hesitated a moment. 'Do you know who I am?'

'You're the one who found Joe.'

'Yes. Well—Joe found me. He knew what I do for a living. I think that's why he came to my door rather than someone else's.'

Donna was obviously puzzled. 'What do you do?'

'I find things. Sometimes, I find things out. Like, of all the people who might have wanted Joe dead, who actually stuck his own knife in him? And why?'

She saw an ambivalence in Donna Sugden's eyes. This was territory a working girl would rather avoid. Loomis was her pimp. He probably wasn't the first, and sooner or later, whatever the girls decided, there'd be another. It didn't do to get emotionally attached. Yet Brodie felt it there, hanging in the dusty air between them—the unwise affection she'd felt for him.

'Shouldn't the police be doing that?'

Brodie snorted derisively. 'Seen a lot of the police since it happened, have you? Keep tripping over forensics teams and technical teams and guys going through the books—*both* sets of books—with a fine-tooth comb? I thought not. The police don't care who killed Joe. They think there are more important crimes to solve, nobler victims to get justice for. I'm not arguing—of course there are. But *somebody* should be standing up for Joe.'

'Why you?'

Brodie gave a wry shrug. 'Good question. We weren't friends. Actually, he was trying to scare me off. But now he's dead and nobody cares. I'm not looking for his killer,' she admitted frankly. 'I wouldn't know what to do with him if I found him. I'm looking for something to get CID back on the job. If I can tell them it was a drug deal that went wrong or a border war that got out of hand, they'll take it from there.' She looked the other woman in the eye. 'And I thought, maybe Joe talked to you about things he didn't discuss with anyone else.'

For a moment it seemed Donna was going to deny it. Then the blank expression cracked and she gave a reluctant little nod. Even a woman who made her living the way this one made hers was embarrassed to admit liking Joe Loomis. 'I worked for him for fifteen years,' she explained defensively. 'I may have been the closest thing he had to a friend.'

'What kind of friend?'

'You mean, did we sleep together? Sure.' This admission bothered her less than the other. 'Like I say, we were together a lot of years. Neither of us had anyone else. So yes, we slept together. Sometimes. Sometimes we just talked, and sometimes we didn't even talk. You know someone well enough, you can do that—just watch telly and drink cocoa together. Don't get me wrong.' Her tone sharpened. 'I didn't think he was a nice man. I didn't when he was alive and I don't now he's dead. But we had some nice times. For a basically crap human being, he was OK with me.'

'Then you'll help me?'

The older woman thought a little longer about that. 'If I can. Without stirring up more trouble than I can handle.'

Brodie pricked up her ears. 'Trouble for who?'

'For me; for the girls. I don't know who killed Joe. But if it turns out it was someone after his business, I don't want him thinking I'm a problem. Working girls are vulnerable, you know? I'm sorry about Joe, but not sorry enough to risk having his killer come here one night with a petrol can.'

Brodie was nodding. 'Fair enough. But you could tell me about Joe, couldn't you?'

'What do you want to know?'

'If he was worried about something, would he have told you?'

'Probably,' said Donna.

'And was he? In the week or so before he died?'

Donna shook her head. 'No. I mean, little everyday things— who's creaming the profits, who's pilfering the goods. Nothing to get killed over.'

'Was he at loggerheads with any rivals?'

Donna immediately became wary. 'I don't know.'

'He and Terry Walsh had a longstanding mutual dislike,' said Brodie. 'Any developments on that front?'

That was easier to answer. 'Not that I heard.'

'Did he owe anyone money?'

'Always. No more than usual.'

Brodie was running out of questions. 'What about his personal life? Would you have known if he was seeing another woman?'

Donna laughed out loud. 'Of course I'd have known. He'd have told me. We weren't married—we weren't even living together. If he'd found someone who actually liked him I'd have been happy for him. There was no one. I don't think he was looking for anyone. I think nights with his feet up in front of my telly suited him fine.'

Donna was making it sound like *The Little House on the Prairie,* not a criminal and his cathouse madam. Brodie frowned. 'If he had no enemies, why is he dead?'

'He must have had an enemy,' agreed Donna. 'No, that's stupid—he had lots of enemies. But they were old enemies—he knew them, knew what they were capable of. He wouldn't have let any of them close enough to stick him. Someone took him by surprise. Whoever it was he went to meet.'

'He went to meet someone?'

'Must have done,' said Donna. 'That place where they found his car—there was no other reason for him to be there. But that's funny too, because if he'd felt in any danger—any at all—he'd have taken muscle. He took muscle if he was going down to the betting shop. He took muscle if he was buying a birthday card. If he went alone he knew who he was going to meet and he wasn't expecting any trouble.' She looked up with a tremulous little smile. 'The last mistake he ever made, yeah?'

Brodie twitched her a smile in return. But she was struggling with an incredible image. 'Who the hell did Joe Loomis buy birthday cards for?'

The woman winced as if she'd been struck, and Brodie was immediately contrite. 'I'm sorry, that was rude. It's nice that he bought you a card. It's nice that he had someone to watch television with. I didn't imagine him having much of a home life.'

'He hadn't,' said Donna honestly. 'He spent time with me because there was no one else. He'd reached a point in his life where he didn't even want anything more. Coming to me was easy, cheap, comfortable and undemanding.'

'So he had no family.'

Donna's thin eyebrows drew together. 'Actually, he had. He had a kid. But they never saw one another.'

For some reason Brodie was surprised. 'A son or a daughter?' But Donna didn't know. 'Who was the mother?'

But Donna shook her head. 'I never knew her. Before my time, Joe said.'

So it wasn't a baby. It could be a teenager, or a grown man or woman. 'And he had nothing to do with it?'

'That was stupid,' Donna said sadly. 'He could have kept in touch. He should have made the effort. I said to him, "It's not too late. You're the only father that kid's got, and it's not like you've got any others. You should get in touch—get to know one another, make up for lost time." And he said…he said…'

And Brodie watched in astonishment as this tough, intelligent woman wept over the memory of a vicious thug. 'What did he say?'

'He said, *Over my dead body!*' wailed Donna Sugden.

EIGHTEEN

'So JOE LOOMIS HAD A CHILD.' Daniel sounded almost bemused.

'Apparently,' said Brodie. 'It wasn't part of his life. Donna said he wanted nothing to do with it.'

When she didn't get a response Brodie peered at him. But Daniel was off in his own private world and maintaining radio silence. 'Daniel?'

Albert Einstein was asked once to explain how radio works. 'Wire telegraphy is a kind of very, very long cat,' he said. 'You pull his tail in New York and his head is meowing in Los Angeles. And radio operates exactly the same way. The only difference is that there is no cat.'

There was an invisible cat connecting Brodie and Daniel too. When you stroked his back his head purred; when you pulled his tail he spat. Perhaps the cat had got longer and more relaxed than he once was, perhaps whole weeks passed now where you hardly noticed him at all. But there was always a cat. They had a way of knowing each what the other was doing, what the other was feeling, that drove Jack Deacon mad.

And Brodie felt like a hatpin to the heart the thoughts preoccupying her friend. 'Daniel…'

He didn't try to deny it. Not just because he didn't lie, but because Brodie would know what he was thinking whether he lied or not. He gave a painful little smile. 'It's all right. It's just, every so often it strikes me. That even a thug like Joe Loomis can produce something as perfect as a child. And I'm…really good with numbers.'

If this had been about anything else she'd have reached for

his hand. But she was afraid of hurting him. She said softly, 'If that's what you want—children—you have to find someone to have them with.'

Gentle and stubborn as always, he shook his yellow head. 'Nobody gets everything they want. You try too hard, you lose what you have. Yes, I'd like a family—but not just any family. Everyone's choices carry a cost. There's a saying, isn't there?— *Take what you want, says God, and pay for it.* Well, this was my choice, this is the price tag. It's worth it to me. If it wasn't I'd do something else.'

His honesty transfixed her. There was no one in the world, not even him, to whom she would have revealed herself like that. Even when she felt that way, about her husband in the early years of her marriage, she never declared it; and the way the marriage ended seemed to prove her wisdom. Not even to punish him—and there had been a long time when she wanted desperately to punish him—would she have had John Farrell know just how much losing him had hurt. She would have suffered agonies rather than confess her weakness. In Daniel, though, it hardly seemed a weakness. His honesty about wanting something he could never have seemed almost like a strength.

'If there was anything I could do…' she whispered.

'I know.' His smile tore her heart out by the roots. 'Brodie, this is the story of my life. The wrong time, the wrong place, the wrong person. I'm used to it. And wanting more out of this than you do doesn't blind me to the fact that I already get more out of it than I ever expected. I get you. Not all of you, but quite a bit. I get your children. I get people I care about caring about me. Don't underestimate that. A lot of people go their whole lives and never come close.

'And one of them,' he added, giving himself a kind of mental shake and returning to the subject, 'was Joe Loomis. He had a child—but he didn't know it and he didn't want to. How lonely is that?'

'He had Donna,' mumbled Brodie, struggling to move on. 'Without her I think he'd have been entirely alone.'

'Well, I don't think having a child is what got Joe killed. Knowing him and what he did for a living, there have to be grimier secrets in his coal cellar. The mother might have set the Child Support Agency onto him—she wouldn't have stabbed him in the heart.'

Brodie thought he was probably right. Which left her without a lead to follow. 'I've only found two people who had any kind of a personal relationship with him, and one of them was twenty years ago. Both of them thought Joe died because of the business he was in, because that's how gangsters die. I don't think there's anything more I can do. I'm not getting involved in a gang war!'

'I'm very glad to hear it,' Daniel said as if he'd wondered.

'But if that's what's going on, why isn't Jack more interested?'

'Maybe he has bigger fish to fry.'

'Bigger than a gang war?!!'

'It doesn't *sound* like Jack, does it?' admitted Daniel. 'I don't know. Ask him.'

DETECTIVE SERGEANT Charlie Voss had been in tough spots before. He'd been beaten bloody. He'd been threatened with knives, guns and disciplinary action. He hadn't actually been shot before, but in fact the bullet crease to his thigh was not the cause of his current discomfort. This was the first time he'd been interviewed in bed by his senior officer, and even that he could have carried off with some residual dignity if he hadn't been wearing a T-shirt printed with the legend *Policemen do it with caution.* It was his fiancée's idea of a joke.

Someone else might not have noticed. But Deacon scrutinised the inscription as if it might have been a clue. Then he peered at Voss; then for a moment he shut his eyes. Only after that was he ready to move on. 'Tell me what happened. Everything that happened.'

Voss supplied all the detail he could remember. A lot depended on what Deacon did next.

Deacon listened carefully but didn't interrupt, saving his questions until Voss had finished. Then: 'Was Daoud here to blow things up?'

Voss hadn't realised there was a doubt. 'He was a bit trigger-happy for a guy visiting friends!'

Deacon nodded ponderously. 'I'm getting two stories, Charlie, and I don't know which is right. The Dhazi cousins are telling me they were into drugs, not explosives. That they didn't know Daoud was a terrorist. He came to Dimmock from Pakistan with a suitcase full of heroin which they were going to sell to Joe Loomis.

'But Dave Salmon is telling me—mostly by sign language, he's got so many tubes stuck in him it's like talking to a pipe organ—that Daoud graduated from drug trafficking a long time ago. That the only thing big enough to bring him here now was the prospect of killing infidels. That the Dhazis are lying—their house was being used by a terror cell, only they were still waiting for the stuff they were going to need and they think they can bluff their way out if they just keep insisting they know nothing about any bombs.'

Deacon pulled up a chair with his foot. 'And I don't know which story's right. I know the Dhazis have every reason to lie and Salmon's telling me what he believes to be the truth. But lives depend on getting this right. Forensics say there's been no HMTD in the house. But if Daoud came to set up a bomb factory, until he got started there wouldn't be anything for Forensics to find.'

'Then, if Daoud's dead and the Dhazis are in custody…?'

Deacon finished the sentence for him. 'Are we in the clear? Maybe we are, Charlie Voss, maybe we are. Maybe it doesn't matter what Daoud was up to, maybe whatever it was died with him.

'But the other possibility is that it didn't. That there's another house in Dimmock where intense young men think it's more important to kill other people's children than live long enough to raise their own. Maybe all that's necessary to flatten the town centre is sitting in a garage somewhere right now, just waiting for someone to do the chemistry. When word gets back to whoever sent Daoud, they'll send someone else. So yes, it matters that we know what we're dealing with. I know what Salmon thinks. I want to know what you think.'

Voss didn't want to say. He didn't want to be part of a decision that could cost lives. But it was his job. He took a deep breath and forced himself back to Romney Road.

'He didn't know there was a problem until he came upstairs. We were behind the bedroom door, just waiting for him to pass before we took him. But something warned him. I don't know what: good instincts, I suppose. Anyway, he knew we were there, and he knew he was in trouble—he didn't think we were just the Dhazi boys waking up. He came through the door gun first. He was ready to deal with any trouble he met.'

Something occurred to him. 'If you're smuggling drugs, you know you're going to be in trouble if you're caught—but only if you're actually carrying them. Was he?'

Deacon shook his head. 'Nothing. There was nothing in his rucksack but a change of clothes. According to the sniffer dog, there'd never been any drugs in there. Mind you, the *other* sniffer dog said there'd been no explosives in there either.'

'OK,' said Voss. The point he was getting to was this. 'A drug runner is only a drug runner if he's carrying drugs, but a terrorist is still a terrorist if all he's carrying is a well-formed idea. There was no need for him to react as he did if he really had got separated from a suitcase full of heroin.'

Deacon was watching him intently. 'You think he was here to make things go bang?'

'Yes,' said Voss. 'That's what they were talking about—him and DI Salmon. Dave told him I was an IRA bomb expert, and he questioned me about that. Why didn't he just day, "Leave me out of this, all I'm interested in is the drugs?" Why get involved in a conversation about the relative merits of HMTD and Semtex if your specialist subject is the opium poppy?'

Finally Deacon exhaled. There was no sense of relief in it. 'So we still have a problem. We may have knocked them off their stride, we may have won a bit of time, but there are still young men living in the quiet streets around Romney Road who want to advance the cause of world peace by wiping out half the population of Dimmock.'

NINETEEN

DANIEL'S PHONE DIDN'T often ring in the small hours of the morning. So when it did he had a pretty good idea who it was going to be. 'Hi, Brodie,' he yawned.

'Did I wake you?'

He considered. But he was too sleepy for wit. 'Yes.'

'Sorry. I've been thinking.'

'Yes?'

'I know who Joe Loomis's son is.'

He realised she was waiting for a fanfare. But he was still having trouble making the words connect, couldn't provide a musical accompaniment as well. 'Who?'

'Dev Stretton!' Somehow, she knew that the silence which followed wasn't awestruck admiration. 'Daniel?'

'Dev Stretton's father is Asian.'

'But do we actually know that?' demanded Brodie.

'I *thought* I knew that,' said Daniel. 'There's his name, for starters. And what Faith Stretton said to Loomis before he slapped her.'

'But it works,' insisted Brodie. 'She had a relationship with Loomis back in the eighties, and Dev's—what? Twenty-five? He even looks like Joe.'

'Brodie—he's Eurasian. He *looks* Eurasian.'

Unseen at the end of the line, Brodie was shaking her head. 'No. He's olive skinned. Joe was olive skinned. A lot of Irish people are—there's Spanish blood from the wreck of the Armada. They call them the Black Irish. Joe Loomis and Faith Stretton could easily produce a child with Dev's colouring.'

'Well—maybe.' Daniel sounded less than convinced. But he did sound more awake. 'So what are you suggesting? When Dev found out who his father was he went and stuck a knife in him?'

'Maybe,' said Brodie warmly. 'Maybe that's what Faith and Joe were arguing about when you saw them—she wanted him to stay clear of Dev. But maybe Joe thought a bit more about what Donna had said and decided he wanted to get to know his son. Faith told him—you *heard* her tell him—she'd rather have people think Dev's father was someone else. That's when he slapped her.

'Daniel, maybe that's what started the ball rolling. Maybe until then Dev didn't know who his father was. It was only when she had to explain her bruises that she finally told him the truth. It would have come as a terrible shock. Particularly when he found out he was a different race to what he thought. And then he found out that his long lost daddy was a sleaze-ball who'd been living a few miles away all his life.'

She was developing the theory even as she talked. 'Suppose he called Joe and asked to meet him. Anyone else he expected trouble from, Joe would have taken backup. But he's not going to take heavies to deal with his son. He thinks there may be shouting, even fisticuffs, but he's no reason to expect anything worse. He won't admit he needs protection from his own child.'

Almost against his better judgement, Daniel was getting drawn into the hypothesis. 'Or maybe he does,' he said slowly. 'He was the one who brought the knife, after all.'

Brodie was nodding. She had Jonathan on her knee, the phone cradled between her shoulder and her ear. 'And he was glad he had. The meeting went badly. Dev's a lot bigger than Joe, and he was angry about the way his mother had been treated—not just that week but for twenty-five years. Joe thought he was going to get a thrashing so he produced his knife.'

'But Dev's been around a bit too,' suggested Daniel. 'He's worked on construction sites here and abroad. He must have learnt how to look after himself. Instead of backing off he grabbed for it. They struggled, and it ended up in Joe's side.'

'And Dev found himself wondering how much it really mattered,' continued Brodie. 'If Joe survived he wasn't going to tell the police he'd been stabbed with his own knife by his own son. And if he didn't, who cared? We'd all assume that one of Joe's deals had come back to haunt him. No one but Faith even knew there was a connection between him and Joe. So Dev walked away, leaving Joe in a rapidly spreading pool of his own blood, and thought there was a good chance no one would ever ask him about it.'

There was silence as they pondered it. There was no proof. But so many things, things of no consequence, things no one would have thought to fabricate, made sense if this was how it happened.

Daniel frowned. 'Why did she call him Dev? It's not an English name.'

'She *told* you why,' said Brodie impatiently. 'She didn't want people to know she'd got up close and personal with Joe Loomis! She was breaking the trail. From before that baby was born, she didn't want it linked to Joe. And boy, was that a good decision!'

Starting with not much more than a gut feeling, Brodie was startled at how far she'd travelled in the space of a phone call. Of course, this was Daniel. They were two minds so well attuned they were capable of networking like computers, and the thinking power produced was greater than the sum of the parts. 'I'd better call Jack,' she said.

'Brodie, it's the middle of the night. It's waited a week, it can wait till morning. Go back to sleep.'

'I wasn't asleep,' she said carelessly. 'Jonathan was a bit restless. I made us both a snack, then I started thinking. No, I'll call Jack while this is fresh in my mind.' And with devastating thoughtlessness she added impishly, 'He's woken me up often enough. Now it's my turn.'

DEACON HAD ROLLED into bed, with some of his clothes still on, and immediately fallen unconscious forty minutes before. When the phone rang it split him in half. Half his brain knew it had to be hugely, urgently important or Battle Alley would have let him sleep. The other half decided *nothing* was that important, and tried to go on sleeping anyway.

The dichotomy left him imperfectly prepared for a conversation with Brodie about Joe Loomis.

'I think I know who killed him,' she said without preamble. 'I think I know how it happened, and I think I know why.'

Deacon felt like a spectator at a tennis match suffering a mild concussion from a wayward smash. 'What?' he mumbled. 'Who?'

Brodie breathed heavily at him. 'Joe Loomis. For heaven's sake, Jack, try to keep up! I'm telling you I've solved your murder case. Well—manslaughter, probably. Or since this was Joe, rat-slaughter, but it'll still look good in the crime statistics. The least you can do is concentrate.'

Deacon blinked owlishly at the phone. And then he replied. He didn't tell her of the night he'd had, or how recently it had ended. He cut straight to the headlines, which were that (a) right now he didn't care who killed Joe Loomis, and (b) he was pretty sure she was wrong anyway. Only he didn't say *pretty sure.*

'That's nice language to use in front of your son!' she said indignantly. 'If he grows up to stick a knife in *you,* don't blame me! And don't expect me to turn him in, either.'

If she'd had an ounce of sensitivity in her she'd have heard the exhaustion in his voice. 'Brodie, I'm past knowing what to expect of you. You seem to think my job is a kind of party game and anyone can have a go. These are real people we're talking about. If it turns out it wasn't the butler with the candlestick in the dining room, you don't just shrug it off and have another guess. You can wreck people's lives. You don't go round accusing people because they look shifty and you don't know that they *couldn't* have done it.'

Brodie was piqued by the criticism—the more so, probably, because he was right. It was the difference between his job and hers. If she was hunting for a lost painting, she did the detective work pretty much the same way—but if, when she snatched

aside the curtain triumphantly, it turned out to be not an early
Alma-Tadema but a Beryl Cook print she could wipe the egg
off her face and leave. No one went to prison. No one's family
were left thinking, *But maybe he DID...*

She said snidely, 'I thought that was exactly how you worked.'

He yawned. 'Brodie...'

'So you're not prepared even to listen? Someone died and
someone else killed him, and I've a good idea who, and you
don't want to know? You're the senior CID officer in this town,
and you'd rather catch up on your sleep than solve a murder.'

Old acquaintances were amazed at how Jack Deacon had
learnt to bridle his temper around Brodie. It had to be love, they
decided, or something like it. Which was not to say there were
no limits to his newfound patience, and he reached them sooner
when he was tired than when he was fresh. When he was tired he
didn't care that, rigid with umbrage, she could one day stalk out
of his life. When he was this tired he almost wished she would.

'Brodie, I can't deal with this right now. I have to get some
sleep. If things calm down in the next day or two, I'll give you
a call and we'll discuss it. But not in the middle of the night.'

'The next day or two!' exclaimed Brodie, astonished.
'We're not talking about a parking ticket here. We're talking
about a killing!'

'No,' said Deacon forcibly, 'we're not. You want to go on
talking about it, talk to someone else. Hey—call Daniel, he's
never anything better to do at four in the morning. Talk to
Daniel, work out exactly who did what, then nip round and ask
the murderer to sign a confession. And tell him I'll be round in
a day or two.'

THE NEXT DAY was Wednesday. About half past eight Brodie
trotted upstairs to ask Marta Szarabeijka if she'd mind Jonathan
till Daniel arrived. She could have taken him with her when she
took Paddy to school, but then she'd have had to bring him back
and Daniel would want to know where she was going next. And

she didn't want to tell him. She wasn't expecting trouble—she wasn't actually going to ask Dev Stretton to sign a confession—but Daniel would try to dissuade her.

Marta glanced at her watch. It was an oversized man's watch that covered much of her strong, bony wrist, but Marta didn't do dainty. As a young woman she left Poland two steps ahead of an arrest warrant for political agitation. Now in her mid-fifties, still refusing to bow to convention, she wore her long grey hair in a plait, had a toy boy in Littlehampton and bought watches she could read without putting her glasses on.

'I got Graham in half an hour.' Then, relenting: 'He got no talent. He rides a motorcycle—give him a spanner and he knows what he's doing, give him a nocturne in D-major and it might as well be "Chopsticks". I can rock the baby *and* teach him more piano than he's ever going to play. Sure, bring him up.'

Jonathan had finally settled down about six o'clock and now wasn't waking for anyone. Brodie hadn't gone back to sleep: she'd spent the rest of the night considering her next move. She could wait until Deacon was in a better frame of mind, or at least had fewer distractions, and try again to tell him the conclusion she'd reached. She could shrug if off as none of her business. No one who knew her even slightly would have expected her to take either course. She didn't pander to Deacon's moods, he pandered to hers. And she never, ever thought that anything was none of her business.

And Deacon's manner on the phone still annoyed her. She accepted that he'd been tired. She knew—a sanitised version had been released to the media—that Charlie Voss and another officer had been injured and a third man killed in an accident in Romney Road the night before, and that meant he'd hardly slept for forty-eight hours. But his dismissive tone still rankled, and the best revenge she could think of was to sew his case up for him. An act of subversive kindness, that would sting and sting and leave him nothing to complain about.

Everything depended on her intuition having been right—

that Dev was the result of that brief, unwise, regretted relationship between Faith Stretton and Joe Loomis. If he was, everything else made sense. But she needed to know for sure before
she put this in front of Deacon.

She was going to ask Faith. She believed that if she asked
face to face, woman to woman, Faith would tell her.

TWENTY

THERE WERE BAGS PILED in the hallway. Brodie's heart lurched and raced in the five seconds it took her to realise that one of them was pink and had glitter stickers on it, and however desperate he was to flee the scene of a murder Dev Stretton would probably still rather be caught than make a run for it with girly luggage.

'Evie not off yet?' asked Brodie.

Faith looked terribly harassed. She mopped her brow with the back of her wrist. 'She keeps thinking of something else she's going to need. I swear to God, Drake circumnavigated the globe with less baggage! When I was her age, I was hitching across Australia with all my worldly goods in a backpack. Evie's luggage is bigger than she is!'

The girl appeared at the top of the stairs. 'Mum, I need…'

'No,' said Faith immediately. 'You don't.'

'But…'

'Evie! What you need is to get finished and get off. If you've forgotten something vital you can buy it at the other end. If you've forgotten something trivial you can manage without it.'

The girl turned away with a flounce. Brodie supposed she was about seventeen: a child and a woman at the same time. Old enough to reproduce, not old enough to vote. Old enough to drive, not quite old enough to understand that trains and aeroplanes won't wait for you the way parents—however bad-temperedly—will. 'How's she travelling?'

'A friend's taking her,' said Faith distractedly. She gazed at the pile of bags in despair. 'Lord knows where this lot's going.'

Abruptly she turned her back on it, headed out through the kitchen. 'Come into the studio. We can get a bit of peace.'

Faith's studio was smarter than Brodie had imagined. Her wheel and workbench were in one corner, a powerful modern kiln in another, and the rest of the space was showroom. Faith indicated a couple of chairs beside a coffee table, but Brodie couldn't resist looking round first. There were commemorative plates and rustic dinner services and art pieces whose method of construction was not at all obvious. 'They're lovely,' she said, genuinely impressed.

'Thank you,' said Faith. 'Is that what you wanted to see me about?' She sounded hopeful.

''Fraid not,' said Brodie honestly. 'It's more personal than professional. And you're going to think it's none of my business, and you're right. The only thing is, if you talk to me now you might avoid having to talk to the police later.'

Faith's expression shut down like a firewall. She volunteered nothing, left Brodie to doggy-paddle through an icy sea of silence. 'Look, Faith, we haven't known one another very long, but we have a lot in common. I think we talk the same language. Believe me when I say it's time to talk about this. Keeping the secret any longer can only make things worse, for you and your family.'

Still there was no response from Faith Stretton. She might have said, frostily, *Talk about what?* But she wouldn't offer even that much encouragement. She sat rigid in her chair, implacable-eyed, challenging her visitor to say what she had to.

Brodie sighed. 'OK, make it hard. I know you want me to go away. I will, but not till you answer me a straight question. Or refuse to, which will tell me as much.' This time she waited.

'What question?' Faith's voice was rough, the words dragged from her.

'Was Joe Loomis Dev's father?'

Faith Stretton blinked. Brodie thought, with sinking heart,

that her surprise was genuine. '*Dev's?* You think Dev is Joe's son?' And then she laughed; though in truth there wasn't much humour in it. 'Mrs Farrell, you have *met* my son, haven't you? He's Eurasian. Of mixed race. There are paint cards the same colour as Dev, and they're called things like *Bombay Nights!*'

'Joe wasn't exactly lily-white either.'

'You can say that again!'

'I mean, he was dark—dark hair, olive skin. He could have had a child with Dev's colouring.' Even to herself Brodie sounded like she was fighting a losing battle.

'Maybe that's what I saw in him,' said Faith sardonically. 'I got one nice kid with a dark-skinned man—maybe subconsciously I was looking for another.'

Brodie's teeth had caught a corner of her lip and her nose wrinkled in embarrassment. 'You're telling me I'm wrong.'

'*Yes,*' said Faith with heavy emphasis. 'That's exactly what I'm telling you. Dev is twenty-five years old. He was at school when I met Joe! Look.' She took Brodie's hand fiercely in her own and dragged her to the desk in the corner. 'See those photos? That's Dev in Kashmir. He spent two years there, helping after the earthquake. A hundred thousand people died, and two and a half million were made homeless. And Dev's a civil engineer, he knows how to clear wreckage safely and build bridges and buildings that don't fall down when the ground shakes. So that's what he did. Three days after the earthquake Dev was on a plane heading for Pakistan, and he stayed for two years.

'And my point is this,' she said, turning Brodie to face her. 'Not that Dev's a good guy, although he is. Not that he's a good engineer, although he's that too. My point is, how many young men do *you* know who'd give up two years of their life, at the crucial early stage of their career, to help a bunch of strangers?'

'Well, I don't know any either. Those people freezing on their mountaintops weren't strangers—they were Dev's family.

Kashmir is where his father came from, and that's why he went. Dev is exactly what he appears to be, and his father and I are very proud of him.'

Brodie hardly knew what to say. She didn't often get things this wrong. And she'd been so sure. She and Daniel both… And then she remembered that, actually, all they'd been talking about in the early hours were possibilities. The theory had been entirely hers. All Daniel had done was agree that the sums added up. He never said she'd given him the right figures in the first place.

'I'm sorry,' she mumbled. 'It seemed—I thought… I was barking up the wrong tree, wasn't I? Faith, you'll have to forgive me. I've been thinking too much about this, the shadows started looking like something real. I should leave now, and let you finish Evie's packing. I hope by the time I see you again this is starting to look funny. At least to you…'

She felt her cheeks flaming all the way back to her car.

PHONE LINES CRACKLED between Dimmock, Division, Scotland Yard and the Home Office. No one in the loop was confident that the threat had passed. At the same time, no one was happy to issue a public warning. This wasn't hypocrisy but a recognition that the threat of terrorism makes ordinary people panic, and panicky people hurt themselves and one another.

But while the authorities were still debating the pros and cons behind closed doors and over scrambled phones, events overtook them.

There are places in the world where you can fire guns in the early hours of the morning and the neighbours just pull a pillow over their ears and go back to sleep. But Dimmock wasn't one of them. By six o'clock on Tuesday morning, Tom Sessions of *The Sentinel* was phoning his story to the national media. He wrote about drug-runners and policemen in a dead-of-night battle, and how it ended with two in hospital, two in custody and one in the morgue. And he thought that was pretty much the whole story.

Thirty hours later, having talked to people in Romney Road and elsewhere, he was beginning to think he'd had the wool pulled over his eyes.

The last thing Deacon wanted to do right now was talk to Tom Sessions. And he didn't have to. He could send word to the front desk that he was too busy and the reporter would leave. But he wouldn't stop being a reporter. If CID refused to talk to him, that would be the story. Keeping the secret was no longer an option. And letting people in on it an inch at a time, by means of rumour and speculation, was no way to ensure calm and cooperation. If you can't contain news, Deacon had long ago learnt, the next best thing is to manage it.

'Send him up,' he growled.

Sessions was a tall thin man in his late thirties who always wore a tweed jacket. Deacon had known him for ten years, and except for once a year at the Civic Ball he'd never seen him wear anything but cords and a tweed jacket.

And a succession of ambivalent expressions: interesting combinations like polite authority, amiable determination and open-minded obstinacy. This morning his expression said clearer than words: *You don't have to talk to me, I don't have any strings to pull to make you talk to me, but I'll do my job with or without your help and this is your chance to have some input into the story I tell and how I tell it.*

Deacon got right to the point. 'What do you know already?'

'You *know* what I know already—it was on the TV yesterday! Today I'm starting to think half of it was lies. You want to tell me I'm wrong, Mr. Deacon?' He sounded angry.

'I can't tell you that,' rumbled Deacon. 'It may be the truth. I'm hoping it is. But there's a possibility that there's more going on than that. I needed time to try and find out: that's why I didn't tell you everything. I *still* need time, and I'm still not going to tell you everything. I'll tell you what I can. I'd like to think that'll buy me some cooperation.'

Sessions was starting to look mollified. 'You know *The Sentinel*'s position—that if we can help you do your job without compromising ours, we will. But I don't like being lied to. Even more, I don't like discovering that I've lied to other people.'

Deacon nodded. 'I understand. But I have higher priorities than being frank with you, and in a minute you're going to understand *that*. Some of what I'm going to tell you would have some reporters writing excited headlines with lots of exclamations marks. Are you one of them?'

'Not usually,' said Sessions. 'I can't promise until I know what we're talking about.'

He could pussyfoot around it first, but in the end Deacon would have to come out and say it. 'Terrorism.' And, as Sessions's eyebrows soared, he added quickly, 'We think. There is actually some doubt. Which is why I don't want this going off half-cocked. If I tell you as much as I can of what we know, what we think and what people ought to do about it, is that what you'll write?'

'Yes.'

'And that's *all* you'll write?'

'Well, that's harder,' said Sessions. 'Other people may have things they want to say.'

'Is it your job to do everything anyone wants?'

'No. But then, it's not my job to do everything you want either.' Undeterred by Deacon's scowl, he went on: 'Superintendent, you and I have worked this town for a lot of years. There may have been times you wished I was working some other town, but on the whole we've been on the same side. Dimmock needs us both. This sounds like one of those occasions when you need to look back over the last ten years and decide whether you trust me or not.'

Deacon went on scowling at him for perhaps twenty seconds,

then he snorted a little laugh. 'Mr Sessions, I wouldn't choose to trust anyone with this. But I don't have much choice. So I'll tell you what I can. But let me draw your attention to one consequence of that. Up till now, if this thing went pear-shaped and people got hurt, it was going to be my responsibility. After you leave this office, it could be yours.'

IT WENT OUT WITH the lunchtime news. The man shot dead the previous day in a small south coast town had been linked to al-Qaeda. Police were seeking the assistance of the local community in assessing the terrorist threat.

By five past one the phone lines into Battle Alley were jammed. By half past the roads were growing busy as people who felt they ought to be doing something checked up on friends and relatives and—always the first reaction to any crisis—stocked up their freezers. At ten past two the first unprovoked attack on a person of Asian appearance was reported.

He was Ashok Gul, a twenty-two-year-old trainee accountant, and he was returning to work after lunch when he was set upon by four or five white men with fists, boots and his own briefcase. It was all over in three minutes, after which they ran away leaving him shocked and bleeding on the pavement. Onlookers dialled 999.

Sergeant McKinney despatched a couple of constables, then went upstairs to see Deacon. 'It's started.'

Deacon heard him out, answered with a disparaging sniff. 'It's not the first time someone's been done over for the colour of his skin. Dimmock isn't exactly the beating heart of liberal democracy.'

'True,' agreed McKinney. He knew parts of Dimmock where you got grief for having a Scots accent. 'This was different. It wasn't drunken yobs on their way home on a Friday night. It happened in broad daylight, in the middle of town, with people watching. The guy was wearing a suit. All that tells me it happened because of what was on the news an hour ago. And if I'm right about that, this isn't the end of anything, it's only the beginning.'

'Is he all right?' asked Deacon. 'Gul?'

'I think so. Cuts and bruises, shock, and it didn't do his suit much good. But it's a warning, Jack. Not to him—to us. People are scared. And scared people do stupid things.'

Deacon glowered at him. 'What do you want me to do about it?'

Sergeant McKinney was one of the few people in Battle Alley Police Station who wasn't intimidated by Jack Deacon. He was older than Deacon, he'd been doing the job longer, and he was still in uniform because he chose to be. He'd seen scarier things than Deacon every day when he worked in Glasgow.

'Wrap it up,' he said firmly. 'Until we can tell people the danger has passed, things like this are going to keep happening. In fact, they're going to get worse.'

He was on his way back to the stairs, but turned and said over his shoulder: 'Do you know the really stupid part? Ashok Gul is a Hindu. He's about as likely to belong to al-Qaeda as you are.'

THINGS ONLY got worse after nightfall. All at once the bands of young men, and some of young women, who always hung about on street corners in the evening stopped looking merely idle and started to look menacing. After the Gul incident, the ones who felt most menaced were young Asians, who in consequence made a point of sticking together when they went out. The consequence of *that* was worried phone calls to Battle Alley about gangs of al-Qaeda bombers taking over the streets. It didn't matter how often Sergeant McKinney explained that that's not how bombers work, people were too nervous to listen. Police patrols saturated the town centre, keeping apart people whose mere proximity was making one another anxious.

That wasn't the only problem. Although two days remained of the school week, dozens of uneasy parents decided this was the perfect time to pay unscheduled visits to out-of-town grannies. Dimmock had a perfectly good road system for all normal purposes, but the ebb-tide of people carriers heading anywhere that wasn't Dimmock soon turned into traffic jams.

As a catalyst to this volatile mix of genuine concern and un-justified panic, around midnight a bunch of teenagers had the bright idea—as bunches of teenagers will: there's no situation so fraught that it can't be made worse by a bunch of teenagers—of setting off some fireworks. Mayhem ensued. People stuck in traffic abandoned their cars and ran for shelter, and after that the traffic lights changed and changed in vain—nothing could move. The air was abuzz with the wails of exhausted children, frightened parents shouting instructions no one was in a position to carry out, and volleys of screams as triple-strength bangers went off in the side streets. The sounds melded and mounted to a crescendo that poured over the town in a tidal wave of fear.

Police reinforcements were drafted in from neighbouring towns. In a stroke of ruthless genius the normally mild-mannered Superintendent Fuller, senior officer at Battle Alley, commandeered a bulldozer to shift obstructing vehicles and get the traffic flowing again. The roving bands were shepherded homeward, the stranded were helped, the frightened were re-assured and anyone found in possession of a bit of blue touch-paper was slung in the back of a police car. Gradually the chaos gave way to some semblance of order. By three-thirty in the morning the town was quiet.

Jack Deacon, who'd been directing traffic for the first time in twenty years, slumped exhausted in Superintendent Fuller's office. 'It's official. They're all mad. We work for a commu-nity of lunatics.'

Fuller lacked the strength to smile. 'Go home. Get some sleep. Tomorrow will be worse.'

TWENTY-ONE

TURNING THE MEDIA spotlight on Dimmock changed everything. It was no longer possible to weigh competing evils one against another. Public opinion demanded that *Something must be done,* even though there was no consensus as to what or how it would help.

It wasn't that anyone had done anything wrong. It was the job of *The Sentinel* to report what it knew, however disconcerting. It's the job of the national media to pick up the big stories. And it's the job of governments to protect their citizens against threats, so when the front desk at Battle Alley was inundated with phone calls from people demanding to know if the danger was real, if it was imminent and what the police were doing about it, the callers weren't doing anything wrong either.

With the superintendents too busy to talk, the sergeants field most of the calls—which is pretty much the way police stations work normally. They agreed on a tone of cautious reassurance, telling people that the risk of an attack is still a long way short of an actual attack and advising them to be watchful as they carried on with their normal routines. But even as they said it they knew they were wasting their breath.

Because to the people of Dimmock—to most people in the civilised world—the world *terrorism* that had once meant an IRA bomb in an English pub now conjured images of a city block in ruins. Of innocent, uninvolved, undeserving people slaughtered not by the handful, not by the score, but by the thousand. Of tall buildings full of men and women, most of whom had never done or wished harm on anyone, burning and falling.

They say a picture speaks a thousand words, and it's true. A powerful image etches itself on the retina as if with acid. But you can't tell a story with pictures. There are no nuances, no balance, often not much information. So people see and remember, but what they remember is—quite literally—a snapshot of a moment. A falling man who never lands.

The people phoning Battle Alley were desperate to know what they should do. They needed information and guidance. They turned to a bunch of mostly middle-aged men in blue serge because, say what you like about them when you've had a window broken, in a real emergency most people feel they can count on the police.

But they didn't want to hear that they should carry on as normal. They remembered the pictures and thought they were on the brink of an apocalypse. And though they listened attentively to what Sergeant McKinney and his colleagues told them, after they put the phone down and thought for a bit, and discussed it with their other halves, they all came to the same conclusion. They were getting the hell out of Dimmock. They packed clothes, dogs and—incomprehensibly—bottled water into their cars, locked their houses and hit the road.

A properly organised evacuation proceeds at walking pace. The roads are full of cars with top speeds of a hundred miles an hour; but when the roads are *that* full the cars bump into one another and the drivers get out to argue. Quarter of a mile further back someone's engine overheats; and because they can't move, no one behind them can move either. Three miles an hour is about as fast as you can shift a big body of people, however urgent the need.

If it had been a proper evacuation, people would have been told which roads to take. In the absence of a plan, people living in the Woodgreen estate on the east side of Dimmock decided to visit relatives living in the West Country, and people living in the leafy suburbs on the west side of Dimmock thought they'd try their luck in Dover. They passed one another in the middle of town. But by lunchtime on Thursday it was taking anything up to an hour for two cars heading in opposite directions to get out of one another's sight.

By eight o'clock that morning Brodie had decided against taking Paddy to school. By nine she'd decided against going to her office. Daniel arrived at Chiffney Road at ten past: the chaos in town was such that even walking had taken him twice as long as usual.

'What do they think's going to happen?' demanded Brodie, watching the cars filling Chiffney Road in a doomed attempt to find a short cut out of town. 'The tallest structure in Dimmock is the monument in the park. I suppose you could fly a hang-glider into it, but it wouldn't make much of a bang if you did. It's crazy! All these people would be much safer in their own houses than out on the roads, jammed in and at the mercy of idiots.'

'They're frightened,' said Daniel simply. 'They're afraid that if they stay something terrible will happen to them. Of course they want to leave.'

'Something terrible *will* happen,' agreed Brodie tersely. 'They'll *make* it happen.'

'THIS STUPID TOWN!' fumed Deacon. 'This stupid, stupid, ignorant, *stupid* town!'

He had no need to be so emphatic. No one was arguing.

'*Now* we've got an emergency! Before, we didn't have an emergency. We had a threat—which was probably contained, because two of the only three guys we know about are in custody and the other's dead. There's every chance that any real danger ended when Daoud hit the lino.

'But do people heave a sigh of relief, congratulate us on a job well done and get on with their lives? Do they hell! First they blame us for not being psychic. Then they decide that some town where the police *haven't* thwarted a bomb plot is safer than one where they have. They all pile in their cars and play dodgems till the roads seize solid—and we can't get through, and the fire engines can't get through, and neither can the ambulances to treat all the heart attacks they've given themselves! They're stupid, all of them. They *deserve* to die.'

He didn't mean it. The last bit—he'd meant all the rest. But everyone in the Battle Alley conference room knew, and when he wasn't this angry Deacon knew too, that if he had to he'd put his life on the line to save any one of those stupid little people whose names he neither knew nor wanted to, and to whom he found it difficult to be polite on Community Policing evenings.

'No, they don't,' said the Assistant Chief Constable calmly. 'They deserve to be looked after by those of us whose wages they pay. And they need looking after *more* when they're scared than when they've got all their wits about them.'

Deacon muttered rebelliously. He wasn't muttering anything in particular, just muttering on principle. He didn't react well to authority.

'So how do we handle it?' asked Superintendent Fuller. 'I imagine a decision has been taken higher up?'

ACC (Crime) nodded, a shade ruefully. 'With all the publicity, we couldn't keep it tactical. We couldn't even keep it strategic. It's gone political.'

'*That'll* help,' Deacon muttered savagely.

'So what do you want us to do?' asked Fuller patiently. 'We can shut the town down if we have to. That doesn't necessarily make it a good idea.'

Emily Blake blew out her cheeks unhappily. She knew as well as any of them that whatever counter-terrorism measures they took would hammer at the wedges splitting Dimmock's communities, and that schism was now the greatest danger facing the town. But people were demanding that *Something must be done,* and the difference between policemen and politicians is that politicians need re-electing. Doing nothing isn't always an option, even when it's the right choice.

'We're instituting a no-fly zone,' she said. 'Fifteen miles' radius of Dimmock. There are no airports in that circle, so it'll provide a lot of comfort for not much inconvenience. We want to stop vehicles parking outside any public buildings, or anywhere large numbers of people gather. We want you to divert all vehicles away from the town centre and keep them out until further notice. And we want…' She had the grace to hesitate.

'A curfew? Checkpoints? Photographic ID?' hazarded Superintendent Fuller; and Deacon suggested, 'We should nuke the bastards?' in a hopeful *sotto voce*.

'You're not helping, Jack,' said ACC with a kind of wear severity. 'House-to-house searches, starting at Romney Road.'

That was it. That was where the harmless blue touch-paper met the innocuous match. What Higher Up had decided was that the ninety per cent of Dimmock's population who went red in the sun wouldn't feel safe until someone had looked under the beds of the ten per cent who didn't.

'You want me to round up some foreigners to appease a bunch of mindless idiots?' asked Deacon baldly.

Blake's lips pursed tight. 'I wouldn't put it quite like that, Jack, no. I'd say, we know that some of those foreigners were involved in a plot to inflict death and destruction on this town, and it's in everyone's interests—including all the foreigners who *weren't* involved—to make sure none of the conspirators escaped. I'd talk about regrettable necessities, and apologise like crazy to those we've disturbed for no good reason. And I'd hope like hell to find someone in one of those Romney Road houses who's been up to something we can arrest him for, whether he knows anything about bomb plots or not.'

Superintendent Fuller wanted to say she was wrong, terribly wrong, but he couldn't. He didn't like what he was being asked to do, but he knew that in a crude way it would help. It would reassure those currently fleeing Dimmock that it was safe to return. It would prove to anyone who needed proof that those left in their Romney Road homes had nothing to hide. And if young Hussein from number 23 was still growing birdseed in his grandma's windowbox in the hope that some of it might be worth smoking, they could take him in for questioning in a squad car with the blues-and-twos going and call off the whole ignorant charade. By the time anyone realised the boy had been freed on bail and the worst he faced was his granny's wrath, nerves would be calmer all round.

But that wouldn't be the end of anything. 'We'll be accused of racism.'

'Undoubtedly,' agreed the ACC. 'We'll defend ourselves. The grim reality is that there are people out there right now who pose a significant threat to public safety, and by and large they look different to those they're threatening. Those are the facts—we can regret them as much as we like but we can't change them. You can't call it racism when it's caused by someone twirling a blood great scimitar!'

'A lot of people live in and around Romney Road because it's handy for their mosque,' said Fuller quietly. 'If we do as you suggest we're going to cause distress and anger in a lot of people who've never done anything to deserve it. We may not intend this as a racial or religious slur, but that's how it's going to feel.'

'I agree with everything you say,' said Blake. 'Except that it isn't a suggestion.'

Deacon was thinking it through. It was like watching the business end of a watermill: you could *see* the corn pouring in from above, the stones turning and the flour coming out underneath. You could see every cog moving, every gear changing. And there was a kind of magic to it, because none of those around him felt they could stop the process even though they didn't want it to continue to its natural conclusion.

'You mean,' he growled at length, 'you want us to turn over Dimmock's Moslems not because you think it'll make the town any safer but because it'll make the rest of the population *feel* safer. And you want us to arrest someone—anyone, for anything—because you hope that will be seen as justifying an unnecessary and inflammatory operation.'

Fuller winced. 'Jack…'

But the Assistant Chief Constable interrupted him. 'That's right, Jack,' she said plainly. 'That's exactly what I want you to do. I want you to do it because it'll cause the maximum amount of distress to a vulnerable section of the community, result in letters to the Press and questions in Parliament, and—oh yes—it just might save some lives.'

They regarded one another over the conference table. It occurred to those sitting either side of them that ACC (Crime) Emily Blake and Detective Superintendent Jack Deacon were more alike than probably either of them would care to acknowledge. Essentially, what they were doing was waiting to see who'd blink first.

It was Deacon. 'You'd better be right.'

'Jack—every week I take decisions I have to be right about. This is just another.'

'Except that it isn't, is it?' he said quietly. 'Your decision.'

'No,' she admitted. 'The decision wasn't mine. The job of carrying it out is. And it's your job to help.'

She could have appealed to his better nature, except she wasn't sure he had one. Instead she played the one card he could never trump. The job. Serving and protecting. Jack Deacon had no reservations about serving The People. It was the people who made up The People that he didn't like.

'And if we make things worse?'

'We'll have to try to make things as little worse as we possibly can.'

Deacon shook his head in despair. 'Can I have that on my gravestone? *He tried to make things as little worse as he possibly could.*'

'Superintendent Deacon,' said ACC briskly, 'you can have anything you like on your gravestone. And if I don't see a bit of cooperation soon, you'd better get it ordered.'

The Assistant Chief Constable had been given her orders, and she'd given Deacon his. But giving Deacon orders was a bit like feeding racehorse cubes to a mule—he'd take them all right, they just might not have the desired effect.

He understood Higher Up's dilemma well enough. But he couldn't see that the wrong decision would do anything but make matters worse. Until now the dangerous chaos that had enveloped Dimmock had been the responsibility of a few bad men and a lot of foolish ones. From now on it would rest with the men and women who'd sat in a room and decided that today expediency was more important than justice. That a small number of hurt and angry people could be managed more easily than a large number of frightened ones.

And he understood that the object of the exercise was not to achieve anything worth having so much as to be seen trying. That a visible success mattered more than a significant one. But he wanted someone to come straight out and say it.

'Let me get this right. You're looking for something we can call a result so when we call off the searches it's because they were successful, not because they were stupid in the first place, and a much relieved citizenry can slink back into its pubs and armchairs. We make an arrest and the pin slides back in the grenade. But it needs to be the right kind of arrest. Today the Kray twins would be safe, because they're not the right colour.'

ACC (Crime) was regarding him with no affection whatever. 'This situation is not of our making. But it is up to us to get it under control. Yes, Jack, you're absolutely right. I'm asking you to put on a show. I'm asking you to prostitute your craft for the sake of public safety. Find me a credible suspect, arrest him in a blaze of publicity, apologise for the disturbance to some elderly lady in a headscarf and pull out before there's time for anyone to lose their temper. That way everyone sleeps safe in their beds tonight.'

'Except the guy we've framed!'

'I'm not suggesting you frame anyone! Are you telling me *all* the crime in Dimmock is committed by white people? That you can't find one Arab, Afghan or Pakistani who shouldn't be helping you with your inquiries into *something?* Find him, arrest him and the panic's over. Tomorrow or the day after I'll go on TV to explain how actually people had misunderstood—that the arrested man wasn't a terrorist, he was involved in nothing more sinister than a credit card scam. People aren't going to rush out to their cars and hit the road again. We'll have got through twenty-four hours that could have set this town on fire, and if the worst damage is to my reputation it'll have been worth it.'

Deacon had no illusions about what she was saying. If public safety demanded a sacrifice, it wouldn't be the guy with the recreational amounts of heroin or the unusual number of mobile phones—it would be her. If the questions in Parliament focused on her judgement, her competence, she'd quietly pick up the can and carry it, even if the price was her career.

So he'd go along with it. Somewhere in his files or his memory was someone in the Romney Road area who was overdue a visit from CID. Someone sufficiently disreputable that his neighbours would be glad to see the back of him. He'd get his due deserts, and Romney Road would get a bit of peace, and the rest of Dimmock would turn round at Guildford and be back in front of their tellies by teatime. It was a win/win situation.

And the fact that it wasn't what Deacon thought of as policing was immaterial. Today the priorities were different. Today, this was the only way to go. It was the least worst option. He set his jaw. 'When do we do this?'

'Now.'

TWENTY-TWO

JUST WHEN YOU THINK things can't get any worse…

Any road going anywhere, and some that went nowhere, seized solid. Residents of Dimmock desperate to be somewhere else, anywhere else, were now unable to leave due to (a) the throngs of their neighbours with the same idea, and (b) the national media coming the other way.

There was no Dimmock International Airport. There wasn't even a Dimmock Regional Airport. There was a flying club strip twelve miles north of town, and for a couple of hours on Thursday morning it handled more traffic than it had in the previous nine months. There were helicopters. There were executive jets. One enterprising reporter hired a Tiger Moth and the half-crazed crop-sprayer pilot who came with it, on the basis that if he couldn't get a landing slot at the airstrip he could put down in a field.

With the skies over the Three Downs host to the kind of aerial circus last seen in the 1930s, so that the possibility of a bomb plot paled beside the near-certainty of a plane crash, Higher Up rushed through the no-fly zone. After that the reporters either sat in traffic jams or walked into town. It is a curious feature of the news industry that reporters who will fight their way into a war zone will baulk at walking five miles.

As time passed and nothing much happened—or only the usual things that happen among large numbers of displaced persons: old people got older, children got sick, babies who weren't due for another fortnight got born—the media people grew tired of filming one another getting tired and began to wonder if it was a damp squib. If the absence of black smoke over Dimmock meant that the local Keystones had been right and the situation was contained. If it was time to pick some other crisis off the wire and hope it would prove easier to get to.

Then the front desk at Battle Alley took a phone call from Crichton Construction.

'EXPLOSIVES,' said Jack Deacon, deadpan.

Sergeant McKinney nodded.

'What *kind* of explosives?'

The sergeant gave a grim Caledonian shrug. 'As far as I can make out, every kind. Blasting explosives—they use different ones for different jobs. They're allowed to keep up to two tonnes in a secure bunker on site.'

'But they've got the guy who was stealing it cornered?'

'Aye.' Sergeant McKinney sounded less than enthusiastic. 'That's the good news.'

Deacon's brow lowered suspiciously. 'What's the bad news?'

'They've got him cornered in the bunker.'

WHEN HE GOT THERE Deacon found that there was in fact another bit of good news. The construction site was in open countryside, up on Menner Down six miles north of Dimmock. The main road had already been closed. Since it had been at a standstill since mid-morning this consisted of evacuating the travellers—using the word loosely—across the surrounding fields on foot. There were surprisingly few arguments. Even apart from this new peril, the mood of the evacuees had changed in the cold, boring hours on the road. Most were now content to abandon their flight, their cars and their role in the decision-making process.

Which left a construction site, ankle deep in mud as all construction sites are, with huge arcane machines standing guard like forgotten dinosaurs around the block-built bunker. The only people Deacon could see as he picked his way, swearing, through the mud were other police officers, surrounding the little building at what they fervently hoped to be a safe distance.

'And he's still in there?'

'Yes.' Superintendent Fuller, who had been trying to sort out the chaos on the Guildford Road when the call came in, reached the construction site while Deacon was still trying to get out of Dimmock. 'We can't see him—there are no windows—but he yelled something through the door ten minutes ago and we know he hasn't escaped since then.'

Deacon nodded. 'What did he yell?'

'"I don't want to hurt anyone",' reported Fuller.

Deacon blinked. 'Slightly odd comment from a man stealing high explosives, isn't it? I mean, what *does* he want them for—shifting a tree stump off his lawn? Do we know who he is?'

'Yes, we do,' said Fuller. 'He works here. He helped design the new sewer system they're laying from the villages. His name's Stretton.'

Deacon's eyebrows shot into his hairline. '*Dev* Stretton?'

Fuller was surprised at his reaction. 'You know him?'

'Dev Stretton? D-d-d-Dev? Damn right I know him,' snarled Deacon. 'And I'd take what he shouted with a pinch of salt. Maybe he didn't want to hurt Joe Loomis either, but he killed him just the same.'

HAVING STRETTON holed up with the explosives he was trying to steal at least put an end to the charade at Romney Road. Detective Constable Jill Meadows made the conciliatory noises that would normally have been DS Voss's task. People liked Voss, and they trusted him. When he said he was sorry for a disturbance they believed him and quite often tore up the letter of complaint they were penning. Jill Meadows was good at it too. Whereas Detective Constable Huxley could be counted on to throw metaphorical petrol on any conflagration he encountered.

All in all, Deacon found himself thinking, the situation could have been worse. When Dev Stretton left here, in handcuffs or a bucket, the clear-up column in the month's crime statistics would get an immediate boost. One murder solved, one terror plot foiled. And that wasn't the best of it.

If responsibility for the chaos of the last few days had settled on the shoulders of an Islamic fundamentalist, those residents who'd fled Dimmock would never have forgiven those whose reaction had been to gather about their mosque. And if it had all been a massive misunderstanding, if there never was a bomb plot and half Dimmock had turned gypsy because the drugs subculture that was always simmering away out of sight had turned nastily visible, the residents of Romney Road would never have forgotten that they were blamed for something that was in no way their fault.

But Dev Stretton was the perfect...*scapegoat* was the first word that came to mind: Deacon replaced it with *culprit*. A man of mixed race, neither community could be entirely blamed for him; at the same time, neither could shirk all responsibility. To the precise extent that he was a foreigner and an alien, he was also an Englishman and a local. Deacon gave the guy twenty-four hours before the two communities united in condemnation of him. It could be the greatest unifying event in years. Dev Stretton was a born outsider. And the thing about outsiders is, they make people on the inside feel even smugger than usual, and more ready to throw stones.

And because it was such a convenient solution, Deacon instinctively found himself mistrusting it. *Why?* he wondered. Why would a man like Dev Stretton—a middle-class professional—want to blow up anything? Even if he stabbed Joe Loomis in a fit of anger, why would that incline him to steal dynamite nine days later? But he hadn't time to wrestle with the puzzle. When he got his hands on Stretton he'd ask him why. Unless he was in too many bits to answer.

'We need technical support,' he said to Superintendent Fuller.

'On its way. I called the Army.'

'Did you ask for a negotiator?'

Fuller shrugged. 'There are no hostages involved. I thought he was as likely to tell us what's going on as a bleeding heart.' He stopped abruptly, shocked that—with thirty years of intelligent, thoughtful, firm-but-fair policing behind him—in moments of stress he could sound just like Deacon.

Unaware of his discomfort, Deacon agreed. Clearing up their own mess was always his preferred option; except when it came to high explosives. 'And is he talking?'

'He says he isn't ready to talk yet. He says if we back off no one will get hurt.'

'Does he indeed?' grunted Deacon. 'And he thought that would do it, did he? We'd all go home and watch telly?'

'Lord knows what he's thinking,' said Fuller lugubriously. 'He's a young man of twenty-five sitting on two tonnes of assorted explosives. He must have a reason. But it beats the hell out of me what it might be.'

'Have you asked his mother?'

'I've sent Jill Meadows to fetch her—you may have noticed—the roads are a nightmare. Even if she's at home it could take an hour to get her back here.'

Deacon pulled a face like a shark with indigestion. 'Well, someone's got to talk to the stupid sod. I know most of the background—I think that makes it my job.'

'Be careful,' said Superintendent Fuller. He wasn't joking.

'Aren't I always?'

Fuller thought for a moment. 'No.' And as the big man gave a grim chuckle and advanced across the mud, he raised his voice a little to add: 'Practically never.'

By the time he reached the blockhouse Deacon's boots were leaden with churned up earth. He picked up a stick and a milk crate—there are always milk crates on construction sites though there's never any milk—and sat down to clean them off, leaning his back against the front wall.

For obvious reasons, there were no windows in the dynamite shed. He sensed rather than saw movement through the narrow gap where the door was ajar. He growled, 'After we sort this out, young man, you'll owe me a new pair of boots. Leather. Hand-stitched,' he added, more in hope than expectation.

Dev Stretton gave a desperate little chuckle. 'It's a deal.'

Which Deacon found encouraging. His knowledge of suicide bombers was happily limited, but the videos they left suggested they hadn't much sense of humour. They talked a lot about historic rights and wrongs, and very little about shoe shopping. So maybe Stretton wasn't entirely…

Serious? He'd broken into a powder magazine for a bit of a joke? Because there was nothing much going on and he was bored? No, he was serious enough about wanting the explosives. But perhaps suicide wasn't what he wanted them for.

Deacon gave up picking at his right boot, cranked up his left and tried that. He didn't even turn his head towards the door. 'You want to tell me what this is all about?'

'I will,' promised Dev Stretton. 'Soon. I'm not ready yet.'

'No? Well,' said Deacon, 'there must be something we can talk about. Cars, rugby, real ale? Or—here's a thought—why you stuck a knife in Joe Loomis.'

There was a pause. Deacon couldn't imagine why. If he meant to deny it he'd had a week to think up a plausible story—surely he wasn't trying to make it up as he went along? And it was a little late in the day to be pleading innocence. He'd broken into a shed full of explosives, for God's sake!

'He attacked my mother. He hit my mother. I went round to sort him out. He pulled the knife. We fought for it and he lost.'

'I see,' said Deacon. 'Well, we know he carried a knife. We know he produced it with very little encouragement. What I can't figure is why he'd agree to meet you, alone, in a dark car park?'

Another, longer pause. 'I don't know that either,' admitted Stretton. 'I suppose, because he thought he didn't need any help. He thought it would be me left bleeding in the gutter, in which case he wouldn't want any witnesses.'

Deacon gave that a little thought, then nodded. 'Could be.

Stranger things have happened. But then, why didn't you come and tell me about it?'

Stretton's voice was cold. 'I didn't think you'd believe me.'

'What—that a man who was known for pulling knives on people finally pulled one on the wrong guy? It sounds perfectly plausible to me. And you're a—what?—a civil engineer. A professional man, a man who pays his taxes. A man who pays my wages. Exactly the kind of man who'd normally expect to be believed.'

Wrong-footed, Stretton stammered out a response. 'I…I suppose…I panicked. I just wanted to get out of there. And then, when no one came looking for me…'

'Sure,' nodded Deacon. 'You thought you'd keep your head down and see if we ever thought of you. And we didn't. So nine days later you broke into an explosives shed and took two tonnes of dynamite hostage.'

'That was… I didn't… I thought…' The man inside the blockhouse was getting flustered. Which was very often a good thing in a suspect, but not today. Today if Dev Stretton got flustered he could kill himself, Deacon and most of those maintaining that nervous perimeter.

'OK,' said Deacon sharply, 'OK. It seemed like a good idea at the time. Well, neither of us is going anywhere. Perhaps when you've had another minute to think you'll be able to tell me why.'

For a little while he said nothing more, just sat there cleaning his boots. He wanted Stretton to get used to the idea of having him close and nothing happening. He wanted Stretton to relax. Stress kills, particularly in the presence of high explosives.

Finally he said, 'If that's too hard a question, let's start with an easier one. How long are we going to be here? I might need someone to feed the cat.'

Dev Stretton didn't know how to respond. This really wasn't what he'd expected. Only sheer desperation had brought him here, and when he'd over-ridden the bunker's security with a combination of inside knowledge and brute force he'd believed that the world he'd known ended right there. He hadn't expected to find himself talking to a man who was worried about his cat.

He didn't believe Detective Superintendent Deacon had a cat. Unless it was a tiger.

Deacon was trying to be reasonable. 'What, an hour? A couple of hours? Only, any time after that he'll start killing poodles.'

Stretton was here—they were all here—because it was the only way he could think of to take control of a situation that threatened to destroy everything that mattered to him. It had been an act of despair, a last resort—and now he was committed, still he seemed helpless to prevent that control spiralling away from him. He tried sticking strictly to the point, to see if that would help. 'Maybe you should get someone to feed it.'

'Ah,' said Deacon wisely. 'So we're waiting for something else to happen. Well, I have to tell you, we're not going to let anyone else in here and we're not letting you out. Whatever you're waiting for, you're going to be disappointed.'

'We'll see.' Stretton's tone suggested he didn't see disappointment as his main problem.

'Oh, I see. You're waiting for a phone call. Sorry—that's not going to happen either. We've shut down the mobile networks. You can use a mobile signal to detonate a bomb.'

'But…' Even Stretton could see the flaw in his logic. 'I'm right *here*. Why would I *phone* a signal in? All I have to do is break one of these fuses…'

'All right!' said Deacon quickly. 'I believe you. You probably know a damn sight more about explosives than I do. In fact, I *hope* you know a damn sight more about explosives than I do.

'One thing you don't seem to know, though, is how this is going to end. So I'll tell you. It's going to end with you in handcuffs in the back of a police car, and eight months from now a judge deciding you're a danger to the public and likely to remain so for fifteen years. That's your youth gone, and everyone you know moving on. If you've got a girl you can wave her goodbye. She's not going to wait years for you—you couldn't ask her to. Because this wasn't her idea, was it? She didn't ask you to steal enough explosives to put Dimmock into orbit. That was someone else.'

'No,' said Dev Stretton, as firmly as he could with the images Deacon had conjured crowding his eyes. 'No one asked me. This was my idea.'

'What was?'

He wasn't stupid enough to fall for that. 'I told you. Right now, I'm not prepared to talk about it. All you need to know is, if you leave me alone no one will get hurt. I never wanted to hurt anyone. I'm happy with Dimmock where it is. I'm not seeking to overthrow the government, I'm not a terrorist, I have no agenda, hidden or otherwise. I just need…' For a moment his voice grew thin. Then he took a grip on his emotions again. 'It's just that, right now, I really need to be where I am, doing what I'm doing. I know this makes no sense to you. All I can say is, I will explain. Later.'

'Later may be too late,' grunted Deacon. 'Whatever your intentions, you've triggered a full-scale security alert. You've made the news in Tokyo, you stupid sod! There isn't going to be a moment when you can explain everything and walk away. The best you can hope for now—the best any of us can hope for—is that we leave here in a squad car, not the morgue van.'

'You're not going to kill me,' said Stretton with a kind of shaky conviction. 'I have no hostages. There's no one here but me. And you, and you can walk away any time you want to. You have no reason to kill me. You'll wait to see if I come out of my own accord. And I'm telling you now, Mr. Deacon, I will.'

'When?'

'When I'm ready.'

As stand-offs go, this was unusual in Deacon's experience. Not just because of the proximity of enough explosives to make him the first Detective Superintendent on the Moon. Not because the other protagonist was a well-spoken, intelligent young man who'd begun the confrontation with reassurances rather than threats. Not because, although the danger quotient was high, the number of people at risk was comparatively low. No, what made this siege virtually unique in the history of sieges was that Dev Stretton had no demands. He hadn't asked for political concessions, he hadn't asked for money, he hadn't even asked for a fast car and a head start. He seemed content—edgy, but content—merely to be here, a man sitting quietly on a bomb, unperturbed though the cause of much perturbation in others.

Which told Deacon something. He knew now what Stretton had come here for. He knew why he'd risked being apprehended as he broke into the blockhouse, and worse than apprehended if he'd tripped on his way in. He knew why he had no demands. The only thing he wanted was already being given to him, and he hadn't even had to ask.

He'd come here to buy time.

TWENTY-THREE

'A MAN NAMED locally as Dev Stretton…'

When Brodie heard that on the radio her heart turned over. 'That poor woman…!'

Daniel was beside her. 'So you were right. Dev Stretton murdered Joe Loomis after all.'

'Looks that way.' Her lips were supplying the words but her mind was elsewhere. Daniel could see it in the way her well-shaped brows gathered, in the fathomless depths of her dark eyes.

'But…?' he prompted softly.

'I don't know,' she said, shaking her head like a horse bothered by flies. 'Something… It doesn't add up. Why? Why kill Joe at all—but if he had, why do this nine days later?'

'Perhaps Jack was closer to him than we realised.'

'Jack!' Scorn laced her tone. 'Jack hasn't been remotely interested in who killed Joe Loomis for a week. Of course, I understand that now—if he's known there were terrorists in Dimmock, everything else would go on the back burner. But if Jack was hunting bombers, why was Dev so spooked? And he must have been *very* spooked to hide in a shed full of dynamite!'

It was a good point. It had seemed to make sense: a man suspected of one serious crime had broken cover and committed another. But when you looked closer there was no casual line between these different events. The sums didn't add up. 'Suppose,' Daniel said slowly, 'that Dev Stretton did murder Joe Loomis. Why?'

'Because Faith lied to me and Joe really was his father,' said

Brodie immediately. 'The cow! I would have *sworn* she was telling me the truth, at least about that.'

'Even if Joe was Dev's father, why did he end up with a knife in his lung? Nothing else we've heard about Dev suggests he settles scores that way. And it was Joe who brought the knife to their meeting.'

Brodie was nodding. 'So after the incident on the Promenade, Dev went round to mark Joe's card. Or more than that—perhaps he meant to give him a thrashing. Joe pulled the knife, they struggled and he got stabbed.'

'So why did Dev flee the scene and pretend nothing had happened? If he'd called the police and said it was self-defence, no one would have doubted him. No one who knew Joe.'

Even people who didn't move in criminal circles were aware of the man's reputation. All Stretton had to say was, 'It was his knife—I was afraid for my life,' and his only problem after that would be deciding whether it was in bad taste to actually wear the medal.

'Does it make a difference,' wondered Brodie, 'whether or not Dev was Joe's son?'

Daniel considered. 'I'm not sure it does. If Dev stabbed him, it's not because he was a lousy father. It's because he hurt his mother and Dev was making sure he'd never do it again.'

Brodie was still thinking. 'It *could* make a difference. Not to what Dev did—to what Joe did. He went to that meeting alone. Whoever he went to see, he thought he could handle the situation alone. Joe, who habitually took muscle to change his library books! And he was a much smaller man than Dev. If he'd thought there was any chance of coming to blows he'd have had help.'

'Size isn't everything,' said Daniel with a quick grin. 'Dev's a nicely brought up civil engineer—his idea of a walk on the wild side is exchanging sharp words with a slacking labourer. Joe got where he is—was?—is,' he settled on, because no one could have argued that Loomis got less than his just deserts, 'by being more vicious than a lot of bigger men. In a street fight, even without the knife, he'd have left Dev bleeding in the gutter.'

'So it *was* Dev he went to meet?'

When Daniel screwed up his face like that he looked like a twelve-year-old struggling with long division. 'Dev, or someone like Dev.'

Brodie frowned. 'Meaning?'

'It was personal, not business. If Joe had been meeting someone on business he'd certainly have taken back-up because he'd have expected the other party to take back-up too. He went alone because he didn't expect to need help, but also because he didn't want his minders to know what he was doing. He didn't want them gossiping about a private matter.'

'Donna knew.'

'Donna's different. She was about the closest thing Joe had to a friend. And all she knew was that Joe had a child, and he wasn't interested in it.'

'If he knew about the child, maybe the child knew about him,' suggested Brodie. 'Joe slapped Faith's face in a public place: Dev was bound to ask why. Maybe that's when she told him. That he wasn't who he'd always through he was, he was the son of a vicious little drugs baron instead. Imagine how that made him feel. Before he'd had time to come to terms with the idea, and recognise that Faith had been right all along to keep the pair of them apart, he'd called Joe and told him to meet him. And Joe came because if they couldn't discuss it in private it was going to happen in public.'

'You sound pretty sure that it was Dev.' Daniel was sorry about that.

'I think it had to be,' said Brodie. 'The elements are all there. We know Faith knew Joe back in the Eighties. Well, if you'd had a child by Joe Loomis, you'd want to hide the fact too. So she invented a Kashmiri father-figure, and that worked fine for a quarter of a century. Daniel, you were there when she as good as told Joe that's what she'd done—*I don't mind people*

*thinking I slept with an Asian as long as they don't know I slept
with you!* But then he slapped her, and people saw, and back
home Dev wanted to know why and wouldn't take her evasions
for an answer any longer. So she told him.'

Daniel was nodding slowly. 'But then, why didn't Dev report
the fight to the police?'

Brodie shrugged. 'Shock?' This isn't the kind of situation
he's familiar with. And he's still reeling from the discovery that
he's son and heir to a thug, and his own father's just pulled a
knife on him. Dev wouldn't be firing on all cylinders at that
point. And maybe he didn't realise how seriously Joe was hurt.
Once he'd calmed down a bit, perhaps he'd have gone round
to Battle Alley to explain what happened. Only by then he'd
heard that Joe was dead. If he told the truth now, it was all going
to become public property. Maybe Faith's the one he was trying
to protect.

'And nobody had come looking for him. The only one who
knew Dev was Joe's son was his mother, and she wasn't going
to turn him in. Maybe he thought he'd wait to see what
happened next. He didn't feel like he'd murdered anyone. All
he did was defend himself against an attack.'

Daniel took up the narration. 'And nine days passed, and not
only did the police not come knocking at Dev's door, they lost
all interest in the killing. There's a full-scale terror alert going
on. At that point Dev finishes his packed lunch and breaks into
his employers' explosives bunker? Why on earth would he do
such a thing?'

Brodie couldn't imagine either. 'Is it possible Dev's involved
in terrorism as well?'

'Islamic fundamentalist terrorism?' She nodded. 'But
haven't we just decided Dev is Joe's son? What possible interest
could he have in *jihad?*'

'Well…' said Brodie slowly. 'Because until Faith told him
about Joe a fortnight ago, Dev *thought* he was half Kashmiri.
That's why he went out to help after the earthquake. Maybe he

got involved with fundamentalism while he was there—maybe he was involved in a plot to bomb Dimmock long before he stabbed Joe. Maybe *that's* why he was angry enough with Joe to stick a knife in him—that he'd put his whole future on the line to support a cause he'd come to believe in passionately, only to discover it wasn't his fight after all. He'd been lied to. He wasn't a member of an oppressed culture at all: he was the illegitimate son of an Irish drug dealer.' She considered. 'I can see how he'd be a bit miffed about that.'

'All right,' said Daniel, accepting her version for the moment. 'So he was angry with Joe because he felt cheated. Then he thought about it some more and decided that the accident of his conception wasn't a good enough reason to give up on a cause that, a few days earlier, he'd believed in strongly enough to die for. So he determines to go on with the bomb plot. But Daoud is now dead and the Dhazi cousins are in custody. Is that why he tried to steal explosives? Because the guy who knew how to make them out of common household chemicals was dead?'

'I suppose so,' said Brodie slowly. 'He'd psyched himself up to be a suicide bomber—and even after he discovered he had the wrong genes, he was still crazy enough to want to go through with it. He had to find a new source of explosives—it was all he had left, all that mattered to him. Even if he wasn't who he thought he was, if he went out with a bang he'd always be remembered as an Islamic martyr. He'd had the title stolen from him—he had to win it back. And though he maybe didn't know how to blow things up with hair bleach and chapatti flour, he did know where there was a stock of blasting explosives.'

'So what went wrong?' asked Daniel.

Brodie didn't understand. 'Nothing went wrong. He got past site security because he knew his way round and everyone there knows him. Then he broke into the bunker and…' Now she had it. 'Ah.'

'And now he's sitting there inside a police cordon and while he could make a big bang if he wanted to, blowing up a shed in a field is never going to strike a hammer-blow against Western imperialism. So what has he gained?'

'It went off half-cocked,' said Brodie weakly.

'Sure it did. He broke into an explosives bunker in the middle of a working day, with people who knew him all around. Of course they called the police—what else were they going to do? It was entirely predictable that it would end in a siege. A siege doesn't get him anywhere. So why did he do it that way?'

'He panicked,' Brodie supposed. 'Everything was going wrong, he couldn't carry out the original plan, he thought this was the only way he could carry out any plan at all and he could only do this if he acted before the police caught up with him. He was making it up as he went along.'

But Daniel didn't buy it. 'How panicked would you have to be to do it in broad daylight? He could hardly have drawn more attention to himself if he was trying. At night, knowing his way around, knowing what security there was, he had a chance of getting hold of the explosives and staying ahead of the police long enough to use them. Why didn't he wait until dark?'

'The guy's planning on blowing up half Dimmock and probably himself as well,' Brodie reminded him. 'Maybe getting away with it didn't seem that important.'

'But he had to stay free long enough to do what he planned, or what was the point? It's not the suicide that's the aim of a suicide bombing, it's the bombing. The target. People, important buildings—something that will send shockwaves through the ranks of the enemy. He can't do that on a building site in the middle of Menner Down.'

'So he's a bad suicide bomber.' Brodie shrugged. 'I suppose it's a skill you don't get much chance to practise.'

Daniel thought about that. 'Maybe. But he's been good at everything else he's done. Brodie—what if it's not that he's a bad suicide bomber? What if it's that he's a good diversion?'

Real silence isn't just the absence of sound: it has substance, it expands to fill the space available. That's why we talk of breaking a silence. It isn't nothing. Sometimes it's almost tangible, a physical obstacle to overcome.

This was one of those silences. Brodie's eyes grew round and her lips formed a startled O but no sound came. Like having to fight your way out of a sleep paralysis, she had to force the first meaningless grunt out of her throat before the silence pulled back enough to let her speak.

'You mean—while every policeman within a twenty-mile radius is here, preventing the escape of someone who has no intention of going anywhere, something's going to happen that they might be able to prevent if they were where they should be?'

Daniel gave that awkward little half-shrug that was the souvenir of a broken collar-bone. His plain round face was troubled. 'It would make a kind of sense. It would make sense of some of the things that don't make sense otherwise.'

'But he'll never get away with it! He's surrounded, he isn't walking away from this. The moment the town hall or whatever hits the stratosphere, Jack'll know what he did. He'll spend the rest of his life behind bars!'

'These people are happy to die hurting what they think of as the enemy,' Daniel pointed out quietly. 'I don't think they'd be glad to blow their stupid heads off but draw the line at going to jail.'

'My God!' whispered Brodie. 'Daniel, what do we do?'

There was only one answer. 'We have to tell Jack. Maybe he's already thought of it, in which case he'll shout at us, but if he hasn't he needs to. Phone him. He'll take a call from you.'

She nodded, fumbling for her phone. Only with her finger on speed-dial she hesitated, intimidated by the implications. 'What if we're wrong?'

'What if we're right?'

She nodded and dialled. The network was down. 'I'll try the landline.'

She still couldn't get Deacon's mobile. She tried the other number she knew by heart, that of the front desk at Battle

Alley. This time she got the engaged signal. She tried again. Still engaged.

'Stupid bloody people,' she hissed, dialling again, with the same result. 'It's not enough that they clog the roads for miles in every direction, they have to overload the phone system as well!' She tried again. Still engaged.

Daniel stood up. 'Brodie, this could really matter. If no one else has had time to think it through, we could be the only ones who've stumbled on what's actually happening. What's going to happen. One way or another, we have to get a message through. You keep trying the phones. I'll run down to Battle Alley.'

'*Run* down?' She hadn't intended that note of incredulity. But Daniel wasn't much of an athlete.

'I can walk it in twenty minutes—I should be able to run it in ten.'

'Or give yourself a heart attack in five!'

'Maybe I'll get lucky. Maybe I'll find a policeman with a working radio. We can't just wait for the bang!'

And of course he was right. It might be bizarre that in the communication age circumstances could ensure that vital intelligence could only travel a little over a mile the same way it would have got there two thousand years ago, in the hands of a running man. But that was the situation they faced. And however unfit Daniel was, Brodie was even less likely to finish in the medals.

'OK,' she said briskly. 'Do it. I'll get on the computer, see if I can raise them by email. And Daniel'—he turned back in the doorway—'don't take no for an answer. We might be wrong about this, but it really doesn't matter. That can be sorted out later. If we're right and we can't get anyone to listen, there may not be a later.'

HE'D BEEN RIGHT about the car. At the end of Chiffney Road he met a scene like something from a post-apocolyptic movie. A sea of abandoned cars filled the road from side to side, as far as he could see in either direction. They'd been trying to get out of town up the Guildford Road, but as gridlock began to bite panic had set in and fuelled an inventive reinterpretation of the Highway Code. Cars had tried overtaking on the left, and also on the far right. They'd tried driving up the footpaths, oblivious of the trees growing through the pavement every thirty metres or so. The thing about a big tree is, it barely notices if someone drives into it. Crumpled cars squatted round the trunks like dogs looking for squirrels. It would be a crane job to move some of them—when you could get a crane within reach.

There were still people in some of the cars, but most of those who'd got this far had waited a couple of hours and then given up, returning on foot the way they'd come. It was like a weird mechanical still life, or a metal ocean breaking on a suburban shore.

Daniel turned down the hill towards town and picked up an unpractised jog. People still in their cars watched him pass with a kind of uninterested misery; except for one woman who peered in the direction he'd come from and demanded querulously, '*Now* what?'

It could have been worse, he thought— he could have been running up this hill. Even so, by the time he'd done a few hundred metres he was sweating and his glasses were misting up.

A mile and a bit, mostly downhill. Anyone could run a mile and a bit. Anyone with lives on his shoulders could run it *fast*. With urgent fingers he smeared potholes in his foggy glasses and picked up the pace.

BRODIE FIRED OFF an email with no idea whether it would be read or not. Then she sent another to Division. But they had no reason to take her seriously, while Deacon had. She kept trying to get him, always with the same result. Every failed attempt confirmed Daniel's wisdom in leaving when he did. She kept checking her watch. He'd be a quarter of the way there by now, she told herself. He'd be halfway there. If nothing happened to stop him. If the overstressed officers at Battle Alley, all of them struggling to deal with a situation they were never trained for, all of them worried for friends and family, half of them drafted in for the emergency, would take time out from the crisis and give a fair hearing to a man who thought, just thought, they were doing it wrong.

And there was nothing she could do to help. She was besieged in Chiffney Road by the rock-solid traffic jam, unable to leave or to contact anyone closer to the action. Brodie hated being out of the loop. She hated feeling that events could go on happening without her assent.

Thinking about that, she realised there was something she could do. She could call Faith Stretton. If there was now a police presence at the Stretton house, they could use their radio network to forward a message to Deacon. Even if the police weren't there yet, out in the wilds of Chain Down Faith wasn't subject to the same strictures as Brodie. She was also a lot closer to the Crichton Construction site. If she made her way there and introduced herself as the mother of the terror suspect—in the circumstances *suspect* hardly seemed the right word—she could be quite sure of speaking to Detective Superintendent Deacon.

The phone rang twice before someone snatched it up. 'Dev?' It was Faith. Which meant the police had yet to arrive. If they had, they'd be answering the phone.

'No, it's Brodie Farrell.' Despite the urgency she was trying to keep her voice calm. 'Faith—do you know what's going on at the construction site?'

If they'd been face to face she'd have seen Faith's expression close like a box, tight, impenetrable. Instead she heard it in the quality of her silence. 'You do, don't you?' And as the silence continued, turning to granite, she added softly: 'In fact, you know more about it than I do.'

Faith got the words out like squeezing the last bit of toothpaste from the tube. 'Brodie—stay out of it. This is none of your business.'

This was never a good line to take with Brodie. 'Your son's going to take Dimmock into the space race! That's *everybody's* business!'

'He isn't.' Faith's voice was low. 'Nothing's going to happen. Believe me.'

And, oddly enough, Brodie did believe her. But the truth isn't always reassuring. 'This isn't about Dev and what happens up on the Downs, is it? It's about what happens somewhere else while the police are fully occupied and the population are running round like headless chickens.'

Again the silence. She might as well have said Yes.

'Faith, no one's going to make a distinction! No one's going to say, "But Dev's bomb didn't go off—it was his mates' bomb that killed all those people." They're going to say, "This was a conspiracy to commit mass murder and Dev Stretton's actions were central to it. If he hadn't done what he did, none of the rest would have been possible." They're going to say, "He was one of us. He was born and raised here, he got a good education and had a good career. And that makes what he did worse. He wasn't stupid, he wasn't ignorant, he wasn't desperate. He made a choice. He killed a lot of people, to make a point."'

'Brodie.' Faith's tone had changed again. She sounded genuinely surprised, and genuinely afraid. 'You've got it all wrong. No one's in any danger. Dev doesn't want to hurt anyone. He hasn't got any mates who want to hurt anyone either.'

'Then what the hell's he doing?' yelled Brodie, frustrated beyond endurance.

'What he has to,' said Faith, with a kind of flat despair. 'What he chose to. He's a good man, my son. He puts himself at risk for other people. I know what this is going to cost him. *He* knows what it's going to cost him. He thinks it's worth it. I just hope he's right. I know I'm more proud of him than I can begin to tell you.

'And now I have to go.' And with that she put the phone down, and though Brodie hit redial immediately no one picked up.

TWENTY-FOUR

'WE'VE SENT SOMEONE to the cottage,' said Deacon conversationally. 'Your mother will be here soon. Assuming the Area Car can get through the traffic. You've caused a right old snarl-up out there, you know.'

'I don't want to talk to my *mother!*' exclaimed Dev Stretton through the crack of the door. 'Leave her out of this.'

'Bit late for that.' Deacon shrugged. 'Like it or not, we're all involved. The time to think whether you wanted to embarrass your mother was *before* you broke into an explosives bunker.'

'I mean it,' said Stretton, his voice rising unpredictably. 'I don't want you going anywhere near her.'

'Tough,' grunted Deacon, unimpressed. He wasn't a trained negotiator. Deacon's idea of negotiation was giving people a choice between doing what he said and doing what he said with a bloody nose. But he was the one who was here, leaning his back against two tonnes of blasting explosives, so cards on the table was the only game in town. Criminals—and whatever else he was, Dev Stretton was certainly that—didn't get pandered to on his watch.

'Do you know how big a bang this'll make if I detonate it?'

'Don't know,' sniffed Deacon, 'don't much care. It'll kill you and me, so whatever it does after that will be somebody else's problem. You don't get to say how we do this, Dev. All you get to say is when you've had enough. Say you're coming out and I'll walk you to the car. Say you're staying in and I'll keep you company. That's all the choices you get.'

A trained negotiator would have handled it differently. But

perhaps Stretton would have known how to deal with someone doing it by the book. It wasn't going the way he'd expected. Everything he'd read, every film he'd seen, suggested that people did what they were told to by an armed man. He'd supposed that, if a revolver and a handful of shells would achieve that, two tonnes of high explosive would achieve a great deal more.

At first it had seemed to be working. Then Detective Superintendent Deacon arrived and the script went out the window. Stretton hadn't gone into this lightly. He'd known what he was going to have to pay for it: years of his life or, if he got clumsy, the rest of it. He was ready for even that. He thought what he was doing was that important.

What he hadn't expected was to be taken less than seriously. His sensibilities were offended. He didn't too much mind being thought of as a mad bomber. He did mind being treated like a bolshy teenager who's going to be in deep shit as soon as he puts the class hamster back in its cage. Deacon had sent for his mother, for God's sake! He had to keep telling himself, *That's not the bit that matters. The bit that matters is happening elsewhere—but it wouldn't be happening except for what I'm doing here.* He thought, *When Deacon realises what it was all about he'll see me in a different light...*

In a Damascus moment, suddenly he recognised what Deacon was doing. That off-hand manner was anything but arbitrary. He was goading Stretton. It took a leap of the imagination to suppose that a sane police officer would deliberately annoy a man armed with explosives, but that's what he was doing. He wanted Stretton to feel misunderstood. He wanted him to vent his frustration in the few hot words that would explain what was really going on here.

A chill wave swept up Dev Stretton's spine. He knew that, however much Deacon tried him, he couldn't afford even those few words that would make him feel better. Detective Superintendent Deacon was a cleverer man than he appeared. If he guessed what this was really about, it was all over.

He said deliberately, 'Then make yourself comfortable, because we're staying where we are.'

Disappointment wrinkled Deacon's lip. But if Stretton had figured out his game plan, Deacon had learnt something too. He'd learnt that Stretton had an agenda beyond simply martyring himself. Even without choices, Stretton still considered he had options. That was encouraging. He wasn't going to pull the pin, or whatever you had to do to set this lot off, because he'd backed himself into a corner and couldn't think what else to do.

Deacon shifted his back against the rough hardness of the breeze-blocks and complained, 'My bum's getting cold.'

BRODIE RACED UPSTAIRS. Marta and the children had lost interest in the chaos outside and were playing Scrabble, though not in a form the manufacturers would have recognised. As played by a seven-year-old, a blind baby and a Polish music teacher it sometimes involved stacking the tiles and sometimes having them leapfrog one another, like draughts.

'Marta, I have to go out. Can you keep the kids?'

'Sure.' Unable to leave herself and with students unable to reach her, it wasn't such an imposition. 'But how? You can't take the car. You going to run too?' It was in her tone how improbable she thought this was.

'No. That was my second question. Have you got the number of the world's least talented pianist? You know—the guy who was here yesterday.'

'Graham? Sure. But...*why?*'

'Because he was here yesterday and now he isn't. He can get through this stuff, Marta. He's got a motorcycle!'

Men called Graham who are good at motorcycle maintenance but fancy themselves as Liberace don't often have women like Brodie Farrell riding pillion behind them. His mouth was open to tell her he couldn't help, that he was at work…and then he heard himself and stopped abruptly. 'Be there in ten minutes.'

He stuffed his limbs back into his leathers, all the while trying to think up a plausible excuse for his boss. Then it dawned on him that no excuse would serve as well as the truth. He just might lose his job, but what he'd gain in respect would be worth it. He swaggered out of the garage where he worked to a round of applause from his colleagues.

Brodie was waiting outside her house. His heart skipped a beat. They weren't proper motorcycle leathers, but when a woman looked that good in a black leather jacket and trousers and high-heel boots, who cared? He passed her his spare helmet with a hand that actually trembled.

It was more than ten years since Brodie had been on a motorcycle. Somehow she expected that the instinct would still be there, but in fact she felt wobbly and vulnerable. She clung to Graham in a manner which, had he been there to see, would have made Deacon immediately go out and buy a Kawasaki.

It was no clearway even for a motorbike. But Graham weaved judiciously, and once rode across someone's front lawn, and within minutes the jumble of metal blocking the road began to thin.

The obvious way to Chain Down was up the Guildford Road. But the only traffic on the Guildford Road now was returning to Dimmock: barriers and diversion signs met anyone trying to head north.

Brodie tapped Graham on the shoulder and pointed. 'Try Cheyne Lane.' It wandered round the southern side of Chain Down, serving the various farms and hamlets. The narrowness and the snakelike bends would have kept a car in second gear, but Graham rode with a skill he would never display on the piano and ten minutes later they crested a swell of the Down and saw the cluster of houses grouped about the crossroads that was Cheyne Warren. Faith Stretton's cottage was halfway up the hill on the other side.

Faith Stretton's car was pulling out of the driveway.

Brodie's first thought was that the police had contacted her and she was on her way to the Crichton Construction site. But she was going the wrong way. Brodie tapped Graham's shoulder again. 'Follow that car.'

All his life Graham had waited for this moment. *Tom Cruise?* he thought. *Too short. Tom Hanks? Too old.* Daniel Craig! When they made the film, he wanted to be played by Daniel Craig. He set off in pursuit, and somehow resisted the urge to throw a wheelie.

Hugging Graham's waist, Brodie felt her mind spinning as fast as the wheels—and like the wheels, spitting grit on the corners. It made no sense. *None* of it made any sense. If she was right about Dev, why was his mother now heading for Guildford? Or—no, not Guildford—further west. Basingstoke? Swindon? Her son was trying to blow up the Three Downs because he'd just found out he wasn't a Moslem fundamentalist after all, and she was hightailing it to Swindon?

'What are you *on?*' gritted Brodie inside her helmet; and Graham, chastened, turned his head enough to say, 'Nothing. I always drive like this.'

'Sorry,' said Brodie, 'talking to myself. You're doing great. Just—watch the road. Keep watching the road.'

So Faith wasn't heading for Swindon. With everything that was going on at Crichton Construction there was still something important enough to take her in the opposite direction, north across Menner Down where there was next to nothing. Sheep farms. Wind farms. Little wooded copses, and villages that didn't yet have proper sewage. And that was all, until the swell of the Downs dipped and levelled out and...

And became flat enough to build an airfield.

DANIEL WAS HALFWAY down the long hill into Dimmock before things really started going wrong. Until then all he'd had to contend with was the sweat in his eyes, the knives in his lungs, the leaden ache of his running legs and the fact that his heart was playing 'Chopsticks' inside his ribs.

But halfway down the hill people started taking an interest in him.

Perhaps it was only natural. Everyone else on the road that day was trying to get out of Dimmock. By mid-afternoon, of course, many of them had given up and, abandoning their cars, were trudging back the way they'd come. Still the sight of someone in a hurry to get back to town was enough to attract attention and then concern. People don't behave like that. They don't run towards a known danger. Suspicions were aroused that he was Up To No Good.

Somebody shouted after him, 'Where's the fire then?'

And Daniel, who should simply have ignored him and kept running, tried to reply without wasting either time or breath that he could ill afford. 'There's no fire,' he gasped.

But if he thought that would reassure anyone he was wrong. The Chinese Whispers travelled down the hill faster than he did. 'What did he say? Don't fire? Why would anybody be shooting at him?' 'Jesus—you don't think it's him, do you? The bomber?' 'That little runt? But he's not...' 'That's the bomber? The one on the news?' 'That's him. That man there says so.'

At first it was only that the people he passed drifted together into watchful groups. They followed the running figure with their eyes, with pointed fingers and with nervous challenges Daniel was too preoccupied to hear. He thought lives depended on his ability to keep running. It never occurred to him that one of them might be his own.

Soon after that the little clumps of people gravitated—like star-stuff—into bigger, heavier agglomerations that acquired a momentum of their own. They began to follow in his wake. At first, because he was running, he left them behind. Then some of them started to run after him. And those further down the hill saw a man running towards them with a small crowd chasing him. Primed for disaster and ready to believe the worst, they moved to intercept him.

Daniel didn't realise what they were doing, thought it was just his usual luck that put people in his way on the one occasion when speed mattered to him. He waved his arms frantically at them. 'Please…I need to get through…'

He found his way blocked, unaccountably, by a brick privy. Except that it spoke with a Yorkshire accent. 'What's your hurry?'

Most satisfactory explanations are either very short or very long, a sentence or an essay. A middle-distance explanation can cause more confusion than it resolves. Because time mattered, and he was fighting for breath, Daniel went for the abridged version. 'I have to get to the police station. Or people are going to get hurt.'

For once, brevity wasn't a happy choice. People heard the word *hurt*. They heard the word *police*. They raced, whippet-like and in fact accurately, to the conclusion that Daniel knew more about what was going on than they did, and inaccurately to the supposition that this was because he was involved. The Chinese Whisperers took up megaphones.

'The police are after him!' 'He says he's going to hurt people!' 'Ask him about the bomb. Where's the bomb?' 'He says you planted a bomb!' 'What do you want to bomb *us* for?'

'I don't want to bomb anyone!' yelled Daniel. 'Do I *look* like Osama bin Laden?'

'He says he's Osama bin Laden!' 'He doesn't look much like him. He's got yellow hair.' 'Who's Osama bin Laden?'

'Sonny,' said the Yorkshire privy severely, 'this is not a good day for teasing people. They're ready to beat the crap out of someone, and if they can't find the real Osama bin Laden they may decide you'll do.'

'I didn't *say*…!' Daniel heard the hysteria in his own voice and made an effort to calm down. 'I think I know what's going on. The phone system's down and I need to tell the police. Help me!'

The man regarded him thoughtfully for perhaps another ten

seconds. Then he nodded. 'All right. Mind you, I'm taking a chance. If it turns out you've blown up the town hall after all, you'll have me to answer to.'

Daniel didn't know whether to laugh or cry. 'Fine. It's a deal. Now *please,* let me through!'

One tweed arm spread wide like a door opening. 'Let him through. Let him through, now. The man's got urgent business. Terrorist? Does he *look* like a terrorist? He's a… He's a…' Stuck for inspiration he looked down at Daniel and hissed, 'What are you?'

Daniel hissed back, 'I'm a teacher.'

The man looked shocked. 'Ee, lad, are you sure you want to tell them that?'

A sense of the surreal washed over him and Daniel shook his head. 'No. Silly me. Tell them I'm a competitor on a television game show. Tell them I've got ten minutes to get to Battle Alley. Tell them, if it takes fifteen I'll still get the dishwasher but I'll miss out on the cuddly toy.'

Even the Chinese Whisperers didn't know what to do with that. They stared at Daniel and blinked. Then they stood back.

'Thank you.' He took a deep breath and started running again. A shy voice called after him, 'Good luck…'

Three hundred metres further down the hill he thought he was in trouble again. The log-jam of cars was gradually being broken up, and one of the few he'd seen moving this afternoon slowed to keep pace with him. He stole enough breath from his running to yell plaintively, 'Leave me alone! I'm not hurting anybody.'

And Detective Sergeant Voss leant across the passenger seat and said in a puzzled tone, 'I can see that, Daniel. But what exactly *are* you doing?'

Daniel staggered to a halt against a lamppost, relief all but sweeping the legs from under him. 'Charlie! I was never so glad to see anyone in my life! But why aren't you in the hospital?'

'Because I'm fine,' growled Voss. 'And because, with all this going on, there'd be *something* I could do even if I wasn't. Get in. Where are you going?'

His knees still bending both ways, Daniel fell in rather than got in. 'Battle Alley. Unless you've got a radio.'

'Of course I've got a radio. Why?'

While Voss was raising Battle Alley, Daniel explained.

SUPERINTENDENT FULLER didn't ask constables to do something he wouldn't do himself. When he got the message from the Battle Alley radio room he gave it a little thought, offered up a little prayer and stepped out of the cordon, squelching across the mud towards the blockhouse. It was the longest hundred metres he'd ever walked.

Deacon looked up as he approached. 'Hello,' he observed to the man inside the bunker. 'Developments.' He got up stiffly and went to meet his colleague.

'There's no need to look so nervous,' he said when they were out of earshot. 'He's not blowing up anything.'

'I know he's not,' said Fuller. 'He's the decoy.'

Deacon's eyes drilled into him like diamond-tipped bits. *'What?'*

Fuller passed on the message he'd received, and where he'd received it from. 'They could be wrong, of course.'

'Of course they could,' acknowledged Deacon. 'They very often are. Just, not quite as often as they're right.'

'Is that what he's waiting for? The bang, the puff of smoke.'

'He was waiting for a phone call. When I told him he wasn't getting one, he was a bit put out—but not enough to rethink the whole thing. If Brodie's right, we can guess why. He knows I'll tell him when the middle of Dimmock hits the stratosphere.'

'What do you want to do? If this makes sense to you, we can leave a reduced presence here and pull everyone else back into town. Or we can split our forces and try to cover both scenes.'

Deacon had no idea. 'What's the situation in town? I mean, if it's already empty—if the evacuation is pretty much complete…?'

Fuller shook his head. 'People found they couldn't reach a safe distance and now they're drifting back. I can keep them out of the town centre. I probably can't keep them from returning to their homes. And if there is a bomb, it could be anywhere.'

'Have you told Division?'

'Not yet. I only just got the message. I wanted to ask you how seriously we should take it.'

Deacon frowned pensively. 'They're not jerking you around, if that's what you're wondering. If they went to this much trouble getting you a message, they think it's a clear and present danger. If we can do anything about it, I think we should.'

'All right,' Decided Fuller. 'Will you stay with Stretton? I'll leave you enough men to keep him contained, take the rest of them back to town. If there's an explosion, at least we'll be there to control the situation. Maybe when Stretton sees we've twigged his little game he'll give himself up.'

'Maybe,' said Deacon doubtfully. 'I can't quite make him out. I'm not sure why he's doing this. I'm not even sure what it is he's doing.'

Fuller shrugged. 'We'll get to the bottom of it, one way or another. It just may be too late.'

Deacon's eyebrows climbed. 'Too late for what?'

'Too late for him. When I tell Division, their response will be to send a marksman.'

TWENTY-FIVE

SHE WAS FLEEING the country? Faith Stretton was leaving her son sitting on two tonnes of dynamite and getting away while the police were whistling up a SWAT team? Brodie didn't believe it. Maybe she didn't know Faith well, but she knew her better than that. She was sharp, snippy, independent, defiant of convention, impatient of constraint. She was...

Well yes, she was very like Brodie herself. And Brodie knew there were no circumstances, none, in which she would put her needs ahead of Paddy's.

The road they were on straightened as it dropped off the northern edge of Menner Down onto the rich agricultural levels beyond, the car ahead regaining a little of the lead Graham had been whittling back. The bike picked up speed too, the slipstream whistling past Brodie's helmet and tugging at her sleeves.

By now Faith must know she was being followed. There were only these two vehicles on the road. Someone heading for the supermarket might have put it down to coincidence: someone in the grip of a crisis would know it was nothing of the kind. If it was the sort of crisis that could be sorted out by stopping and explaining, she'd have done it by now. So it wasn't.

Brodie's thoughts ran on with the wheels on the tarmac. Faith was up to her neck in something, all right—something she considered more important than her son's future. Brodie couldn't imagine anything that big, that bad. Yet the evidence was plain. Four miles away Dev was holed up with his explosives while his mother was heading for the nearest airstrip. And on the far side of the Three Downs, Dimmock police were struggling to contain a terror alert. These facts could not be un-connected. If there was a plot to bomb Dimmock, Dev Stretton had to be part of it.

Why? Brodie asked herself then. Because his skin was darker than hers? If Dev had shared Daniel's colouring, would anyone have linked him to a bomb plot? Well, perhaps—if he'd tried to steal two tonnes of explosives! Still… He'd done some-thing desperately stupid, dangerous and criminal, and however inadequate he must have had a reason. But was that necessar-ily the killing of shedloads of English people for the greater glory of Islam? Or was he still acting out the consequences of previous events? Long before there was a terror alert, someone had already put his hand to murder. But for the incident at Balfour Terrace—and if Brodie had understood correctly, the meaning of that incident was still not entirely clear, even to the police—would any of them have dreamt of linking Dev Stretton with a terror plot?

His hand? Or hers? That made Brodie forget what she was doing long enough to lose her balance. Graham shoved her back into place with his elbow.

Most murder victims are killed by people they know. Faith not only knew Joe Loomis, she'd fought with him publicly just days before his death. In any other murder case, that would have been enough to turn the spotlight her way. But when an al-Qaeda terrorist was observed in Dimmock, suddenly the police had more to worry about than the violent but not terribly un-welcome death of a local thug.

And as their inquiries continued, somehow it had come to be assumed that all these events were connected. And maybe that was a mistake. That was why things didn't quite add up, however hard you juggled the figures—even if you got a ma-thematician to do it. They didn't add up because some of them were apples and some were miles to the gallon.

Brodie tried to focus on what she knew or could with con-fidence surmise. Faith was on the run. Dev had been cornered in an attempt to steal explosives that was so cack-handed he must have wanted to attract police attention. It was a diversionary tactic. But he wasn't making a political point—he was trying to protect his mother. Maybe they both thought that when the truth came out he'd be in less trouble than she would. But if Faith killed Loomis, the very least Dev would have to answer for was perverting the course of justice. Maybe he'd think it was worth it, but Faith couldn't believe that. Could she?

The lane swung round to approach the airfield. It wasn't Heathrow or Gatwick; it wasn't even Ronaldsway. It was a flat field with two bits of tarmac on it, one running approximately north to south, the other crossing at an angle. The control tower was rather like the explosives bunker at Crichton Construction, except with a second storey made mostly of glass and a windsock perched on top. There was a hangar—except if you'd seen it in a field with cows in it you'd have said there was a barn—and that was it. No terminals, no restaurants, no Duty Free, no Customs. Just the strip, one car parked beside the squat little tower and a helicopter on the tarmac.

The airstrip was inside the no-fly zone and should have been shut down. But the helicopter was sitting on the tarmac with its engine ticking over.

Paddy would have known what kind of a helicopter it was. She'd have known the engine size, the rotor diameter, the hovering ceiling and quite possibly the test pilot's name. But Brodie never went through a plane spotting phase. The only aircraft she knew by name were Concorde and the Spitfire, and it was neither of those. She supposed it was executive transport for the successful smaller company, a guess in which she was helped by the green and gold livery and the elegant scrawl along the boom: *The Green & Pleasant Leisure Company.*

A man was standing beside it. Over Graham's shoulder Brodie saw him look up at the sound of the approaching car; and again and more sharply when he heard the second engine.

Faith Stretton didn't lift her foot from the accelerator until the man was waving frantically at her. Then she braked hard enough to skid on the grass, and she flung open the driver's door before the car had come to rest.

Even so, she was barely halfway out before Graham had fishtailed to a halt beside her. Brodie climbed down from the bike, slapping her helmet into his chest as if he was the one who owed her an explanation. While the men watched, slightly confused and slightly appalled, the women picked up the argument exactly where they'd left off.

'How *could* you?' yelled Brodie. 'That boy's ready to lay down his life for you! And you're prepared to *let* him?'

'Stay *out* of this!' spat Faith. 'You have no idea what's going on here! Go back to your incomplete tea sets and broken figurines, and let me sort this out!'

'It's too *big!*' cried Brodie. 'You can't sort it out! They think he's a terrorist!'

'Excuse me,' said the man with the plane. 'What is happening? Who…?'

Faith didn't let Brodie answer. 'It'll be all right. We worked it out. Once you reach France it'll all be over. No one's going to get hurt.'

'You reckon?' hooted Brodie, shrill with disbelief. 'Listen to me. I know something about the police. And I'm telling you, some sharp-shooter from Counter Terrorism will have him in their cross-hairs just about now, on the basis that a big explosion in a field is better than a small explosion in a town centre!'

They might have worked it out, Dev Stretton and his mother, in the wee small hours of the morning when anything can sound possible, but they hadn't considered that. They'd thought it was clever to use the terror alert as cover. They hadn't realised how serious the situation already was, or how much more serious it would become. They never guessed that this was one of those rare occasions when, even in Britain, the consequences of acting first and asking questions afterwards were seen as less frightful than doing it the other way round.

Now she thought about it, the implications crashed through Faith's face like falling masonry, taking the colour with them. Instinctively she looked over her shoulder, back the way she'd come. 'No,' she whimpered.

'Yes!' insisted Brodie. 'And *I* know he doesn't want to hurt anyone, but the police think he's a suicide bomber. Even if Daniel's managed to get a message to Jack at the site, they still think it's bombers he's acting as a decoy for. When they get a clear shot they'll take it. This is *big!* They're worrying about hundreds of lives, you stupid woman, and not so much about the guy with the TNT.'

'Ex*cuse* me,' said the man with the helicopter again, still polite but more firmly. 'Will someone please tell me what you are talking about? Things are going on that I am not aware of.'

For the first time Brodie took enough notice of him to identify the accent and, putting it together with the sturdy frame and short wavy hair, to realise she knew him. 'It's Mr Tarar, isn't it? From the country club?' She looked again at the aircraft. 'This is yours?'

'And you are Mrs Farrell, I believe. Yes, the helicopter is mine. That is of no importance. Please tell me, who is believed to be behind a plot to blow up the town centre and for this reason is liable to be shot?' And the tremor barring the words said he already knew the answer.

Her voice a stunned ghost, Faith said: 'Dev is.'

Another of those massive silences stretched and grew. There were three big engines turning over in the immediate vicinity— a car, a bike and an Avco Lycoming aero-engine—but the silence swallowed them all, sucking the sound into itself.

Finally Tarar said to Faith: 'You planned this.' His voice was calm, but it was the same kind of calm as the silence—a calm that had swallowed fury.

Faith didn't know how to answer him. 'No. At least… It was Dev's idea. He thought they'd lift the no-fly zone if they believed they had the mad bomber cornered.'

'Why didn't you *tell* me?'

'Pervez, there hasn't been time!' Then, acknowledging that while it was the truth it wasn't the whole truth, she added in a small voice, 'And I was afraid.'

'Afraid I'd change my mind?'

'Yes.'

He considered. He breathed out a sad little sigh. 'You were right.'

From the way she held his sleeve it was clear that Faith Stretton and Pervez Tarar were old friends. 'No!' she insisted. 'This is what Dev wants—what he's risking his life for. It's his call. Not yours, not mine—Dev's. You don't have the right to refuse him!'

He didn't shake her off. His eyes were compassionate but unyielding. 'I'm sorry. I know what I said. But I'm not going anywhere while my son is in danger.'

'WAS THAT A PLANE?' Through the open crack of the blockhouse door Dev Stretton's voice sounded suddenly alert.

Deacon cast a weary eye at the sky. 'No, a helicopter. Oh…' There shouldn't even have been a helicopter aloft just then.

'Does that mean they've lifted the no-fly zone?'

'Might do,' shrugged Deacon. 'Maybe they've got your mates, and decided the risk of you flying a concrete shed into a tall building is one worth taking.'

The witticism was lost on Stretton. 'I don't have any mates.'

'If you're looking for sympathy, you're doing it all wrong.'

Dev Stretton struggled to make himself clear. 'I mean, this isn't a conspiracy. It's just me. You can't have picked up the other guys because there aren't any.'

Deacon shuffled, trying to ease the ache in his lower back. 'But if there were, I expect that's what you'd tell me anyway.'

Stretton gave a faintly desperate little chuckle. 'I expect it is. Listen, Superintendent. Would you believe me if I told you this was nearly over?'

Deacon considered. 'I might.'

'Good. Because it is. Keep me company for another half-hour, then I'll come out with my hands up or any other way you want, and we'll go back to your place and I'll tell you everything. Including why I killed Joe Loomis.'

Deacon's expression didn't flicker. 'You killed Joe Loomis.'

'Yes. I'll tell you everything that happened. Just be patient another half-hour.'

Deacon didn't really do patient. The closest he ever got was no bloody alternative. 'Give me something to think about while we're waiting. What do you know about Daoud?'

'That won't fill half an hour. I know nothing about him.'

'He is dead, you know,' said Deacon. 'He can't get at you now. Well—unless he comes back to haunt you. But with seventy-two virgins waiting, who would?'

'Really,' said Stretton, 'I don't know him. I don't know anything about him.'

'How about the Dhazi cousins?'

The visible half of Stretton's brow frowned. 'There's a Rafiq Dhazi who works in the building society.'

'That's where you know him from? He runs your ISA?'

Stretton shook his head. 'I don't know him. I've seen the name on his lapel badge.'

'Then tell me this,' said Deacon. 'Are you a Moslem?'

Stretton bristled. 'Not that it's any of your business, but no.'

'You get my town in a muck sweat and *anything* to do with you is my business,' Deacon said forcibly. 'A Christian, then?'

'I'm not an anything. I'm a me.'

Deacon recognised the unconscious arrogance in that. 'I have a friend who's an atheist,' he said. 'The most passionate atheist you can imagine. He goes at it with what can only be described as religious zeal, and I swear to God if the cause ever needs martyrs again he'll be first in the queue. Which makes him a dangerous man. You believe that strongly in anything and you have the potential to be a dangerous man. What is it you believe in, Dev?'

'Nothing,' said Dev Stretton firmly.

But Deacon shook his head. 'No one wakes up one morning and thinks he'll crucify himself because he's got nothing better to do that day. We're all here because you believe there's something more important than your future. If that isn't faith, I don't know what is.'

'It wasn't like that,' insisted Stretton. He sounded desperate for Deacon to believe him. 'I told you, I killed Loomis. After that, I wasn't thinking straight. I just needed a way out.'

Deacon was unconvinced. 'If you cared so much about the death of a petty gangster that you wanted to end it all, you wouldn't have waited nine days. And we wouldn't be sitting here chatting about it when you have the means to do it at your fingertips. No, that's not what this is about.'

'Yes, it is,' said Stretton, his tone growing increasingly urgent. 'I killed Loomis. He hurt my mother. In the street. I let a week go by so no one would suspect, then I went and stuck a knife in him.'

'Then you thought, what a terrible thing to do! And after another nine days you decided to blow yourself up.'

'Yes. Exactly.'

'Go on, then.' Jack Deacon had never done a course in siege negotiation, and it showed.

There was a stunned pause. Then: 'I don't want to kill you.'

Deacon clambered stiffly to his feet. 'Suppose I move off a bit? Let's get it finished, shall we? You tell me you're so ashamed of killing Joe Loomis you want to die. Well, here you are, sitting on two tonnes of blasting explosives. What's stopping you?'

Stretton's voice was small. 'I changed my mind.'

'Yeah, right,' snorted Deacon derisively. 'Dev, you never wanted to die. I think Daniel's right and you're a diversion. The question is, a diversion from what? What is it you don't want me seeing or thinking about? What is it that's worth risking your life to stop me investigating—but only for the next half-hour? And the only thing any of us can think of is, someone needs that half-hour to plant a real bomb. If we're wrong, if there's something else going on, something that doesn't threaten hundreds of lives, you need to tell me. You need to tell me now.'

'I can't,' whined Stretton. 'Not yet. Can't you just wait half an hour?' His voice was a plea.

'Till these co-conspirators you say don't exist have had time to do their job?' Then Deacon's voice softened. 'Or...until whoever it is you're trying to protect is safe?' He found himself glancing at the sky again. But the helicopter had gone.

'There are no bombs! At least,' stumbled Stretton, 'as far as I know there are no bombs. Maybe you know better. You put this town on a terror alert because you thought an attack was imminent, and maybe you were right. But I don't know anything about it. All I know is, it gave me an idea. You're right about me. There is something I believe in more than the future. It's my family. Joe Loomis hurt my family. I had to deal with that.' He gave a despairing little laugh. 'You know how excitable we Asians are. Look at our women the wrong way and you're taking your head home in a sack!'

Deacon gave a knowing little grin. 'Ah yes, but that's them, isn't it, and you're you. I guess that's the advantage of being half one thing and half another: you don't come ready-packaged. You can decide for yourself who and what you are. You can make your own choices—about what's important, and what you do about it. And you're as much your mother's son as your father's.

'Yes, I think you'd take risks to take care of your mother. I think you might have gone to The Rose the day Joe Loomis slapped her, and punched his lights out even if it meant having his heavies on your back as you did it. I *don't* think you thought about it for over a week and then ambushed him in a dark car park—*and* relied on him bringing the knife! And then waited *another* week before making a public exhibition of your remorse.'

'That's exactly what happened,' insisted Stretton. Then, a shade defensively: 'No one's at their best and brightest in this kind of situation.'

Deacon chuckled. 'No, but people don't behave that much out of character either. You didn't kill Loomis. You know how I know? Because if you had you'd have done one of two things. Either you'd have come straight round to Battle Alley and told me what happened, or you'd have kept your cool and waited to see if I worked it out.

'You're a pretty tough character, Dev. Not like Joe—you don't feel the need to pick your teeth with a stiletto to prove it. You're quiet, polite, conscientious—but you're strong. Going to Pakistan after the earthquake wasn't the easy option—you did it because those people needed your time more than you did. I know, and you know, you could do prison if you had to.'

Deacon paused while Stretton worked out that it was a compliment. 'You could also handle being a wanted man. If you'd decided Joe got no more than his just deserts—and who among us would argue?—you'd have gone to work the next morning as if nothing had happened, and carried on as if what happened was nothing to do with you unless I could prove differently. You were never going to panic and draw attention to yourself.

'So like I say, that isn't what this is about. You're not a suicide bomber, and I don't think you're a murderer. I think you *are* here to be a martyr—but not to any cause, least of all a religious one. You told me what mattered to you—your family. You're covering for your mother, aren't you? Faith killed Joe Loomis. And she's doing a runner right now, while every policeman on the south coast is watching this blockhouse.'

IF BRODIE HAD STILL been on the motorcycle, that was the moment at which she'd have fallen off. She felt the jolt travel from the top of her head to the soles of her booted feet, and for some minutes afterwards her brain felt like a crime scene, where intruders had thrown the contents into a pile in the middle of the floor.

So Pervez Tarar was…

Then Joe Loomis wasn't…

Then what the hell were they all doing here?

'Somebody's going to have to help me out,' she stumbled. 'Mr Tarar—I didn't misunderstand, did I? You're Dev Stretton's father.'

'Indeed I am,' said Tarar warmly. 'And I didn't misunderstand either, did I? Dev is in danger. Right now.'

'Yes, he is,' nodded Brodie. 'Real and immediate danger. Not just the explosives, which I imagine he knows how to handle, but the Counter Terrorism arm of the police which I don't suppose he does. They think he's part of an al-Qaeda plot. And he isn't, is he? All he's been plotting is how to get his mother beyond the reach of Dimmock CID, who—when they've a bit less on their plates—will remember they're in the middle of a murder investigation.'

'What?' said Tarar; and, 'Me?' said Faith.

Brodie ran a distracted hand through her thick hair. 'Oh shit. Is that not right either?'

Faith shook her head. 'I'm not going anywhere. When I'm finished here I'm going to the construction site. I'll explain and the anti-terrorist guys can go home. Dev will give himself up and we'll sort it all out. More or less,' she added tiredly. 'There'll be hell to pay, of course. But rather that than…' She let the sentence die away, as if everyone knew what she meant. And they didn't. Brodie didn't. Actually, Graham didn't either, but he wasn't even trying any more. He was admiring the Lycoming engine on the helicopter.

'I'm sorry.' Tarar was looking at Faith with compassion. 'This stops here. I can't do what I promised. Not now. For myself I would take the risk. I told you that, and I meant it. But you haven't been honest with me. You didn't tell me that helping you would mean leaving Dev to face the consequences.'

'It's what he wants.' Faith's eyes were imploring. 'This isn't something I told him to do. It was Dev's idea. His idea to ask you for help—and when the no-fly zone was imposed, his idea how to get it lifted. You have to go through with it, Pervez. Not for me, not for old times' sake—for Dev. If you don't, he'll still pay the price, he just won't get what he wants in return.'

'I am his father,' said Pervez Tarar quietly; and it was clear to Brodie that the plain words meant something very special to him. 'It's not my job to do what he wants. It's my job to do what is best for him.'

And this, Brodie supposed, was pretty much how Daniel had got involved with the Stretton family: watching Faith, intense and committed, trying to move by sheer willpower a man who had no intentions of giving her what she wanted.

She and Tarar had been lovers a quarter of a century ago. And something of that time had stayed with them: an affection, a regard. If she'd needed money she'd have got it. When she needed him to break the law for her, to risk everything he'd worked for to get her out of more trouble than she could handle, he was willing to do that too. But Dev was his son, and fond as he was of the mother he wasn't going to sacrifice his child to save her.

'Well, bully for you,' cried Faith, red hair flying in her passion. 'I don't have the luxury of always putting my son first. I have two children.'

And it was only then, minutes into the confrontation, that Brodie realised there was someone else in the car. She wasn't hiding: she just wasn't very big, and the dark hair fell around her scared little face like a screen. Evie. Of course, Brodie thought then, she should have guessed. If Faith was on the run, she wasn't leaving her teenage daughter behind. That was what all the packing had been about. They'd have been gone days ago if it hadn't been for the security alert.

Evie…

I have two children.

And this was Dev's idea, something he cared enough about to sacrifice his own future. And Faith cared enough to let him.

I have two children…

Moses, hearing the voice of the burning bush, could hardly have been more staggered than Brodie was then as the implications hit her. It had seemed barely credible that Faith would let her son go to jail in order to keep her out. Now Brodie realised that wasn't what was happening at all. Faith Stretton had two children. Dev didn't just have a mother to think about, he had a sister.

TWENTY-SIX

BRODIE HAD HARDLY NOTICED the girl, except as a figure in the background. She wasn't even sure how old she was. Eighteen, nineteen?

Twenty?

She looked at her now, taking in the long straight brown hair, the pale skin, the expression of a frightened rabbit cornered by a weasel. She didn't share Dev's colouring: no anonymous Kashmiri was needed to account for her. It wasn't Dev who was Joe Loomis's child—it was Evie.

And it wasn't Faith who was on the run. That was why Dev Stretton was ready to do hard time and why Faith was ready to let him. Because, much as it was to ask, they both knew that he could cope with it and Evie couldn't.

Evie Stretton killed Joe Loomis? Drove a knife deep enough into his side that he bled to death? Killed her father, and walked away and left her brother to face the music?

Brodie leant down slowly in the open door of the car, and tried to give her a reassuring smile. It wasn't easy because she felt like someone trying to outrun a landslide, with things she'd thought solid suddenly tumbling round her. She fought to keep her voice level. 'Evie—what happened?'

Now Faith was there too, leaning past her into the car as if she could block the question, and the consequences that would inevitably flow from it, with her body. 'Don't answer that,' she commanded. 'It's none of her business. It's none of *your* business!' She twisted angrily towards Brodie. 'Go away. Let me deal with this!'

'But you can't deal with it,' snapped Brodie impatiently. 'I'm not sure anyone could deal with it now. It's not a snowball any more, it's a bloody great avalanche—it won't stop when you say it can. It'll keep rolling, and it'll bury you and Dev and half of Dimmock, and it won't even notice.'

'Then what do you want me to do?' cried Faith.

'He's right.' Brodie jerked her head at Tarar. 'It stops here. Tell the truth—the whole truth. And just hope there's still time to salvage the situation.'

'I have to get Evie away first!'

Brodie shook her head. 'The moment that helicopter takes off, none of you can turn back. I know Dev was willing to do this. That doesn't make it OK to let him.' Something occurred to her. She looked at the girl's pale, frightened face and tried to read behind it. 'Does she even know?'

Fear and fury warred hotly in Faith Stretton's cheeks. 'Shut up! Go *away!*'

She tried to push her, but Brodie was solider than she looked and barely swayed. 'She doesn't, does she? She doesn't know what it's going to cost to get her to safety.'

Evie mightn't have played much part in the conversation till now but she had been trying to follow it. She mumbled, 'Dev said he'd keep the police occupied.'

'Yes,' said Brodie softly. 'And I expect that's all he said, isn't it? Because he wouldn't want you to know what keeping them occupied is going to cost him.'

'What?' She didn't look twenty. Scared, she looked about twelve. But Brodie detected a streak of her mother's stubbornness. Evie Stretton wasn't stupid. She'd worked out that she'd be better not knowing. But she wanted to know anyway.

'Just about everything,' said Brodie honestly. 'He's certainly going to prison. That's assuming he gets away with his life.'

'Ma!' It was almost a scream. Brodie's insides clenched at the distress in it. She wasn't much more than a child, and circumstances had led her to perform one dreadful act that her whole family was going to spend the rest of their lives paying for. And they hadn't told her. Faith and her son had discussed the situation without her, and decided what they had to do. Knowing what it would cost them both, and believing it was worth it.

They were a strong family, a close family. They shouldn't have been in meltdown over the death of a man like Joe Loomis. A man with so much blood on his hands that by the end he hardly noticed the smell.

Brodie turned to Faith, trying to ignore the agony in her eyes. 'You know it's over. Blame me if you want to, hate me if you must, but they had to know. Both of them. It'll be hard getting through what comes next, but you'd have lost them all if you'd done what Dev asked. When they found out that while his father was taking his sister out of the country Dev was playing a game with the police that involved explosives and sniper rifles, and that if he survived he'd take the rap for what she'd done, and *that you'd known,* neither of them would ever have forgiven you.'

Finally she got it right. No one was arguing. All of them looked shocked. Brodie knew she'd hurt them all, in ways that would reverberate long after she'd passed from their orbit, and her only consolation was that there might still be time to prevent a worse disaster. She shook herself, making an effort to take control.

'There'll be time to talk this through later. Between yourselves, to the police, with Dev—all of that. The important thing now is to get word to Jack Deacon at the construction site. The last thing the police were told was that Dev was keeping them occupied while bombers targeted Dimmock. We need to let them know he isn't, he's just looking after his little sister.'

Pervez Tarar stared, thunderstruck. 'But…who would *tell* them such a thing?'

Brodie shuffled uncomfortably. 'Well…actually…it was me. I'm sorry, it seemed to make sense at the time. I knew *something* was going on that wasn't what everyone thought was going on. I put it all together and I got it wrong.' She gave Faith a preemptive glare. 'But not *that* wrong! If you'd been honest with me I could have helped. Now all we can do is try to make sure Counter Terrorism know it's a stupid, overprotective brother they're dealing with, not a mad mullah. Get on your phone and tell Dev to come out with his hands up, and I'll call Jack.'

But the network was still down. Brodie cast around desperately for a solution. Maybe Graham could get her to the site on his bike. Maybe in the time it took to get there, to find someone who'd let her through the police cordon and to convince Deacon that the crisis was over—that there never was, in fact, a crisis— Dev wouldn't have shown enough of himself for the marksman from Counter Terrorism to draw a bead…

'One moment,' said Pervez Tarar. He opened the door of his helicopter and beckoned to Brodie. 'Come with me, please.'

As the rotors began to spin he explained. 'We need to be above the Downs to raise Air Traffic Control. They'll be able to radio a message to the police.'

The aircraft had been ready to depart when Evie arrived. Within seconds it was airborne. Brodie screwed in her seat to see the car and the motorcycle, indeed the whole of the airstrip, falling away below. She'd never been in a helicopter before. It was tiny, noisy, scary and rather exciting.

As soon as he'd cleared the radio blindspot, Tarar raised Air Traffic Control.

Air Traffic Controllers are used to dealing with emergencies. But not this kind of emergency. Brodie had to explain three separate times before the one she was talking to understood what she needed. But he confirmed he could relay a message to the police.

Brodie thought quickly. 'Then get word to Detective Superintendent Jack Deacon of Dimmock CID that Dev Stretton isn't a terrorist and if there's a plot to blow up Dimmock it's nothing to do with him. Tell him no one's in any danger from him. Tell him Dev's mother's on her way, and he'll come out when she gets there. And tell him to please keep the Counter

Terrorism guys from thinking one well-placed bullet could secure the monarchy, the Union Jack and the British way of life for generations to come.'

When Brodie had delivered her message, Pervez Tarar spoke to ATC again. 'Please be advised we are returning to Menner strip soonest. There is no need to scramble the RAF.'

Brodie gave him a disapproving look. 'I'm not sure a joke is appropriate just now.'

His expression was sombre. 'Mrs Farrell, no joke is intended. A no-fly zone is imposed only when there is considered to be a realistic prospect of attack from the air. Not only would RAF fighters scramble to intercept an unidentified aircraft in a no-fly zone, if they couldn't escort it down they'd shoot it down.'

Brodie considered for a moment. 'Did Faith know what she was asking of you?'

The pilot gave a wry little smile. 'No, I don't think she did. But I did. I thought about it and I thought it was worth the risk. I'd have done it, except…'

'Except that by saving her daughter you'd be abandoning your son,' Brodie finished softly.

'Yes.' He considered. 'Does that make me a selfish man?'

Brodie shook her head. 'Just a good father.'

She needed more facts. But Tarar didn't have them. Faith had told him only that Evie had to get out of Britain as quickly as possible and couldn't use public ports or airports. Of course he'd known that something bad had happened, because people who can't run to the police are usually on the run from the police. He hadn't enquired any deeper. Faith Stretton was the mother of his son. He'd once thought she was the love of his life. He'd been happily married for twenty-two years now to someone else, but the fondness, the sense of attachment, had lasted. When she asked for his help he'd said Yes and then he'd said How?

When they got back to the airstrip Brodie thought the car would be gone. She found it hard to guess Faith's next move, impossible to guess how she was feeling. Both her children in danger, and anything that made things better for one made them worse for the other. A situation she could never have anticipated blowing up round them until it involved Counter Terrorism police and RAF fighters. And with everything she'd risked to get Evie to safety, she was still on the wrong side of the English Channel, just miles from the spot where she'd driven a knife to its hilt into Joe Loomis's side.

Brodie ached to know how that had happened. But she doubted she'd get the chance to ask. Whether Faith was now on her way to the construction site to try to help Dev, or driving wildly anywhere there was an open road in the hope of keeping Evie one step ahead of the police, Brodie thought she'd be gone.

But as the helicopter dropped towards the tarmac Faith's big estate car was clear to see. Brodie supposed she was waiting for Tarar to return, hoping to change his mind. That having done all he could to protect Dev he'd fulfil his promise to Faith. But no one rushed forward as the aircraft landed. Faith remained standing beside the car, Evie sitting inside.

Tarar started to apologise again. Faith interrupted, dull-eyed. 'Evie has something to say.'

The girl's eyes were downcast. Her voice was tiny, as if it was coming a long way, but tucked away at its core was a grain of adamant. 'I didn't know,' she whispered. 'What Dev was doing. He said he'd keep the police off my back while I got away, and I didn't even ask how. I knew he'd do it. He's always looked out for me.'

She looked up. 'But if I'd known what he planned I wouldn't have let him do it. I never thought—I never wanted it to be him or me. I never *imagined* him getting into this kind of trouble. Maybe I should have done. Dev was always willing to go the extra mile for people. And…he's my brother. I love him, and he loves me.

'But I never, *never* thought he'd try to take the blame for this himself. My mother knows that. I want you to know it too.' She was looking directly at Dev's father. 'And I want you to know that I don't blame you for putting Dev first. Not just because he's your son—because he's the innocent party. Because he deserves it, and I don't. I've told Ma I'm not going anywhere. Except to the police, to tell them what happened. I don't want anything else on my conscience.'

Tarar's eyes brimmed and he hardly knew what to say. 'My goodness, what a splendid family you are! And what a tragedy that so much love should lead to so much heartache! Dear child, I know you're not mine. I wish you were. But whatever you need to deal with this, let me provide it. I have an excellent solicitor, I'll contact him as soon as I can. Don't think you're alone. Your mother, your brother and I are with you and will do everything we can to make things easier.'

Evie managed a damp little smile. 'What do we do now?'

With everyone else about to dissolve in tears, Brodie did what she did best—she took over. 'We still can't phone anyone. I think we need to split up. Mr Tarar, take Faith and head for the construction site. When you start meeting police road blocks, tell them who you are and have them radio Detective Superintendent Deacon—he'll wave you through, and he won't do anything else until you get there. I'll take Evie back to the cottage and we'll wait for the police to contact us. OK?'

No one objected. But Faith lingered at the driver's door of her car so Brodie couldn't get in. Pervez Tarar put an arm around her shoulders. 'Come on. Everything will be all right now.'

'No, it won't,' moaned Faith. 'How can it be?'

'No, it won't,' he agreed, chastened. 'We'll all be in a lot of trouble. But we'll get through it. Believe that. We will get through.' He guided her to his car.

Still astride his motorbike, Graham cleared his throat. 'Er…'

And Brodie turned back from the car just long enough to kiss him. 'Graham, you're a life-saver. You can tell your boss I said so. If you have any trouble with him, send him to me.'

But for the life of him, watching her climb into the car and drive away, Graham couldn't remember where he worked or who his boss was.

THERE'S SOMETHING about being in a car that encourages intimacy. The fact that, if one of you is driving, you can't be constantly looking at each other is part of it. The fact that a car is an enclosed shell keeping the rest of the world at bay is another part.

As the airstrip fell behind them Brodie said softly, 'Do you want to tell me what happened?'

Evie twitched her a nervous little glance. 'You mean…

'I know you stabbed Joe Loomis. Do you want to tell me why?'

The girl thought for a minute. 'Do I have to?'

'No,' said Brodie honestly. 'In fact the police, and Mr Tarar's solicitor, would probably advise you not to. On the other hand, the first time you tell someone—someone other than your family—is going to be the hardest. It might help to have a practice run first.'

She only looked like a child: mentally, physically and chronologically she was a woman. She managed a little grin. 'Plus, you'd quite like to know.'

Brodie gave a chuckle. 'That obvious, is it? Yes, I'd like to know. I know some of it. And some of it I worked out, or guessed. But yes, I'd like to know the rest. If you want to tell me.'

She thought a little longer. Then she nodded. 'All right.'

TWENTY-SEVEN

DEACON WOULDN'T WEAR the in-ear radio receivers. He said they were uncomfortable. He said his ear was the wrong shape. He said he couldn't hear the advice they were giving him over the static anyway. None of this was true. Everyone at Battle Alley knew that Deacon wouldn't wear the receivers because he didn't want anyone telling him how to do his job.

Which meant that when there was an important message for him someone had to bring it in person. This time it was Detective Constable Huxley, who walked out to the blockhouse as if through a minefield and took only moderate comfort from the casual way his boss was leaning against it. He didn't look as if he felt to be in danger, though with Deacon you could never tell.

Ten metres away Huxley stopped and filled his lungs to shout. Then he thought better of it. If two tonnes of blasting explosives went up, ten metres wasn't enough to save him. But it *was* enough to damage his cred. He used the breath to stiffen his resolve and walked the rest of the way.

Inside the blockhouse, observing through the crack of the door, Dev Stretton didn't know what it meant that the detective with the rugby playing nose was leaning over, murmuring in Deacon's ear. He couldn't hear what he was saying. But he saw Deacon's eyes flick momentarily wider and his lips tighten. Then he said tersely. 'Tell them I can handle this.'

The younger man shuffled broad shoulders uncomfortably. 'I'll tell them, sir. I'm not sure they'll listen.'

'Tell them from me they'd *better* listen,' snarled Deacon. 'This is my crime scene. They'll do what they're told.'

'Yessir,' said Huxley quickly. 'Only, I got the impression they think it's *their* crime scene now.' He retreated as soon as he decently could.

Deacon vented a fractious sigh. 'OK,' he said to Stretton, 'this just got serious. Counter Terrorism are on site. They don't mess around. They aren't here for a friendly chat about your fears, your ambitions and how you really just want to make a better world. They're screwing tripods to sniper rifles and looking for a chance to take you out. They don't care why you're doing this. They just want to end it.'

Stretton's voice soared in astonishment. 'They'd shoot me? I haven't *done* anything!'

'Now don't be naïve,' growled Deacon. 'You've reduced an entire town to a state of chaos. The longer that goes on, the more casualties there'll be. For everyone's sake, we need to bring this to a close right now.'

Fatally, Stretton was calculating percentages. 'They're not going to shoot at an explosives bunker. And they're certainly not going to shoot at an explosives bunker that has a Detective Superintendent leaning against it!'

Three good strides, thought Deacon. Three good strides and I'd have him by the throat, and I could slap seven kinds of shit out of him under the pretext of subduing him. And probably nothing would happen.

What he said aloud was, 'Dev, I know you're stupid. We wouldn't be here, any of us, if you weren't stupid. But don't make a virtue of it. All you know about this sort of situation is what you've seen in films. Counter Terrorism isn't my field either, but I know more about it than you do. I know that the guys setting up their gear right now are the best we've got. The best shots, armed with the best equipment. They can put a bullet through a man's eye at half a mile. And they have bullets that'll go exactly where they're aimed and then stop. All that will blow apart is your head.'

Stretton's voice quivered as the image Deacon had painted

lodged in his mind. He still thought there was another way. 'I can just shut the door. If they can't see me they can't shoot me.'

'Thinking of spending the rest of your life here, then?' asked Deacon wearily. 'Getting meals sent in, laundry picked up? Getting cable TV? You're right, you can shut the door. That's when I walk away. And still at some point you have to open the door, and that's when they'll nail you. They'll watch all day if they have to, with the patience of sphinxes. But if they've been told to take you down, that's what they'll do.'

It was true, every word of it. He thought Stretton believed him. And still, when he heard the blockhouse door shut, his heart sank like a stone because he thought it hadn't been enough. The young man had painted himself into a corner and couldn't find the way out. Deacon thought he was going to die not because he was wicked, not even because he was stupid, but of indecision.

Then the lock turned again and the crack in the door reappeared, together with a thinner sliver than ever of Dev Stretton's face. His voice was smaller too. 'All right. Get me out of here.'

SHE WAS NO LONGER a child but a woman. Some things she had a right to, and one was knowing who she was—where she came from. For nineteen years Faith had protected her from that. But increasingly since coming of age Evie had asserted her right to her own history. It was the only thing they argued about.

As a child she never even wondered. The family was her mother, her brother and herself. There seemed no need, indeed no place, for anyone else. In an earlier era she might have been alerted to the deficiency by schoolmates—but by the time Evie was at school, half the people there lived in units other than the traditional nuclear family. She was secure, she was happy, and still she had no interest in who sowed the seed she sprang from.

As she grew it occurred to Evie that there were differences between herself and her brother that could only be explained if they had different fathers. Faith had no hesitation about confirming this. She had loved like Othello, she said: not wisely, but too well. The first time, though the relationship ended, she came away with the best possible souvenir, which was Dev. And the second time she was lucky enough to get a daughter she loved every bit as much, fiercely and endlessly. She considered life, and love, had been good to her.

And for a few more years, that was good enough for Evie.

What started her thinking about it afresh was when Dev, five years older than her, preoccupied with his imminent trip to Pakistan and less than usually circumspect because of it, let drop the casual bombshell that his father was helping to finance the expedition.

Evie was staggered beyond belief. Dev knew his father? She felt as if something she'd known all her life was no longer true. The family had been split asunder, someone she'd never met had been admitted to it, and no one had told her. And the man (as it seemed to her) buying his way into her family was nothing to do with her.

She demanded an explanation. Why was Dev permitted to know his father when she wasn't? How long had Dev known? When had Faith planned to tell Evie? *Had* she planned to?

And who was Evie's father, and when did she get to meet him?

Faith found herself in a situation she'd hoped never to face. But she'd always known it was a possibility, and if she'd been just a little braver she might have taken this opportunity to take the skeleton out of the cupboard and talk more frankly to both her children.

But she baulked. Perhaps it was lack of courage. Perhaps she was doing what she genuinely believed was best. At the time Evie thought the former; now she recognised that perhaps Faith had good reason when she refused, even under pressure, to tell Evie anything at all about her father.

What she said was that there were differences between her first love and her second. That Dev's father was a good man and, even from a distance, a good parent; and when Dev was about fifteen an opportunity had arisen and—proceeding carefully, gauging how much he could deal with—she'd told him who his father was. A little later, with both of them well prepared, she'd introduced them. They'd remained in casual but affectionate contact ever since.

'Ten years?' whispered Evie, thunderstruck. 'He's been seeing his father for *ten years?* And he didn't *tell* me?'

'I told him not to,' said Faith. 'When Dev was fifteen you were only ten. Of course you'd have wanted to know when you were going to meet your father, and you wouldn't have understood when I told you that, if I had my way, you never would.'

'I don't understand it *now!*' yelled Evie in a passion of anger, hurt and frustration.

So Faith tried to explain; a little. She didn't want to tell Evie she was born of bad blood. She certainly didn't want her thinking there was anything glamorous about her father's unsuitability. And she didn't want to drop any clues that would help Evie to find him. 'I'm very fond of Dev's father. We never wanted to marry, but we stayed friends. If I needed a friend today, he's the one I'd turn to.

'If I needed a friend, your father's the last man I'd turn to. We didn't part on good terms. I was passionately in love with him, blind to his failings. The only good thing he ever did for me was give me you. Well, I can forgive him a lot for that— but he's not a nice man and I don't want you getting involved with him. You'd end up getting hurt, and I'll do anything to prevent that.'

'But it's not your decision!' insisted Evie.

'Yes,' said Faith quietly. 'It is.'

Regardless of who her father was, first and foremost Evie was Faith's daughter. Strong-willed and stubborn, she wouldn't take no for an answer. When it became clear that neither tears nor tantrums would undermine her mother's resolve, she proceeded by other means.

As Brodie knew better than most, there is almost nothing

that cannot be discovered by an intelligent and imaginative researcher. And Evie had the incentive. It took a little time. She made a comprehensive trawl of all the old photo albums. There were no pictures of Loomis—Faith wouldn't have risked keeping one even if she'd wanted to—but there were pictures of other people her mother knew twenty years ago. Girls and men, close friends and casual acquaintances, some moved on but others still living in the Dimmock area.

By a judicious mixture of ingenuousness and guile, under the pretext of arranging a surprise party for her mother's birthday, Evie contacted those she could directly, and used what they knew to contact others. Over a period of weeks, unsuspected by anyone, she worked her way out to the margins of the group of friends until she found the sister of a friend of Faith's, who'd been just close enough to hear accounts of her pregnancy and just distant enough not to realise she should keep them to herself. When Evie asked, all innocently, if there was anyone else Faith had known at the time, she suggested, 'There was a guy called Loomis. He and Faith were pretty close about then.'

That was the little silver gismo that opens the oyster. She levered on it and the shell began to crack. Other people remembered Faith and Joe, and how they'd gone from hot to not almost over the course of a weekend. Remembered how, a couple of months down the line, Faith had announced the forthcoming expansion of her family. No one came out and told Evie that Joe Loomis was her father, but she could do the math. And so far as she could discover there were no other candidates.

Still, she didn't want to send a Father's Day card to the wrong man. She confronted Faith.

This was Faith's worst nightmare. She knew she'd been careful. She thought no trail led back to the place of Evie's conception. She did the only thing she could: she lied. She said Evie had got it wrong. When she knew Joe she was already pregnant, to a sales rep she met at a party. They'd enjoyed the occasion, the drink and one another's company just a little too freely, and never met again. Joe came along soon afterwards.

Evie didn't believe it. It didn't even fit with what Faith had said previously. She thought—by now she was sure—she was right first time: her father was Joe Loomis, proprietor of The Rose in Rye Lane. And like Dev's father, a man who'd lived just a few miles away all her life.

Further enquiries established that Loomis was a single man and that he had a certain reputation. Though this caused her a moment's hesitation, she refused to worry about it. Successful businessmen were rarely popular, she knew. They became successful by beating rivals at their own game—of course they left a trail of hard feelings. And as a single man with no family to protect, Evie hoped that connecting with his long-lost daughter might mean as much to Loomis as it would to her.

By this time in the telling of her story, she and Brodie were in the kitchen of the cottage, nursing large mugs of coffee, with the radio tuned to the local station in case there was a sudden newsflash.

'So you went to see him.'

Evie nodded quickly, trying to get this done. 'I phoned him. I told him my name but not who I was. I don't know if he worked it out. God, I hope not!'

She asked to meet him. She expected an invitation to his pub, which she thought—not knowing The Rose—would be a good neutral venue. It was a public place, if her revelation didn't go down well she could get up and leave without making a scene.

'It's not that I was expecting a grand fairytale reunion,' she insisted. 'I wasn't. I knew it would be hard to find something safe to talk about. I knew we might not even like one another. I just… It was something I had to do. I'd found him—I had to meet him before I could move on.' The implications of that wrung from her a tortured little sound that was half a chuckle, half a sob.

But Loomis didn't ask her to come to The Rose. He offered

to buy her a coffee at Nettie's Café on Fisher Hill—they could meet in the car park behind Shack Lane. Evie saw no particular problem with that. But then, she didn't know the car park was just a bit of waste ground without a street-light to its name. To the casual stranger, even Shack Lane had a touch of the Dickens about it. She felt her way through the tightening net of lanes, each a little narrower and darker than the last, and kept the car doors locked, and only the imminent prospect of achieving what she'd spent the last six months striving for kept her from turning tail.

And made what followed all but inevitable.

TWENTY-EIGHT

DEACON TOOK IT ONE careful step at a time. The guys watching down the gun-barrels didn't know him the way his own officers did. Today, waving his arms and shouting wouldn't get him what he wanted—it would probably get him shot. All the same, he did wave. He stood up and faced the direction the danger was coming from, and waved both arms across in front of him. Then he stuck a thumb up. Sights that would let you put a bullet in a man's eye at half a mile ought to show a generous thumbs-up. Then he turned his back on the snipers and, keeping himself between Stretton and the guns, opened the blockhouse door.

A little traitor voice at the back of his mind was saying, *This is what it's all about, is it? This is part of the job description?—to be the meat in the sandwich between a lunatic sitting on two tonnes of blasting explosive and a professional with his finger on the trigger of a sniper rifle? Great. Well, I might live to tell the tale, if everybody keeps calm for the next thirty seconds. Starting with me...*

'Take off your coat.' Stretton did as he was told. 'And your shirt.' Deacon sighed. '*And* your vest. Shoes. Trousers.'

Stretton's eyes saucered. 'I'm not...!'

'Yes,' said Deacon heavily, 'you are. *They* think you're a suicide bomber. When you come through this door, I want them to see that all that's coming out is you. You're embarrassed? Tough.'

So they emerged from the blockhouse—Deacon first, coatless, his own shirt flapping in case anyone wondered what it would take to turn a suicide bombing into a proxy bombing. Then Stretton, naked, hands spread wide until Deacon told him to get down on the muddy ground and keep still as if his life depended on it. Because it did.

Across the mud, where the perimeter was being held, slowly men began to break cover and come forward. Last of all the men with the guns took their eyes from their telescopic sights, stood down and stood up.

Another minute and Dev Stretton was securely handcuffed, held by as many officers as could get a hold on him, being marched squelchily across the site to a police van.

'Hang on a minute.' Deacon went back to the bunker for his coat and threw it roughly around Stretton's shaking body. By way of explanation he growled, 'I know he's a stupid bastard. He doesn't have to be a freezing stupid bastard. Now get the silly bugger out of my sight.'

'GO ON,' SAID Brodie quietly.

Loomis was already there when Evie found the car park. Her headlights ran along the flank of the long silver car and a small dark-haired man got out. He was on his own. There were no other vehicles in the car park and no passers-by.

She pulled up beside him, wound down the window and said, 'I'm Evie.' And Joe Loomis opened the door for her.

She'd wondered just when she should break her news. If she should declare herself right away, so they both knew what they were talking about, or if she should wait until they had the coffee in front of them and she could see his reaction. She was still wondering when Joe took the initiative. Putting an unexpectedly proprietorial arm around her shoulders he steered her towards his car and said, 'So you want to be a hooker.'

'He thought… He thought…' Evie could hardly get it out. Her voice shook, and her hands shook on the kitchen table, spilling the contents of her mug. Brodie fought the urge to help. The girl needed to do this. It wouldn't be the end of the nightmare. But it might be the beginning of the end.

'He thought I wanted to work for him. Because he was a

pimp and I was a prostitute. I'd gone there to meet my father, and he was talent-spotting for his cathouse!'

'Why did he pull the knife?' asked Brodie softly.

Evie shook her head despairingly. 'I don't know. There *was* no reason. It was like…like that was what he did with his hands. Smokers play with a cigarette, drinkers toy with a drink, geeks play with a computer mouse, and he took out a knife because he'd nothing better to do with his hands. He wasn't threatening me with it. I mean, I *thought* he was, when he reached into his coat and out it came. I thought, *Dear God in heaven, he thinks I'm here to blackmail him and this is his answer!* But I think I was wrong.'

Brodie nodded. 'A woman who knew him told me he'd do that. That it didn't mean anything. He used the knife instead of his finger—to make a point, to keep his place on a page, to touch things… She said it was mostly a habit, and a bit of power play. He did it because it held people's attention. He'd probably done it so long he'd forgotten it wasn't entirely normal.'

Behind the veil of her hair Evie was struggling with the emotions she'd tried so long to suppress. And the battle went on because each was as strong as another. Was that good news or bad, that though her father had drawn a knife on her he often drew them on other people too? Was it better to believe that he wasn't threatening her or worse, because that made what followed worse? If she'd turned and run away, would everything have been all right? Was that all she'd have had to do to keep the sky from falling?

'So what happened?' Brodie prompted her gently.

Shocked and frightened, the girl had tried to explain the misunderstanding. Tried to get out the magic words: 'I'm not a whore, I'm your daughter.' But she'd rehearsed this so often in the privacy of her own head, and it was different on a quantum level from this. She'd watched the puzzlement turn to hope and delight in his imagined face as she built up to her revelation. And she was reluctant to let that go. To admit that it wasn't possible to salvage it from where they now stood.

Loomis had stood grinning at her tongue-tied stammering. He used the point of the knife to lift her hair away from her face. 'It's OK to be nervous. Ask anyone who's been for a job interview. Get in the car, we'll do the practical, then if you measure up we can talk terms and conditions.' He still had his left arm about her shoulders, the tip of the knife against her cheek.

'What happened?' Brodie murmured again.

'I elbowed him in the belly,' whispered Evie. 'And stamped on his foot. And his arms flew out as he lost his balance, and I grabbed the knife out of his hand.'

If she'd been a sixteen-stone bouncer with a tattoo he'd never have let her close enough to hurt him. But he wasn't expecting trouble. He'd thought all he had to do was put the fear of God into her. But Evie was her mother's daughter; and actually, she was her father's daughter and her brother's sister as well. Pushed like that, her instinct was to push back. She held the knife out at arm's length, crouching behind it, keeping him at bay. 'Keep your fucking hands off me!' she yelled. 'I'm not what you think! I'm your…'

But if Joe Loomis had been scared of kids waving knives he'd never have got where he was today. He lifted his narrow shoulders in a negligent shrug. 'I know what you are.' He didn't keep his distance. He came towards her, reaching for the knife.

The long car was at her back: she couldn't have run now if she'd tried. Doing anything would have involved lowering the knife, and then he'd have had her. She swung at him.

She thought, she really thought, he'd dance back out of range. That he'd see she was serious and back off. When the knife buried itself in Joe Loomis's side, they were staring at one another from a range of inches and it was impossible to say which of them was most surprised. Evie gave a little yelp, and letting go of the knife cringed back against the car. Loomis went on regarding her in mute astonishment until he sank to his knees.

'And I ran,' whispered Evie. '*Then* I ran. Two minutes earlier I could have run, and he probably wouldn't even have chased me. Now when I ran I left my father on the ground with a knife in him, and I didn't even call for help! I ran back to my car, and I drove home, and it was two days before I even told my mother!'

Brodie found herself fighting back sympathetic tears. 'Listen to me. There are two things you need to know. What happened wasn't your fault. You were defending yourself against what you believed to be an imminent assault. Joe Loomis died with his own knife in his lung not because of what you did, but because of who he was. He was *always* going to die pretty much like that. If it hadn't been you, it would have been someone else.

'And the other thing is…' She paused. But the girl had a right to know. It wouldn't make things easier now, but later it might. 'Evie—Joe knew who you were. He knew who you were when you phoned and asked to see him. He knew because your mother told him. Do you remember that day Dev brought her home? She was upset and had a bruise on her face. Did she tell you why?'

Silently, Evie shook her head.

Brodie sighed. Secrets, secrets; and between them they'd destroyed a decent family. 'She'd been to see him. She knew you intended to approach him, and she didn't want him drawing you into his world. She warned him off. She wanted him to lie to you. To say you'd got it wrong. To laugh in your face, and send you away so embarrassed you'd never want to see him again. She thought she was protecting you.'

Evie's eyes were perplexed. She didn't understand. And if it was true, didn't it make it worse? He was going to *rape* her…!

Brodie reached across the table and folded her hands over the girl's. 'I think she succeeded. I think Joe recognised that, though he'd been no father to you for twenty years, at least he hadn't done you any harm. And that could be about to change. I think he decided the best thing he could do was scare you off. Everything he said and did was to that end. He thought you'd scream and run a mile, and avoid him like the plague ever after. Evie—I think he was trying to help.'

They were still sitting there, holding hands across the table,

eyes locked—Evie's hollow pits of slow comprehension,
Brodie's tear-bright with compassion—when there was a knock
at the door. After a moment Brodie freed her hands and stood
up. 'That'll be the police.'

THERE WERE NOW THREE separate parties converging on Battle
Alley: Detective Superintendent Deacon and his prisoner;
Stretton's mother and, apparently, his father in the care of Detective Constable Huxley; and his sister and, to no one's
surprise at all, Brodie Farrell accompanied by Detective Constable Jill Meadows. But free flow of transport was still a
problem. It was going to take time for any of the cars to find a
way into the town centre, and only when they could get
together, under one roof if not in one room, could all the little
bits of information be glued together into something that—if
it didn't actually hold water—at least looked like a pot.

   (Detectives and archaeologists have a lot in common. Both
dig deep in awkward and often dirty places, and may not know
how the sherds they find will fit until the very end. All the same,
Deacon hadn't the patience to be an archaeologist. It's hard to
intimidate a midden.)

   At the same time Superintendent Fuller had his people on
the streets, actively promoting calm and breaking up any gath-
erings large enough to look like a target. Even with Stretton in
custody, it was too soon to say there would be no bombing here
today. So the police station was manned essentially by Sergeant
McKinney and the radio room staff when SOCO called in from
Romney Road. McKinney was wondering what to do with the
call when DS Voss limped up the back stairs and became the
station's CID presence. He waved the earpiece at Voss and
Voss took it.

   Daniel was still with him. He'd no reason to go anywhere
else and in any event no way of getting there. But he could make
no sense of that half of the conversation that he could hear.

   Voss said: 'Where had it been? Which is pretty much what

he told the cousins, of course. So when it turned up they sent it to the address on the label. What's it like—soft, rigid?'

There was a pause in which Daniel could hear the sound of the other voice without being able to pick out words. Then Voss said, 'Not until I'm sure it's necessary. The state this town's in, an Army truck driving up Romney Road will send it ballistic. Don't handle it. Put it somewhere it won't be disturbed— and if Hux turns up, don't let him in the same room! I'm on my way.'

Finally: 'No—I'm not an ATO, and I don't have a death wish. But I don't want to throw petrol on the flames if it's just a souvenir-stall camel from the family back home. Do nothing. I'm on my way.' He was heading for the door as he gave the earpiece back. Daniel fell into line behind him. They'd reached the steps before Voss realised. 'Where do you think you're going?'

'I have no idea,' said Daniel honestly. 'But you're not exactly overmanned at the moment. I may not be much help, but I ought to be better than no one at all.'

Voss gave a grin and gave up. 'Come on then. There's no reason to suppose you'll be in any more danger there than here.'

'No,' agreed Daniel. 'Er…where?'

Scene of Crime Officer Billy Mills had still been working in the Dhazi cousins' house when the parcel van drew up outside. 'Package for Mr Salma.'

Mills frowned. 'Who's that, then?'

The courier shrugged. 'Beats me. But this is the address on his suitcase.'

There was a covering note from the airline. The case had been found on a carousel in Luxembourg. There was nothing to be gained by speculating how it had got there. They were now returning it, with their apologies and some complimentary air miles, and hoped its temporary absence had not impacted too much upon Mr Salma's holiday.

Before he was a civilian SOCO, Billy Mills was a uniformed sergeant at Battle Alley. He'd learnt the science stuff, but he'd always known about crime. After the courier had gone he turned to Reg Vickers who was helping him. 'Salma is Daoud?'

Constable Vickers had no ambitions to be a detective. He liked dealing with what Deacon referred to as 'The bastard public'. But Uniform see a lot of criminals too, and criminal practice is second nature to any police officer who's been paying attention. 'Well, he wasn't travelling as himself or he'd have been picked up. Did you find a passport?'

Mills shook his head. Usually it takes surgery to separate law-abiding travellers from their passports. If Daoud's wasn't found on his body it was because he'd hidden it somewhere.

'And this is his bag.' Vickers thought back. 'The cousins said something about a missing bag. They thought he was ripping them off—that he'd never had their heroin.'

'And maybe he hadn't,' rumbled Mills. 'Maybe what he had was Semtex.'

'Oh shit,' said Reg Vickers fervently, taking a step back.

Which is when they radioed Battle Alley.

THEY STOOD IN A CAUTIOUS circle round the table Mills had placed it on, watching the suitcase closely, listening for ticking.

'If it's Semtex,' ventured Vickers, 'shouldn't it have been picked up at the airport?'

'If it's heroin it should have been, too,' said Voss. 'But we know security measures only pick up a fraction of what comes in.'

'It's a battle of wits,' said Mills heavily. 'The smugglers find ways round the measures we have in place; we find ways of improving those measures to catch them next time. And so on, ad bloody infinitum. Whatever else he was, Daoud was no amateur. He could have protected either of those substances against a routine airport inspection.'

'Or it could still be his underwear,' murmured Daniel.

The others regarded him sourly. But it was true. Even mass murderers are doing other things most of the time.

'I'm going to have a look,' decided Voss.

'What?!' Vickers' voice climbed. 'Not while I'm standing here you're not.'

'Fair enough,' said Voss. 'But I'm not calling in the Army, and having guys with robots and body armour sealing the street off while they go through a dead man's smalls. This town has been on the point of meltdown for forty-eight hours. One more incident—in particular, one more incident *here,* where people look more like Daoud than they do like you, Reg—and we'll have a race riot on our hands. Well, if I crack open that case and see wires I'll risk it. But if it's heroin—or underwear—we can handle the situation ourselves. At least we won't make it any worse.'

'It's a gamble, Charlie,' rumbled Mills. 'If it got through airport security, there are no tests I can do on the outside to tell you what's on the inside. If it's a bomb, opening the case a crack might be all it needs to detonate.'

'But why would it be a bomb? It was supposed to be on the same flight he was—why would he risk carrying an armed device? Even if it is explosives, surely he'd get them safely here and arm them at this end. This house isn't the target, it's the factory—or not, as the case may be, but Daoud had no interest in blowing it up. I don't think it's a bomb.'

'I don't think it's a bomb either,' said Billy Mills. 'But I wouldn't want to bet my life on it.'

Voss gave a nervous grin. 'OK. This isn't going to take all of us.' He glanced at his watch. 'Goodness—it's time for tea and doughnuts! You want to get them, Reg? And maybe Billy could help you carry them. And Daniel…'

'And Daniel,' said Daniel firmly, 'has no intentions of explaining to Detective Superintendent Deacon what happened to his sergeant, his crime scene and half a square mile of his manor. You open that case, Charlie, you do it with me here.'

In the end, no one went for tea and doughnuts.

Vickers watched the door. Any more delivery men, window cleaners or elderly ladies collecting for charity would be hustled

away to a safe distance with the time-honoured explanation:
'We think it's a gas leak.'

Daniel held the case steady on the table. He kept saying to
himself, *Underwear. It's just underwear. Even terrorists need
a change of underwear when they travel.* Once he saw a worried
expression cross Voss's freckled features and was horribly
afraid he'd said it aloud.

Billy Mills produced a variety of small cutting tools and
some plastic gloves. 'Whatever's in it, I'm going to want to
swab it when we're finished. I don't want the DNA tests showing that it was put together by a ginger Irishman.'

'I'm only half Irish,' said Voss defensively; but he pulled
the gloves on.

'And I might not have enough fingers left to swab anything by then,' muttered Mills, 'but let's look on the bright
side.'

In one respect they were lucky. Daoud's bag was not rigid
fibreglass but soft-bodied, made of well-used leather. This told
them two things. That whatever it contained was not very
volatile—if it had been, the ordinary rough-and-tumble of
baggage sorting would have set it off. And that it would be
possible to peep inside without disturbing the lock and hinges,
two prime sites for anti-handling devices.

After some deliberation Mills chose a little craft knife with
a non-magnetic blade. The blades didn't stay sharp as long but
were a safer option when you didn't know what you were
looking at. He ran his fingers over the outside of the bag, finally
picking a spot—away from the corners, which would be a good
place to locate something a bit delicate, but not in the middle
which would be an obvious place to catch out someone who
knew to avoid the corners. He made a sliver of a slit that at first
didn't even penetrate the leather. Then he pinched an edge of
the cut in non-magnetic tweezers and lifting it away from the
contents made the first miniscule penetration.

'Pass me the…' He'd laid them all out ready before he started, but Voss didn't know their names. 'Third from the left.' Mills inserted the tip of a fibre-optic probe into the tiny opening.

'Mm,' he said thoughtfully.

'What?' whispered Voss, but there was no reply.

When he'd seen all the probe could show him, Mills, with fingertips as delicate as a girl's, pushed it a little deeper and looked again. 'Mm,' he repeated.

'What?' demanded Voss. 'What can you see?'

'Not sure.' Mills moved the little probe around cautiously. 'Something... A label.'

'Oh shit,' whined Reg Vickers.

'Semtex?' asked Voss. 'Or...Semtex written in...whatever alphabet they use in the Czech Republic?'

'No,' said Billy Mills slowly. 'It's written in English. It's...hang on a minute, I've nearly got it...that's better...yes. It's Marks & Spencer.'

Charlie Voss straightened up slowly. The sweat was running down his face; which was odd when he felt cold to the bone. 'You're saying it really is his underwear.'

Mills shrugged. 'That's all I can see. I don't think there's anything that'll blow my hand off if I open it up.'

Still struggling for composure, Voss nodded. 'Do it.'

For safety's sake he continued the slit across the top of the bag, extending it into a Y-shape he'd learnt by attending autopsies. Then he sat back on his heels. There were no boxes with wires protruding. There were no unreasonable quantities of deodorant cans. There wasn't even a toy camel labelled *A Present from Islamabad*. There were shirts, T-shirts, sweaters, socks, a pair of shoes, a wash bag. Any one of them, packing for a week away, would have thrown in the same things.

'There isn't enough,' said Daniel softly.

Voss looked at him with disfavour. 'We do have shops. If he'd run out he could have gone back to M&S.'

'That's not what I mean. Look at the size of the bag, and what he's got in it. And it's full.'

He was right. It was a big bag and should have held more. SOCO hunted for his tape-measure. 'We're missing about two inches at the bottom.' He might have to work in centimetres but he didn't have to think in them. 'And the bag's…' More measuring, a bit of calculating. 'There's half a cubic foot unaccounted for. That's enough to be useful.'

'To a drug smuggler?' asked Daniel.

'To any kind of smuggler. It could still be Semtex. You could get enough sticks in there to make a nice big bang.'

'How big?' asked Voss uneasily.

Mills considered. 'Not really the right question, Charlie. It's more a case of how many? Three will make you a useful bomb. There's room in there for fifty.' He looked at Voss. 'What do you want to do?'

Voss steeled himself. 'I want to know.'

Billy Mills nodded. 'OK. We'll keep going.'

The same procedure, this time going in through the false bottom of the bag. The blade, the tweezers, the probe, and SOCO venting his pent-up breath in a long sigh. 'Well now,' he said heavily. 'Even at Christmas, even if you've a lot of aunties to visit, how much talcum powder does a man need to carry?'

Daniel finally found a voice. 'It's heroin?'

'It's heroin.'

Heroin doesn't weigh a lot. But stuff enough of it into the bottom of a bag and you'll have a kilo. Voss, typically, had the figures in his head. 'It'll be pretty pure—you wouldn't bother carrying make-weight. One K at ninety percent purity will have cost him forty thousand dollars. Cut to ten per cent, it'll sell on the street for half a million quid.'

Behind the thick glasses, Daniel's eyes were saucers. 'That's quite a mark-up!'

'He took quite a risk for it. His life, in fact. And he lost.'

'But…' Daniel frowned. 'That can't be right.'

Voss nodded grimly. 'I know. He was smuggling heroin. International terrorists don't, on the whole, smuggle drugs.'

'But…'

Voss nodded again. 'Dave Salmon knew him—knew Daoud worked for al-Qaeda. But first time they met he was running drugs. Maybe at some point he became disenchanted with *jihad* and went back to his old career.'

'Then…'

'No,' agreed Voss. 'Take Daoud out of the equation and there is no terrorist plot. It was a reasonable assumption—that's where the intelligence was taking us—but a lot of it was coincidence. Unconnected events that just *looked* like a conspiracy. For the last three days we've been jumping at shadows.'

'Shouldn't we…?'

Voss nodded. 'I'll get word to the chief right away. And Superintendent Fuller needs to start reassuring people. Daniel…'

'That's OK,' said Daniel with a sly grin. 'I know you couldn't have worked it out without me.'

TWENTY-NINE

THE STREETS WERE NO longer empty. No private vehicles were moving in the middle of town, but many of those who'd had to leave their cars on the jammed arterials were wandering round on foot, trying to find out what to do, looking for someone to blame.

Now their numbers were being swelled by a second influx of anxious and angry people, this time from the Romney Road area. They too wanted to know what was going on. They were tired of being blamed for something they knew nothing about. Despite Voss's best efforts, someone noticed fresh police activity at the Dhazi house and saw Voss and Daniel leaving with a large leather case. They wanted to know what was in it. They suspected, at least some of them did, that having failed to find any actual explosives the police had planted some. As Voss's car headed towards the town centre, a number of local residents followed it.

By now Deacon's party had negotiated the knot of traffic on the Guildford Road, by the simple expedient of abandoning his own vehicles and commandeering more on the other side. There they were joined by DCs Meadows and Meredith arriving back from Cheyne Warren with Evie Stretton under caution and Brodie Farrell under the impression that her presence was required. They all arrived in Battle Alley together, filling the narrow street with a harlequin mix of vehicles, and climbed out and immediately began talking, trading snippets of information.

After a minute Deacon, looking over Voss's shoulder and down the street, said suspiciously, 'Who are they?' Everyone turned and looked.

They were a crowd on the cusp of turning into a mob. Actually, two mobs; and little as they liked the police, they liked one another even less. One thought the other was a bunch of suicidal murderers, the second thought the first a gang of racist thugs. One knew the cops had got the al-Qaeda bomber who'd tried to kill them all, the other knew it was a fit-up because what the police were going to claim was the bomb was only delivered to the house in Romney Road an hour earlier. The more they poured into the neck of Battle Alley, the closer the two groups were forced and the angrier they became.

'We need to get inside,' Deacon said tersely. 'Now.'

But there were a dozen people on the police station steps, including some in high heels and one in handcuffs. Deacon wasn't even sure who some of them were but he knew that the street wasn't the place to be working it out. He grabbed people at random and pushed them up the steps ahead of him. One was Brodie, which should have surprised him but didn't. Another was Daniel.

By now the mob wasn't just jostling, it was advancing. And it was shouting. Almost, it was baying. In all the chaos, no one was able to say—even later, after studying the CCTV footage—who, or even which faction, threw the petrol bomb.

It might have been aimed at the police, it might have been aimed at their prisoner. But anyone who knew Jack Deacon could have guessed who would be last into the safety of the police station. People who disliked him with a passion, who disliked his manner and his mannerisms and his approach to the job, and especially disliked his way of being right more often than seemed reasonable, still grudgingly admitted that in a tight corner, needing someone at your back, there was no one they'd sooner have there than Deacon. It was common knowledge—more, it was a matter of faith—that he'd cover your back if all he had to do it with was his own.

So that was where the petrol bomb landed, burst and sprayed its flaming cargo: across Jack Deacon's back.

If Dev Stretton hadn't still been wearing his overcoat he'd have had some protection. But all he had was his suit, and the flames enveloped him.

For just a second. Because if you regularly risk your neck for people, sooner or later someone will return the favour. Several of those above him on the steps, whose own best interests demanded that they get indoors at once, instead turned and—working on instinct because it was faster than thought— headed back towards the angry crowd and the fire-demon that was Detective Superintendent Deacon.

Daniel and Charlie Voss reached him first. Daniel was already swinging his own jacket round Deacon's shoulders to smother the flames as Voss rugby-tackled him, bore him backwards down the steps and rolled him in the street, the weight of his own body flattening him against the pavement. And then the flames were out.

By then the rest of the party had reached them. Strong hands grabbed Deacon and bundled him unceremoniously up the steps and inside. Voss, still dusting dirt and embers from himself, thought he was bringing up the rear—then realising he was not, turned back once more to grab Daniel who was gazing bemusedly at the remains of his jacket held in spark-singed hands. Five seconds later everyone was inside the police station and the door was locked.

And five minutes later there was no one left on the street, just some broken glass, some charred clothing and a black mark in the shape of a man to show what had happened.

'WELL, THIS IS different,' said Daniel carefully.

It takes a man of a certain mettle to glare while lying face-down on a hospital trolley with a burn dressing on his backside. Deacon was that man. He glared as if tomorrow was No Glaring Day, and after that the council were introducing a glaring charge within the town boundaries. His injuries weren't life-threatening, and his dignity was a lost cause, so there was nothing to stop him.

'Spare me,' he snarled, 'the home-spun philosophy. Don't tell me things could have been worse. If you were going to tell me about last time you were here, and which wards have the best beds, and which coffee machines can be relied on to produce something recognisable as coffee, don't. I don't want to hear it. I want a shot for this'—he tried to gesture with his left ear at his singed posterior—'and then I want out of here. You want to do something useful, tell the medics that. Tell them I don't have time to be in hospital.'

'I can tell them,' said Daniel mildly. 'I don't think they'll care. I think you're going to be here for a few days, whether you have time or not. Look on the br…' He stopped himself just in time. There was nothing wrong with Deacon's hands: he'd have shoved the platitude back down Daniel's throat. 'Look at it this way. If you're here, and Detective Inspector Salmon is here, and Charlie Voss is here, to all intents and purposes this *is* CID. Tie up the loose ends while you're healing. Police interviews have been conducted in hospital rooms before.' Daniel knew this as a fact.

'Because the suspect is injured, or maybe a witness is,' hissed Deacon viciously. 'Not because the SIO has a blister the size of the Millennium Dome on his bum!' Belatedly he heard what Daniel had said. 'Charlie's still here?'

'Well—back here. He's all right,' said Daniel quickly. 'They let him out earlier today on the basis that he'd sit quietly at home and watch some television. Wrestling you down the police station steps opened the wound again. They slapped a patch on it and he'll be fine. They're only keeping him overnight to stop him doing it again.'

'That was Charlie.' Deacon's recollection of those few hectic seconds in Battle Alley was understandably fragmented. He remembered the hands, hadn't until now had a face to put with them. Then his brow creased. Daniel, why are you wearing Brodie's jacket?'

'Oh. Er…' Daniel blushed. He'd forgotten.

Deacon was a detective. 'It was you too, wasn't it? Putting the flames out. Yours got burnt and she made you put hers on.' He thought for a moment, trying to remember what came next. Oh yes… 'Thanks.'

Daniel shrugged, embarrassed. 'It was all over in a second. If Charlie hadn't been there, I wouldn't have known what to do.'

Deacon knew better. 'Oh, you would. Or you'd have worked it out. Or you'd have done it while you were working it out. You weren't hurt?'

'No.' Then, more honestly, 'Not much. They've got a spray here. I want to take one home.'

Deacon chuckled darkly. 'That's one idea. Another would be, *Stay the hell out of trouble!*' He heard another echo. 'Loose ends? We're down to loose ends? Not last time I heard!'

Daniel wasn't sure how Deacon would take the news that his case had been solved for him. 'Well, Brodie was talking to the Strettons… And then a courier turned up at Romney Road…'

Deacon gave what he thought was a patient sigh but actually sounded like the venting of an over-stoked boiler. 'Tell me what you know.'

IT HAD THE RING of authenticity. None of it contradicted his own conclusions. Dimmock had teetered on the edge of the abyss as a consequence of coincidence and misunderstanding. 'There never was a bomb plot?'

'It doesn't look like it,' said Daniel. 'Salmon was right about Daoud—he was involved with al-Qaeda for a time. Then at some point he drifted back to drug smuggling. What the Dhazi boys were telling you was the truth. Joe Loomis paid them to find him a new source of supply, and they found Daoud. They gave him Joe's deposit, but then the airline lost his bag.'

'If we'd found the drugs at Romney Road we'd have known which string of his bow Daoud was playing,' Deacon said slowly. 'But last time Dave met him he was into terrorism and we assumed that was still his game.' He frowned. 'So why's Joe dead?'

'Not because of his involvement in the drug deal,' said Daniel. 'We think—with both of them dead we're never going to know for sure—that Daoud went to The Rose to tell Joe the airline had cocked up. No one was trying to cheat him, he'd get his consignment as soon as it turned up. You have him going in and coming out on CCTV, don't you? But he didn't kill Joe then, and he didn't kill him later.'

'Well, Dev Stretton didn't kill him. He wants me to think he did, but he didn't.'

'No.'

'His mother?'

'His sister.'

Deacon hardly remembered that Stretton had a sister. Now he thought, he recalled someone skittering mouselike through the margins of the picture. 'She can't be more than about fourteen!'

'She's twenty,' said Daniel. 'Joe was her father. That's what he was trying to tell Brodie when he died. D was for Daughter.'

Deacon was wresting with the new information. '*Why?* I mean, apart from the obvious reason that most people would rather be known as a murderer than a relative of Joe Loomis's.'

Daniel sighed. 'We think that for once in his life he was trying to do something good. Evie spent months trying to find out who her father was. When she finally came up with a name, she thought there'd be a touching reunion and they'd get to know one another. But Faith was terrified the girl would get drawn into Joe's world. She went to warn him off. That was the meeting I saw.

'And it seems he was listening. He decided the best things he could do for his only child was scare her half to death. He met her in a dark car park and offered her work as a prostitute. He cornered her against his car and pulled out his knife. Evie thought he was going to rape her. She grabbed the knife, and the rest is history.'

Deacon was shaking his head in bemused disbelief. 'My God. And I thought I left a lot to be desired as a parent!'

'It was self-defence,' Daniel pointed out. 'But she didn't think anyone would believe her. By the time Faith learnt about it she thought it was too late to explain and walk away. And then, no one was looking for Evie. No one knew of any connection between her and Joe. We all expected his killer to be another gangster. Faith thought she just had to get the girl out of sight for a bit. She arranged to send her to friends in France.

'Only when Detective Inspector Salmon spotted Daoud and thought a terror attack was imminent, suddenly that got harder. Stations, ports and airports were being watched. You might have been looking for nervous Arabs, but Evie knew she was wanted too—if she'd started twitching at passport control, someone would have wondered why.

'So Faith asked Pervez Tarar—Dev's father—to take her in his helicopter. She didn't tell him why. He knew she was in trouble but he'd no reason to link her with Loomis either. He agreed.'

'And then the no-fly zone was imposed,' realised Deacon. 'If he'd taken off he'd have been intercepted, and even if Tarar didn't know what it was all about I'd have found out.'

Daniel smiled at the unconscious pride in his voice. 'Which is when Dev got involved. Faith only told him what had happened when she thought Evie was going to have to face the music. Until then he didn't even know Joe was Evie's father.'

'He needed to get that no-fly zone lifted. He hoped that if you thought you'd cornered the mad bomber, Evie could get safely away. There's a streak of nobility in that boy that was always going to get him into trouble sooner or later. Faith agreed, but once she'd got Evie off to France she meant to tell the police Dev was covering for her—that she killed Joe. I think she was past caring what happened to her if Evie was safe and you understood the reasons for Dev's actions. Grand gestures seem to be a Stretton specialty.'

'But if you know all this,' said Deacon suspiciously, 'I'm presuming that's not what happened.'

Daniel shook his head. 'Evie had no idea what Dev was up

to. Neither had Tarar. When Brodie caught up with them at the airstrip and told them, Evie insisted on coming back to face the music; and even if she hadn't, Tarar wasn't leaving his son to the mercy of a marksman. They arrived at the construction site just as you and Dev were leaving, and followed you into town.'

So far Deacon had managed to stay abreast of the story. 'So what were *you* doing in Battle Alley?'

Daniel gave a shy little smile. 'Charlie and I were at the house in Romney Road. We opened the bag, and when it was heroin we realised DI Salmon had been wrong about Daoud. Or not wrong but out of date. And if he wasn't involved in terrorism any more, there was no reason to suppose anyone else in Dimmock was either. When it turned out he'd gone back to lining his pockets with drug money, the whole house of cards collapsed.'

'There was no bomb plot,' said Deacon flatly, trying to get his head round it. 'It wasn't just that Stretton had no part in it—there never was a plot.'

'As far as we can work out,' agreed Daniel apologetically. 'We got it wrong.'

'Perhaps you got it wrong. But what you did was right when all the evidence pointed that way. If you'd hesitated and there *had* been a conspiracy to bomb Dimmock, scores of people could have died. And that wouldn't have been your fault either, but you'd have felt a lot worse about it.'

'The town's been in uproar for three days. People *will* have died. The inquests won't record the cause of death as police error, but they'd still be alive if we'd got it right.' Deacon shook his head angrily. 'On top of that, we've thrown fuel on a situation that was smouldering so quietly it might have gone out before it ever caused a problem. We've given the white people of this town reason to fear and mistrust the Asians, and the Asians reason to fear and mistrust the whites. Quite an achievement for three days' work! God knows when that *nasty* little worm will raise its head again.'

Daniel didn't believe in God. He did believe in people. 'Jack, nobody comes out of this with much to be proud of. At least your mistake was an honest one. The people who crowded into Battle Alley intent on defending their own rights so vigorously it required petrol bombs have a damn sight more to be ashamed of. You may find that once everything's calmed down it's in everyone's best interests to shut up about what happened. You may find people being especially polite to one another rather than risk anything like it happening again.

'We were all swept up in the maelstrom of our own prejudices, saw the dangers we expected to see. The horrors we found in the woodshed were the ones we'd taken there, and that goes as much for the people of Romney Road as for anyone else. People can't be forced into factions—they have to choose them.'

He gave a wry little snort. 'The only one who managed to stay above the sectarianism was Dev Stretton. We'—Deacon knew that actually he meant *you*—'thought he was part of a bomb plot because his father's Pakistani. But the Pakistanis thought he was just another white boy causing trouble for them. That petrol bomb you got in the way of was meant for him. But even knowing that doesn't tell us who threw it.'

'What's the situation now?'

'Calm. The roads are getting back to normal. You can get pretty well anywhere you need to. The street cleaners will have their work cut out for a few days, then there won't be much to show for it. Except…' He glanced discreetly at Deacon's posterior.

About then the casualty officer came to have another smirk at it and Daniel left. Deacon shouted after him, 'Where's Brodie?'

And Daniel called back, 'She'll be along soon.'

BY THE TIME Deacon had been transferred, still prone, to a ward she'd arrived. She pulled up a chair to where he could see her. She looked tired. 'How are you feeling?'

'Stupid,' grunted Deacon. 'A bit sore. Nothing killing.' He squinted at her. 'You did it again, didn't you?'

Brodie purported not to understand. 'Sorry?'

'Worked it out before I did.'

She had the grace to demur. 'I had less to worry about. I was just trying to make sense of the bit we'd got involved in—Joe Loomis and the Stretton family. When you stripped away all the trimmings, what was left made no sense until we tried forgetting that Joe was a thug. Most people who get murdered aren't gangsters. Most killings take place within a fairly tight social circle—family and friends. Joe didn't have much of a social life, but it turned out he did have a daughter.'

Deacon blew his cheeks out. 'What a mess! Why in God's name didn't she just *come* to us? He scared the living bejasus out of her. He pulled a knife! She was entitled to defend herself.'

Brodie shrugged. 'You know that, I know that. She's a twenty-year-old girl who'd just stabbed the father she'd spent six months tracking down. She panicked. And all Faith—and later Dev—could think about was protecting her.'

'They almost cost us our town!'

'They didn't mean to. Dev just wanted to distract you long enough to let his sister get away.'

'Instead of which the whole bloody family's going down,' he snarled vindictively. 'Serve them bloody right.'

'You're still cross,' observed Brodie—a world-class understatement. 'You'll feel less bitter when your bottom's not so sore.'

He curled his lip, mostly from habit. Then something occurred to him. 'Next time you come, bring Jonathan.'

At once, by the shadow that crossed her eyes, he knew something was wrong. 'Actually, he's here. Upstairs.'

Instantly, all awareness of his own injuries fled. 'Paediatrics? What's happened?'

'They're telling me not to worry,' said Brodie quickly. 'They're telling me it's not uncommon in small children, and almost never as serious as it looks.'

'What isn't?'

'Convulsions.' Brodie swallowed. 'I left him with Marta

when I went to see Faith. He'd been a bit restless the previous night but he seemed fine by then. Marta says he was fine, until all at once he wasn't. He was twitching and jerking all over the place. She called for an ambulance. It couldn't get through—the paramedics did the last half-mile on foot.

'By the time they got there the fit was over. He was lying peaceably in his cot as if nothing had happened. Marta thought they'd think she'd made it up, but they didn't. They asked…' Her voice cracked on half a sob, half a desperate laugh. 'They asked if he'd been rolling his eyes. When Marta told them his history, they bundled him up in a blanket and carried him back to the ambulance, and she and Paddy went with them.'

'And what are they saying now? What's the problem?' Deacon didn't want to say the words for fear of what the answer would be.

Brodie reassured him as she could. 'They're saying it's probably nothing to do with the retinoblastoma. They say infantile convulsions are usually caused by a fever in the early stages of an infection—you deal with the infection and with luck you never see the convulsions again.'

'That's what they're doing upstairs—treating him for an infection?'

'Yes.'

'Is it working?'

Brodie shrugged. 'He hasn't had another fit. But then, he only got here about the same time you did.'

'You shouldn't…' She looked tired, and fraught, and afraid, and right now she didn't need to be dealing with criticism, justified or not. Deacon smothered the statement half-born. But his eyes finished it. *You shouldn't have left him with Marta. You're his mother: you should have been with him when this happened!*

Brodie heard it just the same, and flinched. *You think I'd have left him for a minute if I'd thought this was going to happen?* asked her gaze brokenly. *Marta did all the right things—there was nothing more I could have done if I'd been*

*there. In spite of which, don't you think I'm beating myself up
enough over the fact that I wasn't? Do you really think you need
to put the boot in too?*

Deacon cleared his throat. 'You shouldn't worry. I'm sure
they're right and it's just a—blip. But, get back to him.'

She'd expected argument and recrimination. His uncharacter-
istic kindness drew a slow tear that slid to the end of Brodie's nose
before falling. 'I wanted to see you. To know you're all right.'

'I'm fine. Go look after our son.'